LIFE ON URTH

To Mum, with love

JOHN KIRKBRIDE

SCHOLASTIC

Scholastic Children's Books
Scholastic Publications Ltd,
7–9 Pratt Street, London NW1 0AE

Scholastic Inc.,
555 Broadway, New York, NY 10012–3999, USA

Scholastic Canada Ltd,
123 Newkirk Road, Richmond Hill,
Ontario, Canada L4C 3G5

Ashton Scholastic Pty Ltd,
PO Box 579, Gosford, New South Wales,
Australia

Ashton Scholastic Ltd,
Private Bag 92801, Penrose, Auckland,
New Zealand

First published by Scholastic Publications Ltd, 1994

Copyright © John Kirkbride, 1994

ISBN 0 590 54167 6

Typeset by Intype, London
Printed in England by Clays Ltd, St Ives plc

10 9 8 7 6 5 4 3 2 1

Prologue

I

Throughout the multi-dimensional layers of the omniverse an infinite number of atoms wheeled and dipped and absorbed energy. Histories rattled by like express trains, possibilities came and went and the fabric of existence wove and re-wove itself. Worlds bobbed momentarily into sight before flickering out like dead candles, and infinite alternatives tossed coins and argued over cause and effect.

Somewhere, deep within the limitless layers of potentiality, someone had an idea. Not a million miles away* and almost simultaneously, someone else had the same idea.

Existence swirled and shimmered, sending undulating ripples of improbability through the very walls of the Universal Mainframe. Pinpoints of non-dark twinkled momentarily, as tiny random holes opened and closed in the very fabric of time and space.

From somewhere, two fingers of light reached out into the blackness, and suddenly the lives of two relatively innocent people were drastically altered.

What follows is the story of those two people.

* One and a half, to be precise

II

Reg sat back contentedly and lit a rare cigarette. That's not to say that the cigarette was of a brand seldom encountered and thus a thing of some singularity. It was simply that Reg didn't often smoke. Puffing away happily, nonetheless, he gazed at the word processor screen in front of him and smiled. He was pleased with himself. Very pleased with himself. Very pleased with himself indeed. In fact, Reg was so pleased with himself that he would have shaken his own hand and slapped himself on the back if he could, and only the vague notion of a possible dislocated shoulder prevented him from attempting it. Instead he simply smiled, although it was such a smug, self-satisfied smile that it might well have made some people want to push a sharpened pencil up one of his nostrils. Reg had that effect sometimes.

He smiled more forcibly and allowed himself a little chuckle.

At last it was finished.

All those endless hours of work: toiling with the characters, tussling with the plot, struggling manfully with the style and getting the shit kicked out of him by the grammar. It was all there on that little word processor disk, a story dragged struggling and cursing from the dark recesses of Reg's imagination. A story of love and literature and cute conversations in comfortable café bars. The story of Nick Chadwell and Rebecca Trent, a novelist and a sculptress, struggling to find their true identities in a cut-throat jungle of urbanity and spritzers. This was the stuff that real life was made of. Smart, slick, witty stuff. True life drama with a sprinkling of added zest. The publishers would love it; the critics would love it; the readers would love it. In fact, the whole world would love it, just as Reg loved it, and the thought caused his smile to expand until there was almost no room left on his face for it.

He dimped the cigarette, stood up and stretched. Thank God it's over, he thought, still grinning like a Cheshire prat. No more slaving over a hot word processor long into the early hours of the morning. He could climb back on board the social roundabout, hang loose with the old crowd and maybe even start dating women again. *Again?* Well, whatever. It would be just like old times, in those halcyon days before 'The Book'. He might even go out that very night and get pissed as a fart.

The latter thought triggered a vague rumbling in the region of his bowels, and he made his way rather quickly to the bathroom.

Sitting there on his avocado green toilet, Reg pondered the future. The first item on the agenda, naturally, was to get his book accepted by a publisher. He had decided on 'Figure of a Man, Bending' as a title, a reference to one of his heroine's sculptures, and was rather chuffed with it. Not obscure, but abstruse, he'd decided, though some people may have found that distinction interesting. He felt it sounded a little like the kind of thick hardback by some bizarrely named author which tended to win the Booker Prize (though he suspected his own book was far too easy to read ever to attain *that* accolade).

As for a publisher, he would certainly have to go for one of the big boys, preferably one with strong American links and positively dripping with cash. It was a first novel, and it was going to take some real high powered promotion to give it the kick start it needed. He could see it now: Waterstones' window, filled with pristine hardbacked copies of his book and huge cardboard displays emblazoned with favourable reviews – 'An incredible first novel', 'An outstanding achievement', 'Sharp, witty and penetrating'. And, of course, a huge black and white photograph of *him*, Reginald Bethel, staring out onto the bustling high street.

Still wearing the smile of an insane goatherd, he finished what he was doing and pulled his trousers up. Wondering what it would be like to be famous, he flushed the toilet and blasted a cloud of Haze at the lightshade. He opened the bathroom door and stepped out, and was a little disconcerted to find that the rest of his house had completely disappeared.

III

Jeannette Higginbottom stepped out of the shower and smothered herself in a huge pale green bath towel. Plucking a matching hand towel from its hook by the sink, she wrapped it around her damp head in the form of an Indian turban. Snatching a third towel from the rail over the radiator, she padded into her bedroom and plopped down on the Laura Ashley quilt cover. She dried her feet thoroughly with the spare towel, then dropped it on the floor. She stood up, walked around the bed and took a fourth towel from the radiator. She dried her lower legs with it, folded it neatly and dropped it on the floor. Peering around, she spotted another towel draped over the wardrobe door, and grabbed it. Unwrapping the one around her head, she dropped it on the floor and proceeded to dry her hair with the new towel. When she'd finished, she dropped it on the floor. She peeled the large damp bath towel from around her shoulders, dropped it on the floor and went in search of another one with which to replace it. Suddenly there were no more towels.

'Why is it,' Jeannette muttered testily, as she waded through a shifting sea of pale green cotton, 'that I can never find a towel when I need one?'

She stopped in front of the full-length mirror and gazed at the reflection of her naked body. Her firm, round, creamy-coloured breasts were round and firm and not at all un-creamy-coloured, and her legs were long, shapely and wondrously pale. The rest of her slender body was equally well proportioned and pleasing to the eye, which made all the more remarkable the fact that no one but Jeannette had seen it for over three years. It wasn't that men found her unattractive – on the contrary, had Jeannette managed to save every wolf whistle she'd ever received she would have needed an extra drawer in her dressing table to keep them in. The real reason for Jeannette's enforced celibacy was the fact that in the company of potential suitors, she had a tendency to turn into a pseudo-intellectual prat, and many a young man's initial attraction had limpened on hearing her theories about 'sociologically aesthetic figurative expression'. Jeannette was a sculptress – rather a good one in fact – but her theories on the art of moulding lumps of clay into interesting shapes were notable only for their astonishing turgidity.

This is not to say that Jeannette wasn't a kind, caring and good-natured person. It was just that she had some rather peculiar ideas about Life, and some positively idiotic ideas about Art. Her latest sculpture was entitled 'Figure of a Man, Bending', and was supposed to reflect the fact that the world, despite the demise of the Cold War, was still living under the threat of nuclear devastation. In exactly what way the image of a man bending over symbolized global nuclear nervousness, no one who had seen it was quite sure – unless of course he was ducking. Disappointingly for Jeannette, the most common reaction to the piece so far had been bewildered sniggering. Undeterred, Jeannette made plans for a second, life-sized version to be cast in bronze, in the hope that some perceptive local councillor would decide to have it officially placed in some prominent position in the village. Outside that quaint little red brick branch of Nat West would be nice.

Jeannette finished dressing and moved back to the mirror to admire the end result. Yes: that would do nicely. Her pale smooth legs were encased in black nylon tights over which she wore a tiny black mini skirt. A sloppy black sweater, black ankle socks and black Doc Marten shoes completed the outfit, which somehow gave the onlooker the impression that Jeannette was a chunk of night that had suddenly sprouted arms and legs. The onlooker wandered away lost in thought. Jeannette shook her head vigorously, and her long dark curls arranged themselves pleasingly around her face. (The only time she used a hairdryer was when attempting to render wearable an article of clothing she had been silly enough to wash an hour before going out.) She pushed her round, steel-rimmed spectacles back up to the bridge of her nose, picked up the huge black rucksack that served as a handbag and straightened her skirt. Walking over to the bedroom door, she opened it and stepped out, and was a little disconcerted to discover that the rest of her house had completely disappeared.

1

Lady Hortensia Westholme surveyed her sumptuous dining room with an air of quietly aggressive satisfaction. Everything was in its place, from the huge arrangement of dried miss anthemums in the centre of the table to the glistening silver cutlery and crisp white linen napkins. The table itself had been polished to within an inch of its life, and new candles stood proud and erect at each end of it, in eager anticipation of their hour of molten glory. Lady Westholme glanced at George the butler, who was standing discreetly to one side, his hands clasped in front of him.

'A marvellous job, George,' she told him, in her deep, well spoken yet surprisingly feminine voice, 'absolutely first class!'

'Thank you, m'lady. I take it everything is to Modom's satisfaction?'

'Perfection itself, George, absolute and utter perfection!'

George winced imperceptibly, his acute butleresque senses faintly offended by this vulgar display of unbridled enthusiasm.

'Just so, m'lady,' he said tonelessly.

'It's going to be simply wonderful, George,' Lady Westholme went on, 'I can feel it in my bones. Or is it my water? I can never quite remember.'

'I suspect it is Modom's bones to which she refers, m'lady.'

'Yes, well, probably. Anyway, it's going to be a positively scrumptious affair. I shall wear my best jewellery and my new hamster hair stole, I think.'

George raised a single eyebrow. 'At the dining table, m'lady?'

Lady Westholme shot George a testy glance. 'Well, perhaps I'll just stick with the jewellery then. Did I tell you I've had the Cullinan ruby set on a beautiful necklace especially for the occasion?'

'I believe Modom has mentioned it once or twice, m'lady,' replied George, the weight of irony in his voice almost causing it to creak.

'It will simply steal the show, don't you think, George?'

'I don't doubt it for one moment, m'lady.'

A sudden twinge of doubt manifested itself as a tiny wrinkle in the centre of Lady Westholme's brow.

'You don't think it's too . . . ostentatious, do you?'

George raised his eyebrow again. 'Certainly not, m'lady,' he assured her, 'on the contrary. Indeed, I venture to suggest that the Cullinan ruby's flawless beauty transcends all considerations of taste.'

'Oh good. Then you think I should wear it?'

'It would almost be a crime not to, m'lady.'

Lady Westholme smiled gratefully. 'Excellent.' She glanced around the room once more. 'Now, George, are you absolutely certain everything's ready?'

'I believe our preparations have been suitably thorough, m'lady.'

'You remembered to order the wine?'

'Four cases of Hinter Valley Soh-Vignon, direct from the region itself, m'lady.'

'Has it arrived yet?'

'Even now, m'lady, it chills below.'

'You mean it's already in the cellar?'

'Precisely, m'lady.'

'And the decanters? Did you fill them all up?'

'To the brim, m'lady. And there are extra bottles in the larder, should Modom require them.'

'Excellent, George. You really are a marvel, you know.'

George gave a slight bow, and allowed himself the merest suggestion of a smile.

'Oh, George, I can't wait, I really can't!'

'I too, m'lady, am trembling with anticipation.'

Lady Westholme, as usual, failed to catch the facetiousness.

'If I might be so bold, m'lady,' George went on, 'it may be of some help to the er, staff, were we to be appraised, temporally speaking that is, of the event's actual occurrence.'

'You mean, when is it?'

'Quite so, m'lady.'

'Well George, I'm afraid I can't give you an exact date just yet. But I'll inform you just as soon as I get confirmation.'

'I see, m'lady. Just so.' George paused for exactly

the appropriate number of seconds. 'Will there be any-thing else, m'lady?'

'No, I don't think so, George. I'll take tee in the drawing room at five.'

'Very good, m'lady.'

George withdrew silently, giving the unnerving impression – like all good butlers throughout the universe – that he had simply dematerialized. Lady Westholme surveyed the room once more, on her face a look of childlike glee, which made her appear considerably younger than her fifty-five years. Lady Westholme had never been a beautiful woman, but sensitive features and an indomitable enthusiasm for life (and dinner parties) had always lent her a certain fey attractiveness. Lord Westholme had certainly been swept off his feet by the twenty-five-year-old Hortensia (although he was now so irredeemably saturated in pink gin that frequently he failed even to recognize her).

This was going to be the social event, not just of the year, but of the decade. It would be the talk of Linniker Falls for months to come. Ariadne Gold-blatt, that pretentious stuck-up battle-axe who lived on the other side of town, would be simply green with envy – all the more so since she hadn't been invited.

Lady Westholme sighed happily, brushed a speck of dust from the table top and retired to the drawing room to await tee.

Geoffrey Archer consulted his watch.

'What's the longest bridge in the world?' he asked it.

'The Verizani-Narrow Bridge over New Fork Harbour, eastern Western Aisles,' the watch told him.
'Why?'

'I just wondered. Someone asked me the other day, and I didn't know.'

'Well you know now,' said the watch rather petulantly, and its little silver lid snapped shut. Geoffrey sighed, and continued to trudge up the dusty track which led to the ramshackle wooden construction he called Norris. (He had tried calling it 'home' for a while, but somehow it didn't seem to suit it.) He had another mile and a half of barren, sandy, windswept terrain to pass through before he got there, and not for the first time he began to wonder if building a house in the middle of nowhere five miles from the nearest town had been a good idea. It had certainly seemed like it at the time. Peace, quiet and tranquillity; somewhere out of the way, where he could pursue his lucrative hobby of hamster shaving undisturbed. He also needed somewhere with a good supply of wild hamsters, of course, and out here on the Mirium Stoppaard Sand Plains they were in positive abundance. In fact, so profuse were the pesky little beggars that when they were on the move, their sandy colouring almost made it look as if the Plains themselves were alive. What a sight it was, a whole herd of wild hamster roving the Plains in search of dried sweetcorn. And there was plenty of that around, too, although exactly where it came from had always been something of a mystery to Geoffrey.

Still, living on the Sand Plains did have certain advantages. For instance, one never encountered problems caused by unpredictable weather, because the weather on the Plains was, well, utterly predictable. On Mondays and Tuesdays it was windy, on Wednesdays there was a sandstorm and for the rest of the week it was completely still and quite sunny (apart from every third Sunday, when from 2.00pm till 3.00pm it snowed). It was also a reasonably safe area in which to live, because it was so barren and bleak and downright boring that very few people ever bothered to visit the place, and those who did rarely stayed any longer than the time it takes to urinate behind a handy rock. (The handy rock in question had, over a period of several hundred years, turned a rather odd shade of green.)

Thus pondering the pros and cons of house-building on the Sand Plains, Geoffrey continued to trudge along the track. 'Only another half hour now,' he said to himself, 'then Norris sweet Norris.'

There was a noise like that of a marshmallow being plucked from a child's mouth, followed by a barely audible 'slap', and the air seemed to shift uncomfortably in its shoes. For a brief moment, Geoffrey thought he caught a glimpse of a tree-lined street full of peculiar red brick houses, and suddenly there was a tall skinny man with long sandy hair and a distinctive nose standing on the path in front of him. For some reason Geoffrey couldn't quite pinpoint, he looked as if he'd just been to the toilet.

*

The Guddohl Boys were in their usual place – although to describe it as their 'usual' place is perhaps something of an understatement. The fact is, the three old men had been sitting on the veranda outside Ma Rainor's Winged Horse Saloon for as long as anyone could remember, and the oldest inhabitant of the town was 107. Indeed, no one had ever seen them anywhere other than in those three wicker chairs outside the saloon, an unsettling sort of fact and one which puzzled a good many of the town's part-time philosophers. The Boys would be sitting there at six o'clock in the morning as the first of the local polythene miners trudged past on their way to work, and they would be sitting there at three o'clock the following morning as the last of the town's late night revellers made their loud and unsteady way home. Several curious townsfolk had even crept past at various times between the hours of 3 a.m. and 6 a.m., 'just to check', and had only been partially surprised to see the three old men ensconced in their creaking chairs, chewing tobacco and sipping never-ending glasses of Bud Wiser's Pale Ale. The Guddohl Boys were as much a part of the town as the iron water pump in the main square, and if anyone ever felt the urge to jump up and down and scream at them or ask them how they managed to survive since they never appeared to eat, no one ever did.

Ned, Heck and Walt chewed thoughtfully on their tobacco. Heck puckered and swilled and spat out a thick jet of dark brown saliva, which arced majestically over the rail of the veranda and landed in the yellow dust of the main street. A young woman in a long white skirt side-stepped gingerly to avoid it. Heck raised his greasy cap slightly and said simply 'Marm,' by way of an apology. The young woman smiled nervously and hurried on. Ned took a swig of his beer then sat back and belched, his wicker chair creaking alarmingly beneath him.

'Fine weather,' he said, to no one in particular.

Walt nodded. 'Ayup.'

There followed five minutes of silence, broken only by the sound of chewing and the occasional slurping of Bud (as Wiser's Ale was affectionately known).

Eventually Ned said, 'Warm.'

Heck and Walt considered the word for some moments, weighing it judiciously in their minds, fondling it with curiosity and finally turning it over to see what it looked like underneath.

'Ayup,' said Walt at last, and Heck nodded.

Walt looked up at the sky. He looked to the right, then to the left, and finally he looked at the large black cat that was curled up in the corner of the veranda. 'Sunny, too,' he said.

Heck and Ned looked up at the sky. They looked to the right, then to the left, and finally they looked at the large black cat that was curled up in the corner of the veranda. 'Ayup,' they said in unison.

There followed another five minutes' silence, which was eventually broken by a noise like that of a marshmallow being plucked from a child's mouth. There was a barely audible 'slap', and the air seemed to shift uncomfortably in its shoes. As one, the Guddohl Boys glanced down uneasily at their beers, but none had spilled. When they looked up again, they were somewhat surprised to see a girl dressed all in black standing in the street in front of them. For some reason they couldn't quite pinpoint, she looked as if she'd just finished dressing.

Heck ejaculated another luscious gob of burnt sienna spit. 'Now where'd she come from?' he wondered.

Walt considered the question carefully from several different angles, none of which proved entirely satisfactory. He postulated and theorized, calculated and hypothesized, bringing into play his considerable knowledge of human nature and the vagaries of the universe. Finally, after several minutes of in-depth surmise and serious chewing, he reached his conclusion.

'Dunno,' he said.

'Waren't thare minnidag'o,' Ned observed.

Heck shook his head slowly, dislodging several cobwebs. 'Safact.'

The three men gazed at the young woman silently, the nicotine-yellowed cogs of their ancient minds turning slowly in a lubricating sea of Pale Ale. Heck spat absent-mindedly, treating the black cat to a rude and somewhat unpleasant awakening.

'Nice legs, though,' he said, eliciting a bout of vigorous nodding and a chorus of 'Ayup, yesiree bob,' from Walt and Ned.

The three men watched as the young woman gazed

around in a state of obvious shock. Her face, at first just ghostly, turned a whiter shade of pale.

'Tell you what though,' Walt said, nodding sagely and just in thyme, 'I reckon she's 'bout to faint.'

There followed a soft 'follathrepp' as the young woman collapsed onto the dirt road, causing a small cloud of dust to gather round her in surprise.

Heck spat again. 'I reckon yore 'bout right, Walt,' he said, and the three men sipped thoughtfully at their Buds.

2

The small blue planet known as Earth has a limited – albeit varied – frame of reference. The reason for this is that the planet's physical laws have been strangulated by Man's innate dogmatism to such an extent, that they have finally given up the ghost and decided to remain – for the most part – logical. In other words, if the scientists say it could never happen, it tends not to. Consequently, truly incredible occurrences are something of a rarity on Earth – not because they aren't physically possible, but because Man refuses to *believe* that they are possible. Hence, any attempt to describe the sensation of stepping out of one's bathroom to find that the rest of one's house has completely disappeared, will inevitably be hampered by a severe lack of things with which to compare it.

Possibly the best analogy, therefore, is that of imbibing a prodigious quantity of Nepalese Black, then having your ears syringed whilst spinning rapidly on a children's roundabout. It is an experience which positively uproots the mind and kicks it viciously across the cerebral field, where it rolls beneath a hedgerow and lies dazed for several seconds. Footballs no doubt feel much like this a lot of the time.

When Reg stepped out of his toilet to find himself standing on a dusty track in the middle of a vast barren wilderness, his initial inclination was to scream. This proved impossible, however, owing to the fact that at that moment his mind was still languishing under a hedgerow somewhere. Following quickly on the heels of the urge to scream, came the urge to dart back into his toilet. This also proved impossible, because as soon as the toilet door clicked shut, what had for a brief moment been a two-way hole in the wall of the Universal Mainframe closed up with an audible 'slap', and Reg's toilet dutifully buggered off back to its own dimension. His third reaction was to wonder just exactly when he had gone mad, because he really hadn't noticed it happen.

*　　*　　*

As Reg's mind sidled gingerly back into his head, bruised and scratched from its run-in with the hedgerow, he became aware of a figure standing a few yards away from him on the dusty track. It was that of a man, quite tall and thin, with long dark hair and a short beard. He was wearing knickerbockers and a badly frayed tweed jacket, and had a large canvas bag slung over one shoulder. He also appeared to be as surprised to see Reg as Reg was to see him.

The man peered hard at Reg, blinked and peered again, then turned slowly full circle, carefully scrutinizing the barren landscape around them. Finally, he came to a stop facing Reg again.

'Where the fick did you come from?' he asked.

Reg racked his ragged brain. 'I erm, I, I was, I'm er, I'm not sure.'

'What d'you mean, you're not sure?'

'I mean . . . I'm not sure.'

The man regarded him suspiciously. 'You're not a hamster poacher are you?'

'I'm sorry, a what?'

'Hamster poacher. We got a lot of 'em round here this time of year.'

'Oh. I mean, no. I mean, I'm the manager of a bookshop.'

'Bookshop?'

'Yes. Hague & Holland's of Dudsbury.'

'Hague & Holland's of Dudsbury,' repeated the man thoughtfully. 'Never heard of it.'

'Oh. Well, it's quite well known in the village.'

'What village is that then?'

'Dudsbury.'

'Never heard of that, either.'

'But that's where we are. I mean, well, that's where, erm . . . I . . . utth . . .'

The sentence wound down like a neglected gramophone.

A sandy coloured hamster trotted past, its pouches stuffed with dried sweetcorn, and Reg began to feel faint.

'You okay, mister?' the man asked doubtfully. 'Only you don't look so well.'

Reg shook his head and took a deep breath. He focused on the stranger and attempted to summon what was left of his composure (which didn't amount to much, since Reg had never possessed a great deal of the stuff in the first place).

'Where the hell am I, anyway?'

'In the middle of the Mirium Stoppaard Sand Plains,' the man explained helpfully, ''bout five miles from Bogwater Creek.'

Reg nodded slowly, and an almost visible air of resignation settled over him like a personal rain cloud. 'Yes,' he said, speaking mainly to himself, 'it's just as I suspected. I appear to have gone completely off my trolley.'

'Ah, so you came by trolley did you? Well I'll tell you what, why don't you come back to my house and you can tell me all about it over a nice cup of tee?'

Jeannette was vaguely aware of low voices somewhere close by, but her bed felt so wonderfully soft and comfortable that she tried to ignore them and go back to sleep. This fervent somnolence was also fuelled by the fact that she appeared to be suffering from a humdinger of a hangover, which was a little curious since she hadn't had a drink for over a week. And what a peculiar dream she'd just had. Something to do with
voices?
stepping out of her bedroom and finding herself
she shouldn't be hearing voices
in the middle of a street
she lived alone
in a funny looking town . . .

She opened her eyes and sat bolt upright simultaneously. Two bizarrely dressed women standing a few feet from the bed stopped whispering to each other and turned towards her.

'Ah, you're awake, honey,' said one of them. 'How you feelin'?'

Jeannette gazed around in cold, creeping panic. This was not her bedroom. Indeed, this was not the bedroom of anyone with whom she had the remotest acquaintance. The walls were papered with deep red and gold Victorian flock, and two remarkably genuine looking oil lamps lent the room a warm, sensuous glow. The bed in which she found herself was iron and brass, beautifully ornate and probably worth a fortune.

'Where, where, where, where . . .?'

'Where are you?' the older woman prompted helpfully.

'Yes.'

'Mother Tracy's.'

Jeannette's face, already pale with shock, became so blank you could have written on it.

'Who's Mother Tracy?'

The older woman smiled bemusedly.

'Well, that's me,' she said, and the girl standing next to her nodded helpfully.

'But I mean, I mean . . . where actually am I?'

'You mean, what town are you in?'

'Well, yes, I suppose so.'

'Why, Bogwater Creek, of course.'

'Ah. Of course. Bogwater Creek.'

Jeannette's head swam and she began to sway alarmingly. Quick as a flash, Mother Tracy darted forward and stuffed a bottle of evil smelling liquid under her nose. Jeannette's eyes immediately abandoned all attempts to look glazed, and a good deal of the colour returned to her face. (It hadn't been having a particularly good time wherever it had been, and it supposed it might just as well be in Jeannette's cheeks as anywhere else.)

Mother Tracy stood back and smiled. 'Better now, hon?'

Jeannette nodded and wondered what the hell was in the little bottle.

'What the hell's in the little bottle?' she asked.

'Oh, just a little something Doc Leghorn rustled up for me. Rather good, isn't it?'

'You're not kidding,' agreed Jeannette, her head still buzzing like a workaholic bee, 'you'd pay a fortune for stuff like that in Soho.'

'Yes, well, you must rest now,' instructed Mother Tracy, gently forcing Jeannette back onto the pillow and pulling the blankets up around her. 'You were obviously overcome by the heat – not used to it I suppose – but we'll bring you up some food in a little while and you'll be right as rain in no time.'

Jeannette settled back against the pillow and took a deep breath. Despite the almost hallucinogenic effects of the 'smelling salts', she still felt rather weak and vague. Perhaps this lunatic in the Victorian frock was right, and a little rest and sustenance was all she needed. But damn it all, where the hell was she?'

'Erm, by the way,' she ventured, 'how did I actually get here?'

'Oh, well, no one actually saw you arrive, but we assumed you came by trolley.'

'Trolley?'

'Yes. The service is pretty good now, though it's a little irregular on Sundays. We get the wrong kind of snow here apparently, and they tend to get stuck on the Sand Plains.'

Jeannette tried not to look gormless, though it wasn't easy. 'Oh. Yes, I see.'

'Now you just lie back and relax, and we'll rustle you up some nourishing vittles.'

Geoffrey Archer wore an expression of polite disbelief, tinged with the kind of faintly nervous look one might adopt should the man sitting next to you on the bus suddenly start to hum under his breath.

'So you come from a place called Dudsbury?' he said.

Reg nodded. 'That's right.'

'Which is near somewhere called Manchester?'

'Yes.'

'And you went to the bathroom and when you came out you found yourself here?'

'Exactly.'

Geoffrey was silent for a few moments, his brow assuming the rippled effect of corrugated asbestos. He glanced at Reg, took a sip of his tee and drummed his fingers thoughtfully on the table top. He peered out of the window, sighed a short sigh and clicked his tongue. Finally he looked at Reg again, his face suffused with suspicion and said:

'Are you a complete nutter, or what?'

Reg sighed. 'Look, I know how it sounds. If someone told *me* that story I'd be thinking exactly the same as you are. But that's what happened. I've no way of proving it and I'll probably never convince you, but it's the truth, and I'd swear to it on my mother's life.'

'You're absolutely sure you're not dreaming?'

'Positive. I pinched myself earlier.'

'What happened?'

'It hurt.'

'Oh. Right.'

Geoffrey peered hard at Reg's long, sincere face, then shook his head. 'Well I suppose I'm just going to have to believe you,' he said at last, and shook his head again. 'Actually,' he went on, 'I remember hearing stories when I was a kid about this kind of thing happening. They say there are holes in the fabric of space and time or whatever, and every now and then people slip through them into other worlds.'

Reg nodded. 'I've read fairy tales where that kind of thing happened, but they were just children's stories, ridiculous fantasies. I mean, I never dreamed it was actually physically possible.'

'Well, if your story's true – and I'm not saying it isn't, because you obviously believe it is, and I'm in no position to prove otherwise – then it would seem that it is.'

'Sorry?'

'Physically possible.'

'Oh. Yes. I suppose it must be.'

Reg gazed out of the window at the barren landscape surrounding the shack, and shook his head slowly. 'So you say this place is called Earth?'

'That's right, Urth.'

'But a different Earth to the one I come from?'

'Well, I like to think I'm pretty hot on geography, but I've never heard of a place called Manchester.'

'What about London?'

'Nope. Although there's supposed to be an island in the Southern Seas called Nodnol.'

'Oh?'

'Yes.'

'Erm, what about it?'

'Good question. Not sure why I mentioned it to be honest.'

Reg was silent and glum for a moment. Then a thought struck him. 'All right then, if we both come from different worlds, how come we both speak the same language?'

'Yes, peculiar that,' admitted Geoffrey. 'Probably something to do with the two worlds actually being the same place, but existing in completely different dimensions.'

'D'you think so?'

'I haven't a clue, but it sounded good, didn't it?'

'Hmm.' Reg frowned. 'The problem now, of course, is how the hell do I get back?'

Geoffrey pursed his lips and sucked in his breath like a mechanic.

'Well now,' he said, 'tricky one that, squire. You're absolutely sure you *want* to go back are you?'

'Well of course I want to go back! I mean, I've got a life there, friends, relations, all that kind of thing. I've just written a book, and if I don't go back it'll never get published.'

'A book, eh? What's it about then?'

'Well, it's a sort of literary social commentary on the foibles of middle class Britain in the 1990s.'

'Yeah? Sounds crap.'

'Oh. Well, I probably didn't give a very good description of it.'

'Sounded concise enough to me.'

'Yes, well, never mind, we're digressing. I still want to know how I'm going to get back.'

'Oh come on, what's the rush? Why don't you stay for a while?'

'What for?'

'What for? Because it's an adventure! I mean, you've fallen through a hole in the wall of space and time and landed in another world! Stick around, have some fun, see the sights . . . maybe meet a few nice Urth girls.'

'Earth girls?'

'Well, whatever. All I'm saying is that this has the makings of the adventure of a lifetime, and all you can do is talk about going home.'

'But home is where my *real* life is.'

'Real, shmeel. Life's life, it doesn't really matter where you live it. I mean, think of the stories you could write when you do get home.'

'But how am I going to *get* home?'

'Ah. Haven't the foggiest, mate.'

'That's what I thought.'

'But if you really do want to get back, I know a man who might be able to help.'

Reg's dejected face brightened hopefully. 'Really? Who? Where?'

'His name's Mahatma Cain. Lives in a cave just the other side of Bogwater Creek.'

'Who is he?'

'Dunno what you'd call him really. Sort of a cross between a wizard and a philosopher. Some say he's got special powers and can see into the future, but *I* heard he got deported from the Silly Aisles for bumping off his brother.'

'How do I find him?'

'Just follow the track straight through town.'

'Right! Great! That's marvellous!'

'Too late now though. It'll be dark in half an hour.'

'That's all right, I don't mind the dark.'

'Oh, the dark's safe enough. It's the things that creep about in it you need to worry about.'

'What things?'

'Don't ask. I'd advise you to stay here the night, then set off early in the morning.'

Reg was itching to make a start then and there,

but Geoffrey's description of the dark being filled with unmentionable creeping 'things' rather tempered his enthusiasm.

'Well, if you think it's safer . . .' he said reluctantly.

'Good. That's settled then. More tee?'

Reg sighed. 'Go on then, I might as well. It's rather nice, actually. What's it made from?'

Geoffrey took a glass jar from a shelf, unscrewed the lid and took out a perfectly ordinary blue golf tee. 'These,' he said, holding up the little piece of plastic.

'Good grief! Where do you get them?'

'Collect them on the Sand Plains. Hevvan knows where they come from, but who cares. Boil 'em up in a pan of water, add a spot of sugar and hey tesco! – free tee.'

'How extraordinary,' said Reg, though he had to admit, the tee really was exceedingly good.

Jeannette was beginning to feel better. She had just eaten a bowl of thick steaming soup accompanied by some delicious home-made bread, and a glass of something which tasted suspiciously like whiskey had raised her spirits considerably.

'Now then,' said Mother Tracy, placing the empty bowl and glass on a silver tray, 'there's a washstand and some eye pencils and suchlike on the dressing table over there. We'll give you fifteen minutes or so to pretty yourself up, then we'll send someone along to see you. All right, dear?'

'Well, yes, but . . .'

'Dandy. Now don't you dawdle. Oh, and by the way, I should leave the spectacles off. Personally I think they're cute, but, well, you know how it is.'

Mother Tracy winked and flashed her a smile, then glided out of the room and closed the door behind her. Jeannette sighed, threw back the covers and climbed out of bed, feeling rather less unsteady than she'd expected. As she approached the mirror on the dressing table she stopped dead and stared. It took her a moment or two to realize that this was indeed her own reflection, for she had never before seen herself in a white bodice trimmed with lace, matching French knickers and white silk stockings, and the effect was rather startling.

'My God,' she thought, 'if this is what these people wear in bed, what do they use for underwear?'

She gazed at her reflection a little longer, fascinated in spite of herself, and even adopted a provocative pose or two. Maybe she ought to wear this kind of thing more often. True, plain cotton underwear was cheap and lasted for ages, but when you got right down to it (not that anyone had for the last three years) it was pretty basic.

Abandoning the mirror with reluctance, she washed her face in cold water, then dried it with a soft fluffy towel which she promptly consigned to the floor. She sat down in front of the dressing table and applied a little powder, eyeliner and lipstick, then leaned back to admire the result.

'I look like a French tart,' she said to herself, and giggled.

Her heart suddenly leapt into her mouth as someone rapped on the bedroom door. She swallowed hard, forcing the recalcitrant organ back to its proper place. She couldn't answer the door dressed like this! Where were her clothes? She leapt up from the chair and began frenziedly pulling out drawers and opening cupboard doors, but could find no trace of her black skirt and pullover. There was another knock, louder this time.

'Just a minute!' she called out.

A long satin dress hanging in the wardrobe provided a flicker of hope, but its fastenings appeared to consist almost entirely of ties, buttons, and hooks and eyes, and it would take at least five minutes to get into.

'Shit!' she hissed.

'I'm coming in, ready or not,' said a reedy male voice, and Jeannette had barely enough time to fling herself into bed and pull the covers up to her chin, before the door creaked open and a small bald head appeared round it. The head was followed by a small bald body in a dark grey suit and waistcoat, which waddled uncertainly into the room. The little man spotted Jeannette hunched up in bed, and a huge cheesy thing broke out on his face, which after a few seconds she managed to identify as a grin.

'Ahaa, there you are!' said the little man, spreading his hands in a gesture of discovery. 'You naughty girl, keeping me waiting like that.'

Jeannette blinked. 'Who are you?'

'Who *am* I? Well now, I really don't think you need to know that, do you?'

'Yes I do,' Jeannette insisted, a note of anger and frustration creeping into her voice. 'I need to know who you are, I need to know exactly where I am, and I need to know how the hell I got here.'

The little man tutted. 'My my, you are a feisty one, aren't you. Now come along, dear, I haven't time to play games today, so let's get on with it, what do you say?'

'Get on with what?'

'Ah, I see, the innocent type, eh? Well, well, no matter. Let's just see what secret delights you're hiding under those covers, shall we?'

A cold sweat broke out on Jeannette's brow as the little man advanced towards the bed, his chubby fingers wiggling in anticipation. He made a grab for the covers and began trying to tug them away, Jeannette tugging equally forcibly in the opposite direction.

'What the hell d'you think you're doing?' she yelled.

'Now come along, dear, less of this silliness. I'm a very busy man you know, and time is money.'

'What are you talking about? Leave me alone!'

'Come, come, child, this is ridiculous,' wheezed the little man, and climbed onto the bed. Jeannette let out a shriek and jumped out of the other side, the covers still clutched tightly around her.

'What on Urth?' shouted the little man, 'Why, this is outrageous! I demand an explanation!'

'*You* demand an explanation?'

'I am one of Mother Tracy's most valued customers! Mark my words, she shall hear of this, and you, young lady, will be out on your ear before you can say Robert Robinson!'

'Customers? Ear? What the hell are you talking about?'

'I'm talking about the fact that when a gentleman visits a young lady at Mother Tracy's establishment, he expects to be greeted with rather more, shall we say enthusiasm, than I have been afforded here today! That's what I'm talking about.'

Jeannette stared and almost dropped the blankets. 'You mean ... you mean ... you mean this is a brothel?'

'Well of course it's a ficking brothel you silly little tart! What did you think it was?'

'Oh my God!' wailed Jeannette. 'When I left my house I was a sculptress, and now all of a sudden I'm a ... a ... a prostitute!'

'Please, my dear girl, such language!'

Jeannette shook her head slowly. 'I don't believe this is happening to me. I must be going mad.'

The little man's expression became puzzled. 'I say,' he said, 'are you, I mean, am I to understand that you were not aware of your, erm, circumstances?'

'Yes you are, I mean, no I wasn't, I mean ...'

'Yes?'

'What I mean is, I have no idea how I got here, and I am definitely not a prostitute.'

'Ah. I see. Well now, that does put rather a different

complexion on the matter. So how, in fact, did you come to find yourself in one of Mother Tracy's bedrooms?'

'That's just it, I don't know! All I remember is walking out of my room at home and finding myself in the middle of a kind of street. I, I think I fainted, and the next thing I remember is waking up here.'

'Indeed, is that so? Well, well. May I enquire whether there is any history of mental disorder in your family by any chance?'

'No!'

'Just so, just so.'

The little man climbed gingerly off the bed and began to edge backwards towards the door.

'Well erm, under the erm, circumstances, I think it might be better if I erm, if I left.'

With surprising agility, the little man swung around, opened the door and flung himself through it, and the sound of footsteps pelting along the carpeted landing could be heard fading into the distance. Jeannette sat down heavily on the bed, close to tears. Her head throbbed with a dull pain as it tried to assimilate the situation in which it found itself. There were really only two possible explanations, she decided. Either she had simply gone completely off her rocker, or somewhere along the line she had opened the wrong door, walked through the wardrobe and landed in Narnia. So where was Aslan when you needed him?

She was startled out of her contemplation by the

sound of the door bursting open, and the rapid influx of Mother Tracy.

'What's the meaning of this?' she demanded. 'I've just had Mr Hatters-Lee (who for your information is one of Bogwater Creek's most respected citizens) rushing down the stairs to inform me that one of my girls is stark staring mad!'

Jeannette gazed at her sorrowfully. 'He could be right.'

'What d'you mean, girl? What's the matter with you?'

Jeannette roused herself and tried to summon a modicum of dignity. 'Mrs Tracy,' she said, 'or whatever your name is, it is entirely possible that Mr Whatsisname is correct about my being stark staring mad. The fact is, when I woke up this morning I was Jeannette Higginbottom, of Wishington near Manchester. I got up, had a shower and got dressed with the intention of going out to meet a friend for lunch. When I stepped through my bedroom door, however, I found myself in the middle of a dusty street being stared at by three old men in wicker chairs. I can only assume that at that point I passed out, and the next thing I remember is waking up here.'

Mother Tracy stared. 'So you're not – hang on a minute.' She fumbled around in a pocket of her dress and produced a crumpled piece of paper, which she consulted. 'You're not Lavinia Lafayette of Drudge City then?'

Jeannette shook her head. 'No, I am not.'

'And you weren't sent here by Madam Twoswords of Tivolli Gardens Gentlemen's Club?'

'Definitely not.'

'Ah. Well now. That puts an altogether different colour on things, doesn't it?'

Standing in the middle of the windy street, Jeannette was profoundly thankful that she had at least managed to retrieve her own clothes. Quite apart from the fact that they were considerably warmer than the under-wear would have been, her former attire might well have exacerbated what was already a pretty predicament. Suddenly finding yourself in an alien world apparently populated by lunatics was bad enough, without having to wander through the proceedings dressed like a *Fiesta* centrefold.

She peered up the street towards Ma Rainor's Winged Horse Saloon, and the Guddohl boys stared implacably back at her. It was dusk, and oil lamps flickered in the upstairs windows of the stores on either side of the wide thoroughfare that was Main Street, Bogwater Creek. Now what? She'd been turfed out of Mother Tracy's with a flea in her ear, she didn't know where she was or how she had got there, and she was scared – not so much for her life, as for her sanity. None of this seemed real, but by now she was fairly certain it wasn't a dream. That left madness or Narnia, and no matter how unbelievable the latter, she felt reasonably confident that she hadn't gone crazy over-night. But where *had* she gone?

Whatever explanation transpired to be the truth, she realized she would have to do *something*, and slowly, reluctantly, she began to make her way up the street towards Heck, Ned and Walt.

As she came to a halt in front of them a few moments later, they nodded, and Heck raised his greasy cap.

'Marm,' he said.

Jeannette managed a faltering smile. 'Hello,' she said, 'I wonder if you could help me?'

'Be a pleasure, marm,' Heck informed her. 'What can we do fer yuh?'

'Well, erm, this town is called Bogwater Creek, right?'

'S'right, marm.'

'Okay, well, where is it exactly? I mean, what country is it in?'

'Country?' said Heck, and the three men looked at each other curiously.

Heck turned back to Jeannette and scratched his head. 'Weell, this here's what we call the Western Aisles. Way over yonder 'cross the Big Water is the Eastern Aisles.'

'Upaways is the Northern Aisles,' added Ned helpfully.

'And I suppose down there,' Jeannette guessed, pointing to the ground, 'are the Southern Isles.'

'Nope,' said Heck, 'there ain't no Southern Aisles.'

'Oh.'

'Just water.'

'Though according to legend,' added Walt, 'there's a place called the City of Para d'Ice, right there in the middle of the ocean.'

'It's where Goat lives,' Heck explained, 'assuming He exists, of course.'

Jeannette nodded. 'Of course.'

The three old men were obviously in an advanced state of senility, and Jeannette found herself peering around anxiously in search of someone – anyone – who didn't look as if they'd just escaped from a top security mental institution. The street, however, was deserted. She turned back to Heck.

'Look,' she said, a note of desperation creeping into her voice, 'is there anyone around here who might be able to help me? The thing is, you see, I don't think I . . . *belong* here, and I need to get back to where I came from.'

Heck chewed thoughtfully and stroked his chin. 'Weell,' he said at last, 'judgin' by the way you arrived here, that ain't gonna be easy. Reckon you'd best go talk to old Mahatma.'

'Not Gandhi?'

'No, Cain. Lives in a cave just outsida town. Just keep followin' the track thataway, and you can't miss it.'

'Oh, well thanks. Thanks very much,' said Jeannette, and hauling her bag onto her shoulder, she set off in the direction of the cave of Mahatma Cain.

And so it was that the paths of the only two people on Urth who came from Earth were destined to cross.

3

Jeannette had been walking for about ten minutes – although it seemed much longer – and was becoming a little alarmed at how quickly the light was fading. The houses and stores of Bogwater Creek were now some distance behind her, and the landscape was becoming increasingly barren and unfriendly. It hadn't actually said anything, but its very bleakness was somehow threatening and belligerent. In and among the sparse bushes and misshapen boulders on either side of the track, she could hear unpleasant rustling, scratching sounds, and once or twice (she fancied) some heavy breathing. Whenever she turned to look, of course, there was nothing to be seen and the noises would stop for a few seconds, but as soon as she turned away again they would return, this time louder than before.

Up ahead was a rocky outcrop, oddly shaped and somehow reminiscent of an elephant with Nina Miskov on its back. As she approached it she saw something else – colours, deep rich shades of pink and purple, apparently fluttering in the breeze. It looked for all the world like a wizard's washing line.

'I suppose you think that looks like a wizard's washing line,' said a quiet voice beside her. The shock of this was so powerful that Jeannette actually jumped two feet to the left, and losing her footing on an inconveniently placed rock, landed on her bottom in the dust.

'I'm sorry, did I startle you?' said the voice. Jeannette looked up and discovered that it belonged to an incredibly tall, thin old man, with long grey hair and a straggly grey beard. He was wearing a flowing purple robe and what appeared to be a kind of purple velvet fez, and was carrying a basket filled with tiny objects which looked suspiciously like plastic golf tees. The man's face was narrow, pointed and haggard, but his eyes, which were of the deepest and most beautiful blue Jeannette had ever seen, were somehow kind and reassuring. He held out a bony wizened hand and helped Jeannette to her feet.

'My name's Cain, Mahatma Cain,' he said, and smiled.

'Oh. I'm Jeannette Higginbottom,' Jeannette told him, brushing the dust from the seat of her skirt. 'Actually, I was looking for you.'

Mahatma nodded. 'I suspected your wanderings were not completely without aim. This track is rarely used, save by those wishing to consult Mahatma.'

'Ah. I see.'

'And, of course, people setting out to cross the Sand Plains.'

'Right.'

'And the odd door to door salesman.'

'Aha.'

'Oh, and the polythene miners – they come this way,

too. In fact, come to think of it, it gets fairly busy on the quiet.'

'Yes, well, the thing is, I was told you might be able to help me.'

Mahatma smiled again. 'And so I may. Come, we will go to my cave and discuss your problem over tee.'

Mahatma's dwelling turned out to be more like a small cavern than a cave, and was considerably more comfortable than one might have expected. Beautiful soft rugs covered the cold stone floor and the walls were decorated with ornate mystical tapestries. Intricate mobiles hung from slender silver threads, twisting and turning in the warm glow cast by several oil lamps, and the smell of burning incense made Jeannette feel quite light-headed.

Mahatma boiled a pan of water over a small brick fire and added several of the little plastic golf tees. Jeannette watched in fascination, and was quite astonished when he finally presented her with a cup of something which tasted very much like Earl Grey. They sat down opposite each other on two small embroidered pouffes, and sipped their tee.

'Now then,' said Mahatma, his eyes twinkling like sapphires, 'how may I assist you?'

He sat back in silence, frowning slightly, listening to the tale of Jeannette's abrupt arrival, and her narrow escape from a life of harlotry in Mother Tracy's house of ill repute. When she had finished, Mahatma remained silent for several minutes, and Jeannette fancied she could almost hear the cogs of his unusual mind turning inside his skull.

At last he spoke. 'Well well,' he said.

Jeannette's shoulders sagged. 'You don't believe me, do you?'

'On the contrary, my child, I have no doubt that your story is true.'

'Oh. Well, can you help me then?'

Mahatma sighed. 'Alas, I can do no more than point you in the right direction. I myself do not have the power to send you back from whence you came.'

'What do you mean by the right direction?'

'It is the opposite of the wrong direction. As I have said, I myself cannot send you back, but I know a man who can – if it is at all possible, that is.'

'You mean, I might not *ever* get back?'

'That is an eventuality you must be prepared to deal with.'

'But why? I mean, I *got* here easily enough – just opened the door and poof! here I was. If there's a way here, there must be a way back.'

'You forget, dear girl, it is not through simple time and space you have travelled, but through the dimensions, a different kettle of marine life altogether.'

'Is it? What a nuisance.' Jeannette sipped her tee thoughtfully. 'So who's this man you mentioned?'

'Ah yes. The Omnipotent Roopert of Murdok. The greatest thaumaturgist on Urth. If *he* cannot send you back, then no one can.'

'Did you say Earth?'

'Yes, Urth.'

'But that's where *I* come from.'

'Indeed? But according to your story, that isn't possible. It would mean . . . wait a moment. How is it spelt, this Urth of yours?'

'E, a, r, t, h.'

'Ah, it is as I suspected. Our own is spelt u, r, t, h.'

Jeannette's face fell in disappointment.

'Be of good cheer,' Mahatma told her, 'for this may be to your advantage. It means that dimensionally the two worlds are probably very close, which may make it easier for you to return.'

'Really? Oh, well that's all right then. So how do I find this Roopert of Murdok?'

'You must undertake a journey—'

'Somehow I had a feeling you'd say that.'

'—a long and arduous one. The perils will be many and the hardships great, but it is a journey you have no choice but to make.'

'Okay. When do I start?'

'Patience, my child. You will need provisions, and things to . . . protect you. You must stay here tonight so that I may prepare you, then you will set out after breakfast on the morrow.'

The mention of breakfast triggered a peculiar empty sensation in the pit of Jeannette's stomach.

'By the way,' she said, glancing around, 'I don't suppose you've got anything to eat, have you?'

*

All that evening, Mahatma described in great detail the
perils and possible pitfalls of Jeannette's journey, an
exercise rendered somewhat pointless by that fact that
Jeannette herself fell asleep five minutes into the mono-
logue. For all his special powers and inward vision
Mahatma appeared to be singularly unobservant, and
failed completely to notice Jeannette's inattentiveness
even when she started snoring.

When at last he stopped speaking, late into the
night, Jeannette was awoken by the unaccustomed
silence.

'Oh,' she said, rubbing her eyes, 'erm, is that it,
then?'

'Yes,' replied Mahatma gravely, 'you are prepared.
Now you must sleep, for tomorrow will be a long day.

'Righty ho,' said Jeannette, and promptly dozed off
again.

The next morning, Jeannette found herself being tugged
gently from slumber's soft embrace by a pleasant musi-
cal tinkling sound. For the first few seconds she was
completely disorientated, and then she saw a beautifully engraved glass mobile glinting in the sunlight that
was pouring in at the entrance of the cave, and remembered. She sat up. Mahatma was busy poking about in
a pan over his little brick fire, and the mouth-watering
aroma of fried something or other wafted into her
nostrils.

'Good morning,' said Mahatma, without turning. 'I
trust your repose was satisfactory.'

'Oh, absolutely,' Jeannette assured him, rubbing her eyes and stretching. 'I slept like a log.'

'But logs do not sleep.'

'Oh, don't they?'

'Certainly not. Granted, they rest much of the time, but they are constantly sentient, I assure you.'

'Oh, well, I must remember never to insult one,' quipped Jeannette.

'Yes, you must,' said the old man seriously. Jeannette managed to resist the temptation to enquire whether the old coot was taking the piss, and instead asked him what he was cooking.

'Sand Snake,' Mahatma told her.

'Oh,' she said, her enthusiasm knowing many bounds, 'that sounds nice.'

In the event, Sand Snake turned out to be rather delicious, fried – as it was – with a peculiar variety of blue onion which Mahatma had picked fresh from his allotment that very morning.

As they were finishing their meal, they were startled by the unexpected appearance of a stranger at the cave entrance. He was wearing a pair of faded jeans, a white tee-shirt and a mustard coloured corduroy jacket, and (thought Jeannette) in an odd, lanky, dishevelled sort of way, was rather handsome.

'Oh. Sorry,' said the stranger, 'I'm not interrupting your meal, am I?'

'Not at all,' replied Mahatma. 'Please, come in. You are welcome.'

'Ah, thanks very much.'

The man strode cheerfully into the cave and extended his hand.

'The name's Reg. Reg Bethel. I'm looking for a chap named Mahatma Cain.'

Jeannette turned to Mahatma. 'That's you,' she said.

The old man nodded solemnly. 'You have learned much during your time here.'

'Ah, so *you're* Mr Cain, are you? What jolly good luck.'

'You wished to consult me about something?'

'Well, yes. Bit of a sticky prob really. This is going to sound pretty weird, I can tell you that now, but the fact is, I'm not from this world. As far as I can gather I've fallen through a hole in the wall of the universe and landed in another dimension – or something – and I've been told you might be able to help me get back.'

'Two of you! Why, this is most unusual.'

Mahatma stroked his beard thoughtfully and strands of it came away in his hand. Jeannette stared agog at Reg.

'Are you saying that you're from Earth?' she asked.

Reg nodded. 'Yes, but not this Earth. I come from a place called Dudsbury, near Manchester.'

'I don't believe it!' Jeannette cried. 'I'm from Wishington!'

'Good grief! How did you get here?'

'I walked out of my bedroom yesterday and just sort of . . . landed here.'

'My God! That's exactly what happened to me!

Only it wasn't my bedroom, it was – well anyway, that's what happened.'

'This is most peculiar,' Mahatma said, his beard becoming sparser by the minute. 'These things do happen, but they are rare, very rare. Never before have I heard of two Charring Crossers arriving at the same time.'

'Charring Crossers?' queried Reg.

'The man who first identified the phenomenon of inter-dimensional travel was called Nobby Charring,' explained Mahatma. 'Consequently, when one passes from one dimension into another, one is referred to as having made the Charring Crossing.'

'Oh.'

Mahatma shook his head thoughtfully and continued to pluck his beard. 'Two of you at the same time, this is most unusual. Perhaps the Universal Mainframe is becoming unstable. There hasn't been a nuclear war on your planet has there?'

'Not yet,' Jeannette told him.

'Then there must be instability in the very fabric of the space-time continuum.'

'Perhaps it's frayed,' suggested Reg.

'Perhaps so,' agreed Mahatma. 'It is very old.'

Reg scratched the back of his head. 'I'm beginning to feel like I'm stuck in the middle of a Douglas Adams novel.'

Mahatma suddenly stood up. 'Come, we must prepare for your journey.'

'Oh? Where are we going?' Reg asked.

The old man turned to Jeannette. 'Perhaps you would explain to our friend, whilst I make up your provisions.'

Jeannette looked startled for a moment. 'Oh, right, yes. Erm, yes.'

Mahatma pottered off into the depths of the cave, took two large rucksacks from a selection hanging on the wall, and proceeded to pack them carefully with various necessary items. Reg and Jeannette smiled at each other awkwardly.

'Yes, well,' Jeannette began, 'about this journey. Apparently we've got to find someone called Roopert of Murdok—'

'The *Omnipotent* Roopert of Murdok,' corrected a voice from the back of the cave.

'Yeah, right, Omnipotent. He's supposed to be the greatest what-d'you-ma-call-it—'

'Thaumaturgist!'

'—thaumaturgist in the world.'

'What's a thaumaturgist?' Reg wanted to know.

'A miracle worker,' supplied the voice of Mahatma. 'He is a sorcerer of the highest order.'

Reg and Jeannette looked at each other and grinned.

'So anyway,' Jeannette went on, 'we've got to go off and find this chap, and hopefully, he'll be able to send us back.'

'To Manchester?'

'To Manchester.'

Mahatma appeared abruptly from the shadows. 'Who said anything about Manchester?' he asked.

Reg and Jeannette stared at him.

'What, exactly, do you mean by that?' Reg enquired politely.

'I mean that if it is within his power to send you back – and even that I cannot guarantee – you may not necessarily arrive at the point from which you departed. Dimensionamatics is a highly theoretical science. You might even find yourself back in your own dimension, but at a completely different point in its history.'

'So what you're saying,' said Reg, 'is that this journey to find this Roopert chap is really nothing more than a long shot. And a *bloody* long one at that!'

'It may be bloody, yes,' admitted Mahatma, 'but if you *don't* find him you may *never* get back. At least this way there is a chance.'

'He's right, Mr Bethel,' Jeannette pointed out.

'You can call me Reg.'

'Oh, right, thanks. I'm Jeannette, by the way.'

'Oh, well, pleased to meet you – Jeannette.'

'So whereabouts in Dudsbury—?'

'Children, please!' interrupted Mahatma. 'You will have time to discuss geographical synchronicity on the journey.'

'Sorry,' said Reg and Jeannette simultaneously, and giggled.

Mahatma shuffled off into the depths of the cave and returned with the two rucksacks he had filled, one of which was bright purple and orange, the other a luminous green. Both were made of a substance which looked and felt suspiciously like nylon.

'I say, they're a bit bright aren't they?' observed Reg. 'I expected them to be made of old worn canvas or leather or something.'

'They were once,' said Mahatma mysteriously.

'What about this?' Jeannette asked, indicating the huge black sack which served as her handbag. 'I can't carry both.'

'Empty what you need into the rucksack.'

'Will it all fit?'

'My dear, these are no ordinary rucksacks. Several items of household furniture would fit easily into just one of them, with room to spare for six months' supply of food. The contents of your handbag should not present a problem.'

'Good grief!' exclaimed Reg. 'D'you mean to say they're . . . *magic*?'

'In a way, yes. Frankly, it has more to do with molecular physics than sorcery, but it's a useful trick.'

Jeannette opened the orange rucksack and peered inside, but could see nothing unusual or magical about it. As she emptied the considerable contents of her handbag into it, however, she couldn't help noticing that its shape altered not a jot. She closed the flap and fastened it, then slung it over her shoulder. Reg picked up the green one and weighed it curiously.

'Light as a feather,' he announced.

'But by no means empty, I can assure you,' Mahatma said. He moved over to a delicate twisted leg oak table, and from a collection of mysterious looking odds and ends, selected two small objects.

'It is my hope,' he said gravely, 'that you will not be required to use these, but if occasion should arise, be assured they will serve you well.'

He gave to Reg what looked like a small wooden handle of some kind, brass trimmed and with a tiny brass button on one side. It was solid and heavy, and as Reg turned it over in his hand he felt an odd sensation creeping up his arm, not unlike a mild electric shock, though pleasant rather than painful.

'Press the button,' Mahatma said. Reg did so, then stepped back in alarm as a ten-inch steel blade shot from the end of the handle with an intensely satisfying metallic zing.

'My God, that's lethal!' he exclaimed.

Mahatma smiled. 'Isn't it?'

'But I wouldn't be able to use it. I could never stab another human being.'

Mahatma raised one eyebrow. 'Who said anything about human beings?'

Reg opened his mouth. Words gathered, then appeared to change their minds, and retreated. He closed his mouth again.

'And for you, my dear,' said Mahatma turning to Jeannette, 'a little something which might one day save your lives.'

He placed in her hand a small glass bottle filled with a peculiar green substance which looked like washing-up liquid. It was encased in leather and had a silver cap and a long, thin leather strap, and looked for all the world like a tiny hip flask.

'What is it?' she wanted to know.

'A tiny hip flask,' Mahatma told her.

'But what's in it?'

'Ah. A little concoction of my own. It took me years to develop, and – I don't mind telling you – one or two of the earlier recipes had some rather worrying side effects. (I never did find out what happened to the cat.) But at last I perfected it.'

'Yes, but what is it?'

'I call it Elixir of Shergaah. A tiny drop rubbed into the skin on the back of the hand will immediately render you completely invisible.'

'You're joking!' said Reg.

Mahatma looked puzzled. 'No I'm not.'

'Are you trying to tell me that if we rub this stuff on the back of our hands, we'll become completely invisible?'

'I think that was the gist of the information I was attempting to impart, yes.'

'And you expect us to believe it?'

Mahatma's puzzlement deepened. 'Erm, well, yes.'

Reg opened his mouth, and yet again words failed him. After all, why *would* the old man lie to them? He seemed a decent sort of seer on the whole, albeit a little eccentric. And besides, what choice did they have but to trust him? The alternative might well involve spending the next few years walking through every door on Urth in the hope that one of them would lead back home.

'What the hell!' Reg said at last. 'If I can believe I've fallen through a hole in the wall of the universe and landed in another world, I can believe anything. So how long do we stay invisible?'

'The effects last for around fifteen minutes.'

Jeannette slung the little bottle around her neck, and decided that it made rather a nice ornament.

'What would happen if I *drank* some of this?' she wondered aloud.

'I'm not sure,' Mahatma admitted, 'but I suspect everyone else would become invisible whilst you yourself remained plainly in view.'

'Oh,' said Jeannette, and shrugged.

'Now then,' he went on, leading them to the cave entrance, 'you must leave. I have prepared you as far as I am able. Keep to the track at all times and only stop if you really have to. I have sent out messages, and about five miles from here you will be met by some Plainsfolk friends of mine.'

'Plainsfolk?' said Reg.

'Dwellers of the Plains,' Mahatma explained. 'They have lived there for many generations, and are well acquainted with the sacred places ... and the dangers. They will guide you safely through to New Fork (or the Big Tomato as it is colloquially known). When you reach the city, make your way to the quayside and ask for a man named Ty Tanyick. He has his own boat and will take you across to Le Half on the Eastern Aisles.'

'That's all we need,' muttered Reg, 'a captain called Titanic.'

As they stepped out into the sunlight Mahatma handed a piece of paper to Jeannette. 'This is the Omnipotent Roopert's address. When you get to Le Half you must ask for directions – but be careful, for the Eastern Aislanders can be a wild and uncivilized people.'

Mahatma turned to Reg and grasped him firmly by the hand. 'Farewell, my friend,' he said, 'and good luck. May your journey be fruitful and without incident.'

'Oh, er, thanks. Thanks a lot.'

Turning to Jeannette, Mahatma clasped her by the shoulders.

'Farewell, my sweet Jeannette. I pray that Goat will favour you with safe passage.'

'Thanks ever so much, Mahatma, you've been brilliant.' She stood on tiptoe and planted a noisy kiss on the old man's bony cheek, and he blushed.

'It has been an unexpected honour to meet two people from another dimension,' he told them. 'May you both live long and prosper.'

With a final sad smile, he turned and disappeared back into his cave. Reg and Jeannette looked at each other.

Reg shrugged. 'Oh well,' he said, 'I suppose we'd better get started.'

'Yes,' Jeannette agreed, 'I suppose we had.'

With a last, wistful glance at the cave entrance, the two reluctant adventurers hitched their rucksacks into position, and set out on the most important journey of their lives.

* * *

Mad Rolf Hilter paced the length of his private study in a state of considerable agitation, pausing only briefly to gaze through the huge picture window which looked out over Birchingley Gardens. He turned and paced the other way, his pale skin glistening under a sheen of cold sweat and strands of black hair hanging lank and greasy over one eye. His hands were clasped behind his back, and he stared intently at the floor as if expecting to receive inspiration from the expensive oriental carpet that covered it. The large and rather pallid looking man who had for the last half hour been sitting in one of the carved wooden chairs at the side of the room, looked on apprehensively.

'Weapons!' exploded Rolf, suddenly turning on his one-man audience. 'I need weapons, Herman, do you understand? How can I fight a war if I don't have weapons?'

'I understand, Mine Fury, I—'

'I am Rolf Hilter, the greatest leader since Panoleon of Nance! Had it not been for Barber Osser and that ridiculous haircut he gave me, I would now be ruler of all of Ruh Shah!'

'In all fairness, Mine Fury, how was the barber to know that you would catch cold on the journey home?'

'Pah! The man was an imbecile! I ask for a trim and he gives me a short back and sides! What did he expect?'

'Probably not disembowelment,' muttered Herman under his breath.

'I am a warlord, Herman! All I require are a hundred thousand rifles or so, perhaps a little heavy artillery, some tanks maybe – and armoured cars, I must have armoured cars, I like armoured cars – and possibly a thermo-nuclear device or two. Is that too much to ask, Herman?'

'No, Mine Fury, of course not, but you must understand, the world powers have made it impossible. The penalty for doing business with you is not just death, but death by de-genitalization. There isn't an arms dealer on Urth prepared to take the risk.'

'But there must be! Are you sure you've tried them all?'

'Quite sure, Mine Fury. Even the Bastrads of Bloody-ville turned me down flat, and during the Four Hours War they even sold arms to their *enemy*. Mind you, that's why they lost.'

'This is intolerable!' Rolf declared. 'Here am I, Rolf Hilter, The Fury, leader of the most superbly trained army on the planet, and all I have to send them into battle with are pieces of wood shaped like guns!'

'I'm sorry, Mine Fury, but what can I do? I cannot

force the dealers to trade with you.'

'Why not?'

'Well, I mean, what would I threaten them with?'

'With, with, with . . .' Hilter's shoulders sagged. 'With pieces of wood,' he finished lamely.

'Precisely, Mine Fury. We are caught between a rock and a hard place, as the Northern Aislanders say.'

At that moment there was a tentative knock on the door.

'Enter!' bellowed Hilter, and a tall, thin, bird-like man insinuated his way into the room and gave the Nasti* salute.

'What is it, Gobbles?' demanded Hilter, returning the gesture perfunctorily.

'Mine Fury, I have a message from Professor Von Brown.'

'Von Brown, eh? Has he designed a new gun for me? Or perhaps he's found a way of turning gold into lead?'

'I'm afraid not, Mine Fury.'

'Well, what is it then? Come on, man, spit it out!'

'Well, according to the professor, two people from another world have just made the Charring Crossing.'

Hilter looked puzzled. 'The Charring Crossing? I thought that was a myth.'

'Apparently not, Mine Fury. According to Von Brown, he was investigating the practical possibilities of an inter-dimensional matter bomb, when his instru-

* NAtional unSociable and Terribly Irritable (Party)

ments picked up some unusual readings. He has been studying them for the last few hours, and has reached the conclusion that the only possible cause is the transference of matter from one dimension to another. His calculations indicate that two separate crossings occurred, one after the other, and weight, mass and configuration suggest that the matter in question is human.'

'Humans from another world,' murmured Hilter thoughtfully.

'So it would seem, Mine Fury.'

'Where? Did he say where they came from?'

'Well, apparently it's only a theory, but Von Brown thinks they may be from a world which co-inhabits the same orbit as our own, but within a completely different dimension. Separated only by the thin membrane of reality which comprises the wall of the Universal Mainframe, he says the two worlds would be manifestly different, yet in many ways the same. Mind you, it's possible he's been taking those drugs again.'

Hilter stroked his chin thoughtfully. 'Two separate worlds, different, and yet in many ways the same.'

Gobbles nodded. 'That would seem to be the gist of it.'

'Then they must have weapons on this other world!'

'Well, yes, I suppose . . .'

'Of course they must! If they're humans they have wars, and if they have wars, they must have weapons!'

'That seems logical, yes . . .'

'And on another world there would be no international agreements banning the sale of arms to Rolf Hilter!'

'Well, no, but . . .'

'And consequently no limit to the number of weapons I could buy!'

'I suppose not, but—'

'What, what? But what?'

'Well, I mean, how would you get there?'

Hilter smiled maniacally. 'Why, the same way *they* got *here*, of course.'

Herman and Gobbles glanced at each other briefly, their eyebrows raised. The idea was, after all, logical enough. The two Charring Crossers had obviously found a way through, and in theory, if you could go one way, you could go the other way, too.

Gobbles turned to his leader and smiled. 'Once again, Mine Fury, your genius has shown itself.'

Herman nodded with forced enthusiasm. 'An arms deal with another world. It's brilliant! I love it!'

Hilter grinned triumphantly, and his left eye twitched.

'All we need to do now,' he said calmly, 'is discover exactly how these humans from another dimension got themselves here.'

Gobbles grinned. 'I think, Mine Fury,' he said slyly, 'that we need to speak to these two Charring Crossers.'

Hilter returned the smile, imbuing it with an added dimension of nastiness. 'I think, my dear Gobbles, that you are absolutely right. And if they won't talk, we'll torture them. Hell, we'll torture them anyway. Inform my chief of secret police that I wish to see him. Now!'

'You mean . . .?'

'Ssh! Remember, walls have noses. Let us just call him "the man in the black hat".'

'Very well, Mine Fury, but—'

'His methods are crude, Gobbles, I know, but he has the knack of inducing people to do things they would normally never dream of doing. To find the Charring Crossers he will need information, and if anyone can squeeze the truth out of people, *he* can.'

'As you wish, Mine Fury.'

Gobbles clicked his heels and snapped his arm forward in a smart salute, then turned and strode out of the room.

Hilter turned to Herman, his face green with avarice. 'At last,' he said softly, 'we shall have our weapons. And who knows what methods of mass destruction these humans from another world have devised? Yes, Herman; finally the Urth will know what it means to cross swords with Mad – I mean, with the great Rolf Hilter.'

He paused, his eyes glazing over dreamily.

'It will be total war, Herman,' he went on, his voice rising gradually in volume and pitch. 'Our armies will roll back the map of Urth like an old worn out carpet, trampling our enemies under foot, burning bridges, bombing buildings, annihilating every beast and barnyard animal, slashing, smashing, raping, pillaging—!'

He stopped, foam dribbling from the corners of his mouth.

'But justly and humanely, of course,' he added calmly. 'We wouldn't want the rest of the world to get the wrong idea about the Nasti Party, now would we?'

'Of course not, Mine Fury,' agreed Herman, 'and if anyone asks me, I shall just say I was following orders.'

'Quite right,' said Hilter, 'you were just – *what?*'

'Nothing, Mine Fury, just clearing my throat.'

4

Reg and Jeannette had been striding out briskly for around an hour and a half, exchanging amiable smalltalk and attempting to get to know each other, when they spotted a little group of people on the track up ahead.

'Aha,' said Reg, 'the Plainsfolk, I presume.'

'I hope so,' Jeannette muttered, fingering the tiny bottle around her neck.

In the distance they counted five people, all quite small in stature and rather unusually dressed. At first they thought they were children, but as they grew closer it became apparent that these were in fact the full grown variety of what was obviously a decidedly diminutive species. The other thing that became apparent as the distance between them lessened, was that the Plainsfolk were made of leather.

As Reg and Jeannette approached, one of the little group broke away and came towards them, a buckskin-like hand raised in greeting. Like the others, he wore a pale blue denim smock and what appeared to be denim shoes, and had the kind of thick long blonde hair that has shampoo advertising executives drooling into their Aqua Libra. His skin, which was the texture of a well-used wallet, was a deep chestnut brown, his eyes a vivid and startling green. In an odd, rugged, sinewy kind of way, thought Jeannette, he was rather attractive.* The only visible differentiation between male and female that Reg could detect, was the configuration of a number of little bumps under their smocks, which more or less corresponded to the position of human sexual appendages.

'Greetings,' said the Plainsman, in a voice like Louis Armstrong. 'We are friends of Mahatma. You are the two Charring Crossers he spoke of?'

'Er, yes,' said Reg. 'This is Jeannette, and I'm Reg.'

'Greetings,' said the little man again, 'my name is Morgon Free Man.'

'Ah, pleased to meet you.'

The Plainsman pointed to the others. 'That is Alan Free Man and his three wives, Gwennol, Gwenog and Gwynifor. David Free Man was going to come with us, too,' he explained, 'but he has thirteen wives and, well, you know how it is.'

Reg nodded sympathetically, although he really had no idea how it was at all.

'Are you *all* called Freeman?' asked Jeannette.

'Yes,' Morgan told her. 'The title was bestowed on us many years ago by the great chieftain, Nelson Free Man Dayla.'

Jeannette nodded and raised one eyebrow. 'I should've known.'

---

* The reader should not infer from this that Jeannette was the kind of girl who fancied anything in trousers – the Plainsfolk didn't wear trousers.

'I am led to believe it is the Omnipotent Roopert of Murdok you seek,' said Morgon.

'That's right,' Reg told him, 'but apparently we have to catch a ship first.'

'That is so. The Omnipotent Roopert resides in the Eastern Aisles across the Big Water. We will guide you as far as the outskirts of New Fork, but then we must leave you.

'Oh? Can't you take us to the docks?'

'Alas, we cannot enter the Big Tomato. We were banished to the Plains when the flesh settlers came three hundred years ago, and now we are outcasts. Occasionally bands of rednecks ride out from the city and try to hunt us down, but we have grown cunning and know the Plains too well.'

'The city folk don't sound a very pleasant lot,' Reg observed.

'They are like city dwellers everywhere,' Morgon said. 'Some are decent, some are wakners.' The little man shrugged philosophically. 'Such is life.'

The other Plainsfolk gathered round, smiling and eyeing Reg and Jeannette with friendly curiosity. It was obvious that they had never seen people from another dimension before and they were anxious to get a good look – it would make a fine story for the little leather grandchildren in years to come.

'We must leave this place now,' said Morgon. 'We have far to go before nightfall if we are to make camp at Bedrock.'

'Bedrock?' queried Reg. 'Don't tell me the Flint-stones live there.'

'No one lives in Bedrock. That is why we maké camp there. The Cave of Yabadoo will provide good shelter and protection.'

'Protection against what?'

'The night creatures, of course.'

'What exactly are these night creatures?' Reg wanted to know.

'Don't ask,' Morgon told him.

For the rest of that afternoon they trekked across the dusty wilderness under a cloudless deep blue sky, the vast quiet punctuated only by the interminable chatter of Reg and Jeannette. The Sand Plains stretched into the distance on every side, seemingly endless and devoid of any sign of life or vegetation. The Plainsfolk, nevertheless, seemed nervous and apprehensive, their little leather heads swivelling this way and that, their vivid green eyes constantly scanning the horizon for signs of ... well, whatever it was they were scanning the horizon for signs of. The wind, though not particularly strong, was ever present, and became a little irritating after a while. Finally, as dusk approached and fatigue and hunger began to set in, even Reg and Jeannette fell silent.

As they trudged along, accelerating occasionally to keep up with the Plainsfolk, Reg began to think about his book. It had been a part of his everyday existence for so long now that he actually found himself pining for it, as a parrot might pine for the fiords. If he didn't get back, all the blood, sweat and tears would have been for nothing – and he needn't have spent all that money on word processor disks and printer ribbons.

Unless this Roopert of Murdok could pull off the stunt of the century, he supposed he would have to get used to the idea of making a new life for himself here on Urth. He only hoped that when his disappearance was noted, someone would discover the rough draft of his manuscript and decide to publish it posthumously (or whatever the word was for publishing a book by someone who has ceased to exist in a particular dimension, but is not actually dead).

He sighed, and wiped a bead of sweat from his brow.

Jeannette plodded on in silence beside him. She would have given anything for a shower and a change of clothes. Even a quick wash and a clean pair of knickers would have been nice. She felt as if she had sand everywhere; her skin itched and her hair was full of it, and there was even sand in her mouth. She was suddenly reminded of her childhood, and the unpleasant experience of eating egg and sand butties on Bridlington beach. She thought of her father, and how he'd taken her fishing with a length of orange nylon wrapped around a wooden frame, and how they'd hooked something heavy and her father had told her it was a whale. She'd believed him, too, but she'd been credulous as hell even back then.

She supposed he'd always wanted a boy really –

that would certainly account for the football kit she'd received on her tenth birthday and the short back and sides she'd been forced to endure until she was fourteen. The haircut hadn't been so bad when she was younger, but as soon as she hit puberty and those two little bumps turned into magnificent ivory globes almost overnight, it began to look a little incongruous to say the least. She supposed that was why she'd worn it long ever since. Now if only she could get this damned sand out of it. . . .

Suddenly the Plainsfolk stopped, and Reg and Jeannette awoke from their contemplation to discover a large stone mass in front of them, which looked a little like a miniature version of Ayers Rock. The stone itself was a deep autumnal red, and over thousands of years, what amounted to constant sand blasting had created wondrous Henry Mooresque sculptures on its surface.

'It's beautiful,' breathed Jeannette, her artistic eye appreciative of the smooth contours and pleasing shapes which nature had seen fit to bestow. 'I can't believe something so perfect happened by chance.'

'Not completely by chance,' Morgon corrected her. 'The wind has a mind of its own; even in your own world, you must have noticed that.'

'I must say,' Reg admitted, 'it does seem to know when I've just had my hair cut and styled.'

'The rock was once a place of worship,' Morgon explained, 'but was abandoned when the flesh settlers came.'

'Why was that?' Reg asked.

Morgon's green eyes grew sad. 'Because they knew where to find us, and so it became too dangerous. It is used only rarely now, on occasions such as this.'

'So this is where the cave is?'

'This is Bedrock, yes. It will be dark shortly. We will make camp here for the night.'

Morgon led them around the side of the mountain-ette and in between a series of smaller stones, to where a crude flight of steps had been hewn into the rock face. These they negotiated carefully, and only when they reached the top did Reg notice a fissure in the rock wall, about two feet wide and five feet high. The little leather Plainsfolk passed through easily enough and Reg and Jeannette followed, crouching slightly because of their height. Inside, the cave opened out into a huge chamber, its ceiling lost in the shadows above them. The walls were decorated with a number of crude but somehow familiar drawings, and dotted about the floor were several large sand-filled denim cushions.

'Oh. It's rather cosy actually,' observed Reg.

Jeannette slipped the rucksack from her shoulders and flopped down on one of the cushions. 'After all that walking I could sleep on a board,' she announced.

Reg unfastened his own rucksack and sat down beside her. 'I must admit,' he admitted, 'I'm pretty shattered myself. I can't remember the last time I walked so far.' He looked around the cave appreciat-ively. 'I'm just glad this place—' He stopped, his eyes riveted to one of the drawings on the cave wall. For a moment he was speechless, as recognition seeped slowly between the creases in his brain. Finally he raised his arm as if in a daze, and pointed. 'That's Fred Flintstone!'

Jeannette looked across the cave and gasped. 'My God! You're right!'

Morgon raised an eyebrow. 'You recognise the people in the drawing?'

Reg nodded vigorously. 'Yes, yes, that's Fred Flintstone and the other one's Barney Rubble. They're cartoon characters from our world.'

Morgon shook his head thoughtfully. 'Curious,' he said. 'Here we know them as Frodo and Bilbo. They were thought to belong to the prehistoric tribe who first settled here thousands of years ago.'

Reg was dumbfounded. 'But who, who . . .?'

'Made the drawings?' finished Morgon. 'I cannot say. All we know is that they have been here for several centuries.'

'But the Flintstones were only created a few years ago. So how . . .?'

Morgon shrugged. 'Who knows? Many are believed to have crossed over into our world over the years, and dimensionamatics being what it is, not all have arrived in the era in which they departed.'

Jeannette's bewilderment was almost palpable. 'Sorry?'

'What I mean is, someone may have passed from your world only yesterday, yet arrived in this one five hundred years ago. Travel in the inter-dimensional states is highly unstable with regard to time.'

'So what you're saying,' said Reg, his brain struggling manfully with this recalcitrant concept, 'is that someone from our present may have travelled into your past, somehow ended up in this cave and drawn the pictures of the Flintstones?'

'Can you think of another explanation?'

'Not really,' Reg admitted, 'and come to think of it, that would probably account for the place being called Bedrock.'

Jeannette shook her head slowly. 'Curiouser and curiouser,' she murmured.

'Now then,' said Morgon, sitting down on one of the cushions, 'why don't we all make ourselves comfortable for the night?'

The other Plainsfolk muttered in agreement and arranged themselves on the remaining cushions. Morgon took a small clay pipe, a tobacco pouch and a box of matches from his smock pocket. He filled the pipe, lit it and sat back contentedly.

'Did you bring any provisions?' he asked.

'Oh yes!' remembered Jeannette. 'I think Mahatma packed some for us.' She opened the flap of her rucksack, reached in and pulled out a very ordinary looking Tupperware-type box. Reg opened his own pack and pulled out an identical one.

'I wonder what's in them?' he said, with the air of one who expects much. 'Probably something really exotic like desert lizard kebab, or whatever it is they eat here.'

They flipped open the boxes excitedly, and discovered a selection of what appeared to be exceedingly ordinary white sliced bread sandwiches. Jeannette peeled back the corner of one of them and sniffed.

'What is it?' asked Reg.

'Egg and cress,' Jeannette said, pulling a face. 'I hate egg and cress.'

Reg examined his own sandwiches. 'Yuch! Ham and piccalilli. Can't stand the stuff.'

'Fancy a swop?' suggested Jeannette.

'Done,' agreed Reg. 'I love egg and cress.'

The formalities of the food duly dealt with, Reg and Jeannette ploughed through the sandwiches with gusto, and both agreed they were the best they'd ever tasted. They also found bottles of water and two flasks of piping hot tee, which cleared the dust from their throats in admirable fashion. As he was about to eat his last sandwich, Reg was struck by a sudden thought and a twinge of guilt. He looked over at the little group of Plainsfolk, who smiled back at him pleasantly.

'Erm, did you not bring any erm, provisions of your own, then?' he asked. Jeannette paused guiltily mid-munch.

Morgon smiled. 'We do not carry provisions,' he told them. 'We have a ceremonial feast once a week on Sundays, and that sustains us until the next one.'

'Good heavens!' exclaimed Jeannette. 'Don't you get hungry?'

'A mite peckish by Saturday night perhaps, but otherwise, no.'

'So we can't tempt you with a sandwich then?' said Reg.

'Thank you for the offer, but I'm afraid it would make us throw up. Our staple diet is Sand Snake and the oil of the jeetiex tree.'

'Oh, well, fair enough then,' said Reg, and scoffed the last butty.

The light from the cave entrance faded quickly after that, and sprawled out on the large sand cushions – which turned out to be surprisingly comfortable – Reg and Jeannette were soon drifting off into a deep, restful sleep. The Plainsfolk, whose habit it was to sleep only one night out of every twenty-four, remained awake. Although outwardly relaxed, their sensitive ears were alert to even the tiniest of sounds, and their eyes darted about the darkness like ricocheting bullets.

Then, all of a sudden . . .

. . . it was morning.

The first thing Reg was aware of was a strange, coiled sensation in the muscles of his legs, as if they were clock springs that had been wound too far. The second thing was an unusually painful stiff neck, and the third was Morgon bending over him and shaking him gently by the shoulder. His eyes popped open.

'What is it? What's happened?'

'Morning has happened,' Morgon informed him.

'We must leave soon if we are to make New Fork before nightfall.'

Reg sat up and rubbed his neck, and noticed that the cushion beside him was unoccupied. A pin of fear pricked his heart.

'Where's Jeannette?'

'Outside,' Morgon told him, 'washing in the rock pool.'

'Oh, thank God for that,' Reg said, a little surprised at the intensity of the relief he felt. 'I thought something had happened to her.'

At that moment Jeannette appeared at the cave entrance, looking annoyingly bright-eyed and bushy-tailed.

'Morning, Reg,' she chirped. 'Ready for another stroll in the sun?'

'You're very bright and breezy,' Reg said, clambering painfully to his feet.

'It's that water in the rock pool. Amazing stuff. I've a good mind to bottle some and take it home.'

'I wouldn't waste your time,' advised Reg, still suffering from the early morning grumps. 'We don't even know if we're going to *get* home yet.'

'Well there's no point in being pessimistic, is there?' said Jeannette, and kneeling down, she began to re-pack her rucksack. As she picked up the plastic sandwich box she stopped, and weighed it curiously.

'I'm sure I didn't leave any sandwiches last night,' she said.

Reg shook his head. 'You didn't. Neither did I.'

'But there's something in here.'

'There can't be.'

Jeannette looked at Morgon, who merely spread his hands and shrugged.

Carefully, and a little nervously, she peeled back the lid of the box and peered inside.

'Ooh!' she exclaimed, and her face lit up.

'What is it?' Reg wanted to know.

'Two slices of bacon and egg pizza,' she said, and giggled delightedly. Reg reached for his own box, opened it and discovered a large sausage sandwich. It was still warm.

'A sandwich box that's never empty!' he declared gleefully. 'Wow!' Then as an afterthought: 'Pity it isn't a wallet.'

The discovery a few minutes later that the flasks were once again filled with fresh, piping hot tee put Reg in an altogether more cheerful frame of mind, and by the time he'd washed his face in the rock pool, he was positively buoyant.

'Right,' he said, slipping his arms through the straps of his rucksack, 'let's get this show on the road, shall we? The sooner we start, the sooner we get to the Omnipotent Roopert, and the sooner we find *him*, the sooner we get home.'

'You still have far to travel,' Morgon pointed out.

'What the heck?' Reg said gaily. 'I'm beginning to enjoy myself!'

Half an hour later they were back on the dusty track.

The muscles in Reg's legs had loosened up considerably by this time, and even the relentless beating of the Urth's sun could not dampen his newfound enthusiasm. There was a decided spring in his step, and on occasions Jeannette actually found herself jogging to keep up with him. The Plainsfolk, on the other hand, seemed even more watchful and alert than on the previous day, and Jeannette wondered exactly what it was they were afraid of. They hadn't passed a soul since leaving Mahatma's cave, and apart from a few low hills and sand dunes, as far as Jeannette could see there was nowhere for a potential enemy to hide.

Danger, however – as someone probably once said – travels on the wings of the wind.

They had been walking for a little over an hour when the Plainsfolk suddenly stopped and cocked their heads to one side, as if listening for something. Reg and Jeannette cast a puzzled glance at each other.

'What is it?' asked Reg. 'What can you hear?'

Morgon looked at him, his eyes wide and alarmed, and Reg felt a wave of warm apprehension in the pit of his stomach.

'Listen,' Morgon said.

Reg did as he was told, and at first could hear nothing. After a few seconds, however, he became aware of a low, distant growl, like that of an approaching swarm of very large bees.

One of the Plainsfolk women suddenly pointed to a large sand dune in the distance, behind which an ominous looking cloud of dust was forming. The low growling sound grew louder.

Alan and Morgon looked at each other. 'The Devils?' Alan said.

Morgon nodded slowly. 'I fear so.'

'The Devils?' Reg said, a note of alarm creeping into his voice. 'What devils?'

'Just keep walking,' Morgon told him. 'They may not come this way.'

The Plainsfolk set off again at a determined pace, and Reg and Jeannette followed, their eyes glued anxiously to the approaching dust cloud. The low growling noise was rapidly becoming a deep throaty roar, and it occurred to Reg that he had heard something very like it before.

Seconds later the first of the Devils surged into sight over the brow of the sand dune, and Reg suddenly understood what it was that had sounded so familiar. Notwithstanding temporal anomalies and certain discrepancies concerning matter, Harley Davidsons sound much the same the universe over. At least, it *looked* like a Harley Davidson; the same low-slung lines, definitive petrol tank and beautifully gleaming chrome. More bikes appeared over the ridge of the dune, and Reg stared in fascination. The riders of these glittering machines were attired predictably enough, in denim sawn-offs, leather pants, jack boots and aviator-style shades. Some wore helmets, several of which bore a marked resemblance to Second World War Nazi headgear, and not for the first time Reg marvelled at the surprisingly homogeneous nature of his own world and the one known as Urth.

As the group of bikers bore down menacingly on them, it occurred to Jeannette that it might be a good idea to run away. It then occurred to her that it might not be such a good idea after all, since the fact that motorbikes are considerably faster than legs would tend to render the exercise rather pointless. In the end, she did what everyone else did, which was to stay exactly where she was.

The leader of the bikers, a tanned, muscular chap with long greasy blond hair and a map of tattoos across his chest, swung his bike to a halt in front of them, raising an impressive cloud of yellow dust. The other riders skidded to a stop, forming an ominous looking semi-circle around them. The leader removed his sunglasses slowly, and regarded them with apparent amusement. He chuckled menacingly, and his gang sniggered unpleasantly in answer.

'Out for a little walk are we?' he asked, his voice adrip with derision.

'We are taking these people to the outskirts of New Fork,' Morgan told him, 'and have promised them safe passage.'

'Have you now?' said the biker, raising his eyebrows in exaggerated surprise. 'Well that was a silly thing to do, wasn't it?'

'No,' Morgon said calmly, 'it is a promise we knew we could keep.'

'Is that so?'

The biker grinned at his grisly crew, who nodded and grinned back at him. One or two of them threw in a menacing snigger for effect.

'And how are you going to keep your promise', he went on, 'if you're dead?'

'We will keep our promise,' Morgon explained patiently, 'because we will not be dead.'

A look of sudden anger flashed across the biker's face. 'You little leather bastrad!' he spat. 'You'll wish you *were* dead by the time we've finished with you.'

He turned off the engine of his bike and kicked the stand into place, and the other bikers began to do the same. At this particular juncture, however, several things happened very quickly. The first thing that happened was that each of the Plainsfolk, who seconds ago had been empty handed, suddenly had a small and rather deadly looking bow and arrow trained on the leader of the bikers. The second thing that happened was a metallic zing and the sudden appearance of a ten-inch steel blade in Reg's right hand. The third thing that happened was that Jeannette completely disappeared.

The bikers froze, and had they not been wearing sunglasses, Reg would have been gratified to note that the amused and menacing smirks had been replaced by expressions of surprise, fear and bewilderment. In the bikers' experience, ordinary women did not simply disappear, ordinary men did not carry ten-inch switchblades, and the Plainsfolk did not have a reputation as remarkable bowmen for nothing.

'Now,' said Morgon, with no trace of a waver in

either his voice or his bow, 'if you turn around, ride away and let us continue our journey in peace, you will be spared. If you do not, you will be dead before you can dismount your machines.'

The biker glanced at his cohorts, his face etched with indecision, and they peered back at him expectantly. He glanced at the Plainsfolk and the short deadly arrows pointed in his direction. He glanced at the ten-inch steel blade in Reg's hand, which seemed to radiate some kind of blue electrical field, and lastly he glanced at the space which moments earlier had contained Jeannette.

What finally clinched it, however, was the soft feminine voice which at that moment whispered in his ear.

'I'd piss off if I were you,' it said. The biker spun around so quickly he almost fell off his bike, but there was no one there. This was too weird. Trashing supermarkets and pushing old ladies around for kicks were all grist to the bikers' mill, but magic switchblades and disembodied voices were a little out of his league. He wagged a slightly shaky finger at Morgon.

'We'll meet again, leather boy,' he said, in a voice by no means as controlled as he might have wished.

'I very much doubt it,' replied Morgon.

'We'll,' the biker said, turning to Reg, '*We'll* meet again then.'

'Not unless you fancy a trip to another dimension we won't.'

The biker continued to wag his finger at them. 'Well *somebody* will meet me again, you can take my word for it.'

'Sod off,' said a voice in his ear, and with astonishing speed the biker kicked his machine into life, swung it around and roared away from them, his spinning back wheel raising another spectacular cloud of yellow dust. His motley crew needed little prompting to follow suit, and within less than a minute the bikers were nothing more than a muffled whine and a series of specks in the distance. Reg raised his fist and gave a little cheer, and the Plainsfolk slipped their tiny bows and arrows back under their smocks. (Just where they hung them Reg never discovered.)

Morgon glanced around. 'Where is the Jeannette girl?'

'Here,' said a voice beside him.

Morgon spun round and peered into the smiling face of nothing. He spun the other way, then twisted around 270 degrees to look behind him and finally returned to his original position. He glanced at Reg.

'Care to enlighten me?'

'Oh, it's just a little potion Mahatma gave her for emergencies. It only lasts about quarter of an hour I think.'

'She is still with us, then?'

'I'm right next to you Morgon,' Jeannette told him.

'Ah. Fine,' Morgon said, trying hard not to look as disconcerted as he felt. 'Then we'd better proceed.'

The little party set off once more along the track, though the only visible signs of Jeannette were the footprints left in the sand by her Doctor Marten shoes.

'That was quite a close shave,' Reg said presently,

his hand still tightly curled around the handle of the switchblade in his pocket.

'It could have been unpleasant, yes,' agreed Morgon.

'Who *were* those guys, anyway?'

'They are known as Hevvan's Devils. They see themselves as modern-day warrior nomads, but in reality are no more than sub-educated social misfits.'

'Ah, right,' said Reg. 'We've got them in our world, too.'

'I have no doubt that they are a universal phenomenon,' Morgon said glumly, 'like so many of the shitty things in life.'

Reg nodded, and they walked on in silence.

Although he attempted to hide it, Reg had to admit to a profound sense of relief some ten minutes later when Jeannette suddenly reappeared, walking nonchalantly by his side. She seemed to have suffered no ill effects from her spell of invisibility, although for the next five minutes she did have a tendency to flicker rather like an early Lumière movie.

They plodded on.

Hours passed and new ones took their place. The sun sidled across the sky like a huge yellow crab, and their shadows lengthened on the sand in front of them. By teatime the spires and tower blocks of New Fork were visible on the distant horizon, and a little over an hour later, the Big Tomato was less than a mile away.

Morgon stopped and turned to Reg. 'My friend, this is where we must leave you.'

'Oh. So soon?'

'In a short time you will reach the suburbs,' Morgon told him, 'and if you are seen with us, it could be unpleasant.'

'Do they hate you *that* much?' asked Jeannette.

'They think of us as they think of dirt,' Morgon said.

Jeannette shook her head sadly. 'It's such a shame. And all because your skin's a different texture.'

'Do not fear,' Morgon told her, 'for though it may take many years, one day we will rise again, and once more become the proud people we were before the settlers came.'

'Well I hope so,' said Jeannette encouragingly, 'because I think you're awfully nice.'

Morgon took her hand in both of his and squeezed it gently. 'I wish you much luck in your quest. Be watchful, always, and may Goat smile on you.'

'Thanks, Morgon,' said Jeannette, and even though she had only known the Plainsfolk for a matter of hours, there was a decided lump in her throat as she spoke. 'Thanks to all of you. You really saved our skin back there.'

'A curious phrase,' said Morgon thoughtfully. 'That is what the flesh settlers do when they capture our kind. I believe it makes excellent briefcases.'

'Well, thanks again, anyway,' Reg put in, skirting tactfully around the subject of leather goods. 'It's been great knowing you.'

The Plainsfolk raised their hands in a gesture of farewell, then turning slowly – and a little sadly,

Jeannette thought – began to make their way back along the track. Reg and Jeannette looked at each other.

'Well, we're on our own now,' Reg said.

Although to the casual observer Reg's statement may well have seemed justified, it was not, in fact, strictly accurate. A mere fifty yards to their left behind a large sand dune was a man with short green hair and three eyes. He was wearing a silver suit and heavy metallic boots, and was currently staring around in profound bewilderment and shock. The man, whose name was Clitrasill, had moments earlier stepped through the front door of his grandmother's house on a distant planet called Erf, only to find that the rest of his world had completely disappeared. At the staggering odds of 3,956,485,872 to 1, Clitrasill had inadvertently stepped through a hole in the wall of the Universal Mainframe and landed in another dimension.

Clitrasill, it should be stressed, plays no actual part in the story of Reg and Jeannette, and I mention him merely to illustrate the fact that the phrase, 'Well, we're on our own now,' is seldom a wise one.

*   *   *

The swing doors of Ma Rainor's Winged Horse Saloon squeaked on their hinges as a tall, dark stranger walked through them into the bar. This was not an especially unusual event – strangers often walked into the bar of the Winged Horse Saloon, and whenever they did so the hinges of the door would squeak. What *was* unusual was the physical appearance of this particular stranger.

The stranger in question was exceptionally tall, thin and gaunt, with a large hooked nose and a narrow cruel mouth. Around his neck was a bootlace tie with a silver clasp, and on his head he wore a soft black fedora. Perhaps the most startling aspect of the man's appearance, however, were his eyes. They were hooded, and appeared to be sunk deep into his skull, and were possibly the calmest and most calculating eyes on the whole of Urth. They were the kind of eyes one can look into for only the merest soupçon of a moment, before being forced to shift one's gaze to something less unpleasant (such as someone having their bowels removed, for example). They were deadly, baleful, inhuman eyes. In fact, we're talking the kind of eyes that would merit a whole paragraph in Roget's Thesaurus under the heading '*malevolent*'. And it was this same pair of eyes that the stranger now turned on Ma Rainor, who was standing at the end of the bar smoking a cheroot.

Ma Rainor had been in Bogwater Creek for as long as anyone could remember, and over the years she had seen a good many strangers walk through the doors of her saloon. She had seen big strangers and little strangers, ugly strangers and handsome strangers, strangers with all manner of physical abnormalities and once, oddly, a stranger she knew quite well, but never before had she seen a stranger with mince pies like this one. She held his gaze for as long as she was able, but the experience was so thoroughly unpleasant that she finally lowered her eyes and brushed a speck of dust from the bar top.

She took a drag on her cheroot and said: 'What can I do for you, stranger?'

The stranger's voice when he spoke was soft and low, and a slight lisp merely added somehow to his aura of menace. Had Ma Rainor heard of Boris Karloff, she would have thought of him now.

'Perhaps you could help me,' the stranger said. 'My name is Mortimer, and I'm looking for two people.'

Ma Rainor glanced at him quickly, then looked away again. 'Is that so?'

'That is so.'

'Any two in particular?'

'Yes, although I'm afraid I am unable to describe them. I wondered if any strangers had been in here recently?'

Ma Rainor considered for a moment, then shook her head. 'Ain't seen any – 'part from you, that is.'

'You haven't seen anyone looking a little . . . confused, perhaps, or disorientated?'

Ma Rainor shook her head again. ''Fraid I can't help you, mister. Maybe the Guddohl Boys seen somethin'.'

'They would be the gentlemen sitting on the veranda, I take it?'

'S'right, mister.'

'I shall enquire.'

'Wanna drink before you go?'

'Thank you, but no. I find that bibulence dims the wit. Good day, madam.'

The stranger raised his hat briefly, turned, and walked slowly out of the bar. Ma Rainor watched him go and shook her head again.

'Now there's an evil son of a whore if ever I saw one,' she muttered to no one in particular.

Out on the veranda the Guddohl Boys were chummering thoughtfully among themselves.

'Strangers you say?' said Walt. 'Well now, come to think of it, there *was* a handsome lookin' woman here 'bout a day or so ago. Dressed all in black, she was, an' wearin' little metal frame eye-glasses.'

'You mean the one with the legs right up to here?' Heck asked.

Walt nodded. 'Ayup, that's the one. There was a feller here, too, askin' directions to old Mahatma's place.'

'What did he look like, this man?'

'Youngish feller. Blond hair down to 'bout here. Had on a brown cord jacket if I r'member rightly.'

'An' blue work pants,' added Ned.

'And you think they may have gone to see Mahatma Cain?'

'Mebbe. Mebbe not.'

Mortimer raised his hat. 'Thank you for your help, gentlemen. Have a nice day, now.'

They watched in silence as the stranger descended the steps of the veranda and set off down the street towards the edge of town. Ned sniffed, and expelled a wad of near-black sputum.

'Now that's what I call one mean lookin' feller,' he said.

Walt nodded. 'Ayup. I don't know what he wants them two young uns for, but for their sakes, I kinda hope he don't find 'em.'

5

Having passed through the outskirts of New Fork, which, like big city suburbs the universe over had a drab, depressing and deprived look about them, Reg and Jeannette finally found themselves in the heart of the Big Tomato. The noise and bustle was mind-throttling, and it was a little like being in the middle of a film lot on which several different costume dramas are being shot at the same time. There were trolley buses from *Meet Me in St Louis* and cars that looked like Chitty Chitty Bang Bang, whilst numerous Victorian horse-drawn carriages rattled up and down the cobbled streets.

The buildings themselves consisted of stone cottages and quaint half-timbered houses and shops, interspersed with small sky scrapers, concrete office blocks and brownstone apartment buildings.

And there were people everywhere.

Women dressed in outfits dating from the fourteenth century mingled happily with serious looking businessmen in smart grey gabardine suits, and on a corner outside a sex shop a group of women in black plastic micro skirts and fish-net stockings stood and chatted. Clouds of steam rose lazily from manhole covers set into the road, and the air was filled with the sound of clattering footsteps and the cries of the chestnut-selling street vendors.

Reg and Jeannette gazed around in unalloyed wonder, drinking in the sights and sounds of the largest city in the Western Aisles.

Eventually Reg remembered why they were there. 'I suppose we'd better ask someone the way to the docks,' he suggested.

'I'd rather like to explore the place a bit,' Jeannette said, 'but I don't suppose we've got time.'

'Not really. The sooner we get to this Roopert chap the better.'

'Hmm.'

'I mean, they're bound to have noticed back home that we've disappeared. They've probably got the police out looking for us by now, and everything.'

In actual fact Reg could not have been more wrong,* since at that particular juncture not a single soul was aware of their disappearance. The reason for this, as C. S. Lewis was one of the first to note, is that travel through the dimensions into other worlds takes up almost no time whatsoever in our own. Consequently, although they had already spent two nights on Urth, to all intents and purposes they had only just that minute left Earth. The cause of this phenomenon is unknown, though a popular hypothesis holds that what you cannot see ceases to exist the moment you stop being able to see it, a theory which has had many a

---

* Not strictly true – he *could* have said Joanna Lumley was a dumb blonde.

philosopher leaping backwards and forwards between rooms in an effort to catch it out.

Jeannette was visibly disappointed. 'There are some awfully interesting looking shops,' she said hopefully.

'There are some awfully interesting looking bars, too,' Reg pointed out, 'but we really ought to find this chap with the boat.'

Jeannette shrugged a little petulantly, and began peering around in search of someone who looked as if they might know the way. After rejecting several possible candidates, including a group of diminutive oriental looking people with cameras round their necks, she settled on an elderly grey-haired man in a business suit standing nearby.

'Excuse me,' she said, moving a little closer, 'could you tell us how to get to the docks please?'

The man regarded her suspiciously. 'What on Urth do you want to go to the docks for?'

'Well, because we need to catch a boat to the Eastern Aisles.'

The man regarded her even more suspiciously. 'What on Urth do you want to go to the Eastern Aisles for?'

'Because we have to find someone, and that's where he lives.'

The man sniffed. 'Primitive uncivilized lot over there, you know.'

'So we've heard.'

'Lack of basic education, that's what it is. Or is it sanitation? I can never remember which.'

'About the docks, though?'

'Ah yes. See that little street?' The man pointed to a narrow opening between two buildings on the other side of the road. 'Follow it for about half a mile until you come to an intersection. Turn left there and walk straight down the hill and it takes you right to the quayside.'

'Great, thanks very much,' said Jeannette, and Reg smiled and nodded at the man in a chummy sort of way.

'Dick'eads,' the man muttered to himself, and began to hum under his breath.

Reg and Jeannette waited for a gap in the traffic, then trotted across the busy road and turned down the little street. As they did so, they failed signally to notice the small, swarthy man in a grubby brown overcoat who followed them down the street a few seconds later.

The man, whose name was Bullseye Sykes, was a well known figure in the sleazier districts of New Fork, and had the kind of reputation it is only possible to acquire by being thoroughly and despicably nasty. It was rumoured among the criminal fraternity that he had once killed a man for having his flies open, and had disposed of the body by forcing it through an industrial mincer and feeding it bit by bit to his dog, Bill.

As he followed Reg and Jeannette down the narrow street, a queer, nasty sort of grin distorted his already grotesque features. Easy pickings, he was thinking to himself. Two backpackers, probably hitching around the Aisles before going off to Ox Bridge or Camford or somewhere like that. They'd never know what hit 'em. If his luck was in they'd be a couple of rich brats, with expensive taste in wrist watches and their pockets stuffed with round notes.* He'd just walk up all casual like, and lure them down one of the side alleys – gullible as hell these young students, they'd fall for any old con – then slit their throats and relieve them of those bulging rucksacks. Easy as pie. He might even give the girl a good seeing to before he killed her. She was a bit of a looker, that one. After it was done, he'd go to Harry's bar and—

At this point the musings of Bullseye Sykes were violently terminated by that final relief from all known ailments, commonly referred to as death. The cause of this untimely (though unlamented) demise was several hundred pounds of Steinbeck, iron frame, upright piano. Eighty feet above the street, the two removal men who had moments earlier been attempting to manoeuvre it through the window of a fourth floor apartment, looked at each other and sighed.

'Mice have been at the ropes again,' said one of them.

'That's this week's wages up the spout,' said the other, gazing down at the shattered piano.

The crimson pulp that had been Bullseye Sykes trickled over the edge of the pavement and ran down a grid.

A little way down the street, Reg and Jeanette turned

* The circular bank notes which form the standard currency of the Western and Eastern Aisles.

at the sound of a loud discordant crash. Reg glanced at the remains of the Steinbeck, then up at the flailing ropes four floors above.

'Good grief! That could've been nasty!' he declared. 'If we'd been a few seconds later we could've been under that thing.'

Jeanette gave a little shudder and pulled a face. 'There wouldn't have been much left of us.'

'Just a couple of rucksacks floating in a sea of tomato soup,' Reg said colourfully.

'Come on,' Jeannette urged, starting down the street again, 'let's find this boat.'

Five minutes later they reached the quayside, which turned out to be a long cobbled promenade lined with warehouses and storage depots, interspersed here and there with a number of shady looking bars and cafés. Even though it was early evening and twilight was fast becoming dusk, the docks were a hive of activity, with ships being loaded and unloaded and motor trucks and horse-drawn waggons trundling to and fro.

A gang of small, muscular, rather scaly looking dwarves, who, owing to a physiological quirk of nature happened to be green, were engaged nearby in the task of transferring bales of spices from one pallet to another. Reg strolled over casually and addressed them.

'Excuse me, chaps, I wonder if you could help me. I'm looking for someone called Captain Titanic.'

The dwarves stopped what they were doing and regarded him with blank green faces. Reg pressed on.

'Erm, I was told I'd find him at the docks . . . somewhere.'

'Dae'kcid ffo ssip,' said one of the dwarves.

'Ah, I see, you don't speak English.'

'Od ew sey,' said the dwarf. 'Dnuor yaw thgir eht ti kaeps ew, senitsilihp uoy ekilnu tub.'

'Right, yes, well, not to worry. I'll ask someone else.'

A hand landed heavily on Reg's shoulder. He turned round slowly to find himself confronted by a large florid-faced man in a navy blue bobble hat and wellington boots. The man didn't look pleased. In fact, the man looked the way people look just before they punch you extremely hard in the face.

'Tryin' to pinch me reptobates are you?' he growled, and Reg couldn't help noticing that his breath smelt strongly of something closely resembling rum. He staggered back a pace.

'No, no, I was just—'

'Know what I do to people who come stealin' me workers?'

'I wasn't, I—'

There was an oddly familiar sounding metallic click, and Reg looked down to see a short, nasty looking blade glinting in the fading sunlight a few inches from his belly. Jeannette, watching from a few feet away, put her hands to her mouth and gasped. Reg, on the other hand, peered up at the florid-faced man and raised one eyebrow disparagingly.

'It's not very big, is it?' he said.

The sailor's florid face became florider and his eyes

bulged, and for a moment Reg thought the man was about to suffer a major cardio-dysfunction.

'What d'ye mean, not very big?' he boomed.

'Comparatively speaking, that is,' Reg said, and in one deft movement, he slipped the switchblade from his pocket and pressed the little brass button. Ten inches of stainless steel, forged more than a hundred years ago in the lush purple valleys of Outer Chefiild, shot from the tip of the handle and zinged to a halt an inch below the sailor's chin. Not daring to move his head, the erubescent mariner lowered his eyes and peered at it. Blue electrical energy seemed to dance around the blade, and the sailor's teeth suddenly began to ache.

'Ah. Yes. I'll be putting this away then,' he said, carefully retracting the blade of his own knife. 'Just a bit of fun, that's all.'

'That's okay,' said Reg, who was becoming ever more impressed by the reaction elicited by Mahatma's little toy. 'No harm done.'

'It's just that reptobates are very sought after,' the sailor explained. 'Best little workers on Urth, and cheap as fick.'

'Work for peanuts, eh?'

'That's right. Half a sack a week each and they'll work every hour Goat sends.'

'Quite,' said Reg, his conscious mind teetering on the edge of bewilderment.

Sensing that the situation was no longer volatile, Jeannette approached cautiously.

'Excuse me,' she said, addressing the sailor, 'you don't happen to know a Captain Titanic, do you?'

'Ty Tanyick? Why sure, everyone knows Cap'n Tanyick. Why?'

'Because we were told he could take us to the Eastern Aisles.'

'The Eastern Aisles? Now why would ye be wantin' to go to the Eastern Aisles?'

'Well, it's a long story, but we have to find someone.'

'Find someone, eh? Aye, well, if ye're *bound* to go, Tanyick's the man for the job, right enough.'

'So where can we find him?'

The sailor turned and pointed down the quayside, to where a long, three-masted ship was moored. 'That's Tanyick's ship,' he told them. 'He'll either be on board, or in McCarthy's Bar across the road. On second thoughts, he'll be in McCarthy's bar.'

Reg and Jeannette thanked the sailor, who touched his bobble hat and nodded at them floridly, and made their way along the cobbled quayside to the ship. The vessel itself, they were unsettled to observe, looked far more sleek and seaworthy from a distance than it did close up. It was obviously very old, built of timber and – in Reg's opinion – badly in need of several coats of Spinnaker yacht varnish. Its design was similar to that of a small clipper ship, and a narrow gangplank led from the quayside to a small wooden gate on the stern. Leaning nonchalantly on the gate was a somewhat louche and unprepossessing looking youth, whose acne-riddled skin seemed in imminent danger of falling off his face and dropping into the sea.

'Ahoy there!' called Reg, slipping ludicrously into what he thought was the appropriate vernacular. 'Is Captain Titanic aboard?'

The young sailor snorted up an impressive gob of phlegm, and pushing it out with his tongue, let it drop into the murky waters below.

'He's in McCarthy's,' he told them, and nodded in the direction of a dingy looking bar across the road.

'Ah. Thanks a lot, shipmate,' shouted Reg. The lad rammed a grubby finger up his left nostril, extracted a pea-sized clod of snot and flicked it into the sea breeze.

'Charming young man,' observed Jeannette, as she and Reg crossed the busy promenade to McCarthy's. The incredibly dilapidated exterior of the bar provided little encouragement for the casual patron, but Reg pushed open the battered wooden door anyway, and the two of them stepped cautiously inside.

The first thing to hit them was the smell, the effect of which was a little like being smothered under a woollen blanket that has been marinading for several years in something lethally alcoholic. It didn't simply infiltrate the nostrils, but invaded them, raping and pillaging as it went. The second thing to hit them was the noise, or more appropriately, the absence of it. Apart from the fact that there was no jukebox, no video sound system and no farting bleeping electronic fruit machines, it appeared that the bar's clientele to a man had stopped speaking as they walked in, and were now regarding them with scantily veiled hostility.

'Don't slam the—'

The third thing to hit them was a large stuffed swordfish.

'—door,' said a voice from behind the bar.

'Ouch!' said Reg.

'Sorry about that, pal,' said the voice, which belonged to a huge bald man with a beard, who turned out to be the innkeeper. 'It falls off every time the door slams.'

Reg bent down, picked up the swordfish and carefully replaced it on two little brackets on the lintel over the door. He turned to the landlord and grinned.

'Heavy, isn't it?'

The innkeeper shrugged. 'Think yourself lucky I didn't mount it with the head facing down.'

The motley collection of wizened mariners and misbegotten stevedores cackled to themselves in appreciation of this witty rejoinder.

'Right, yes,' said Reg, and chuckled politely.

'What can I do for you?' asked the innkeeper, diligently polishing a tankard with a tea towel that was so filthy even germs were afraid to go near it.

'Well actually, we're looking for Captain Titanic.'

The innkeeper glanced across the room to where a short, thickset man was sitting hunched over a large measure of Guttficker's Special Label Premium Blend Rum.

'Hey, Tanyick!' he called. 'Somebody here looking for you.'

The stocky sailor continued to stare into his glass and mumble.

'Tanyick! You're wanted!'

Still the pixilated mariner failed to respond.

'Last orders!' yelled the innkeeper, and Captain Tanyick leapt from his seat and peered around in panic-stricken confusion.

'Over here, Tanyick,' the innkeeper called. 'Somebody looking for you.'

The old salt shuffled across the room towards Reg and Jeannette, his bewildered pink face a sea chart of crow's feet and wrinkles.

'What erm, who er, is it about the jetty fees, or, er . . . hmm?'

Reg attempted to take charge of the situation. 'Captain Ti, er, Tan, erm, Captain, my name is Reg, and this is Jeannette, and we were told by Mahatma Cain that you might be able to take us over to the Eastern Aisles.'

'What was that?'

'We were told that you might—'

'Yes yes yes, I mean, what was that name?'

'Which name? Hers or mine?'

'No no, the one you said before!'

'Oh, Mahatma? Mahatma Cain.'

'That's it, that's it!' The ancient mariner grinned up at them, revealing a lone, discoloured tooth. 'So, Mahatma sent you did he? You'll be Reg and Jeannette then? Wanting to get over to the Eastern Aisles I shouldn't wonder. Ha. Well well. Dear me yes.'

'You knew we were coming then?' observed Jeannette.

'Knew who was coming?'

'Knew *we* were coming.'

'Did I?'

'You sounded as if you did.'

'Did I?'

'Well, yes.'

'Ah. Right. Well then.' The captain shook his head slowly and stroked his stubbly chin. 'How about a drink?' he said, suddenly brightening as the idea occurred to him.

Reg and Jeannette looked at each other briefly, then turned back to the captain.

'Well, yes, that would be . . .' said Reg.

'All that walking in the sand . . .' said Jeannette.

'Good, good, excellent,' said the captain. 'Mine's a double Guttficker.'

Two and a half hours later the three of them emerged from McCarthy's in high spirits. Very high spirits. In fact, not to put too fine a point on it, they were pissed as farts, arm in arm and singing.

It seemed to Reg that the cobbles of the promenade were decidedly more uneven than heretofore, and they appeared to be moving under his feet. This, allied with a severe absence of directional co-ordination resulted in a distinct crab-like motion, as a consequence of which it took them almost fifteen minutes to cross the quayside to the ship.

As they approached the water's edge, Jeannette noticed that the ship appeared to be tethered to the quay by a long, thin strip of wood, and this struck her as odd. Then she noticed that the ship was also tethered by two very strong looking ropes which were tied around a small iron capstan, and this also struck her as odd. Finally it dawned on her that the long, thin piece of wood actually had nothing to do with the ship's moorings, and was in fact the gangplank, and this struck her as appalling.

She shook her head with drunken determination. 'Nat,' she said mysteriously.

Reg and Captain Tanyick turned to look at her.

'What?' said Reg.

'Nat,' she repeated. 'Cahn doot.'

'What?' said Reg again.

'Gangplan',' Jeannette explained. 'Stoo thin. I'll fall in 'n' the water an' be drown' 'n' then'll be dead, and . . . not be 'live. Nat.'

'What?' said Reg yet again.

'She says the gangplank's too thin,' translated Captain Tanyick. 'Says she'll fall in and drown.'

'Ah,' said Reg, swaying like a sunflower in a moderate breeze, 'she's godda point.'

'Nah nah nah,' the Captain said, waving a dismissive drunken hand, 'there's a trick to it.'

Reg swivelled slowly and peered at Captain Tanyick,

his eyebrows making a creditable attempt to rise. 'Yeah?'

'Yeah.'

'What it is, then?'

'Trick is, don't expect to fall in. If you expect to fall in, you'll fall in. If you *don't* expect to fall in, you won't. It's 'imple.'

'Yeah?'

'Yeah.'

Reg nodded unsteadily. 'Hokkay. You go first then.'

'No problem,' the Captain assured them, and lurched towards the gangplank. He approached the task of crossing it with the curiously controlled gait of one whose whole central nervous system is focused on the sole objective of the avoidance of wobble, a phenomenon instantly recognizable to traffic cops throughout the universe. Unfortunately, when the central nervous system in question has recently been subjected to the imbibition of copious quantities of Guttficker's Special Label Premium Blend Rum, success is far from guaranteed.

'Wup,' said Captain Tanyick, and disappeared.

A matter of seconds after the initial 'splosh' came another, quieter 'splish', the cause of which was a large rope net cast over the stern of the ship by the acned young deckhand. Reg and Jeannette glanced up in surprise. The lad merely shrugged.

'He's never made it across yet,' he explained, 'and I'm on fishing out duty tonight.'

Curiously enough, Reg and Jeannette made it safely

across to the ship purely by dint of the fact that they fully expected to fall in at any moment, further proof – were it needed – of the rickety nature of Captain Tanyick's theory.

'You're in cabins 4 and 5,' the boy told them as they teetered onto the deck. 'We sail at 7 a.m.'

After staggering around the bowels of the ship for several minutes, Reg and Jeannette finally located the two cabins, and bidding each other a brief and inarticulate goodnight, stumbled through the doors and collapsed onto their respective beds.

'Bedder ged undressed,' Reg mumbled to himself. He tried to sit up, but his rucksack suddenly felt as if someone had spiked it with a small building's worth of Accrington bricks. He flopped backwards. 'P'raps I won't bother then,' he decided, and drifted into unconsciousness.

*   *   *

The man known as Mortimer strode through the busy streets of New Fork like a man with a mission, which, taking into account the fact that this is exactly what he was, is perhaps not very surprising. Such was the impression of evil emanating from his being, that early morning commuters on their way to their offices on Wail Street crossed to the other side of the road to avoid him. Even as he passed through the tough inner city area known as The Bonx, Mortimer retained his malignant presence, and the little gangs of sub-humans (known locally as 'teenagers') who ruled the back-streets, found themselves giving ground and parting to let him pass. This was not something that came easily to them; under normal circumstances they would have blocked the pavement, unsheathed an array of lethal looking weapons and demanded payment in return for safe passage. (Their interpretation of safe passage, incidentally, involved being allowed to reach the other end of the street without having your thyroid gland removed with a spoon and the resulting cavity filled with broken glass.)

Walking slowly but purposefully, Mortimer made his way through the city and eventually down to the quayside. As he strolled along the dock, his baleful eyes darting this way and that, tattoo-laden stevedores scuttled out of his path and hid in the shadows. Even the little green reptobates stopped what they were doing and regarded him uneasily as he passed.

'Edud gnikool live eno s'taht,' observed one of them.

'Gniddik ton er'uoy,' agreed another.

Mortimer finally came to a halt in front of the dingy exterior of McCarthy's bar. He pushed the pitted oak door open, stepped inside and closed it carefully behind him. The innkeeper paused in the act of polishing his beloved tankard, and regarded the newcomer suspiciously. Having been landlord of McCarthy's for over twenty years, Allyck Gihlroi had encountered his fair share of cruel, violent men, and more than one had found himself on the wrong side of Allyck's vast, meaty fists. Even so, he experienced a pang of apprehension as he gazed – momentarily – into the eyes of Mortimer. It was the man's quiet, inhuman self-assurance that was so disconcerting – that, and those hideous hooded eyes.

'What can I do for you, sir?' he asked, pleasantly if diffidently.

'I'm looking for two young people,' Mortimer purred.

'Oh yes?'

'Mmm. A male and a female. The man has blonde hair; the girl, I believe, wears spectacles.'

'That so?'

'Yes, that is so. I'm led to believe they came here in search of a Captain Tanyick.'

'You're too late, I'm afraid,' the innkeeper said, resuming his polishing. 'The *Iceberg* sailed at seven this morning.'

Anyone watching might have been alarmed to observe the tiniest, merest hint of annoyance flash across Mortimer's otherwise serene countenance.

'How very unfortunate,' he said, his voice cutting through the smoky atmosphere like a Sabatier knife. 'For where is she bound, might I ask?'

The innkeeper shrugged. 'Sorry, squire. Tanyick didn't say.'

'Quite,' murmured Mortimer, his right hand sliding ominously into the pocket of his coat. 'However, I should be most grateful for any information you might have regarding Captain Tanyick's destination. It really is very important, you see.'

Allyck shifted uncomfortably in his wellingtons. He hadn't liked that hand sliding into the coat pocket like that. The trouble with hands sliding into coat pockets was, you never knew what they were going to be holding when they slid out again.

'Weell,' he said slowly, wilting under Mortimer's unwavering gaze, 'come to think of it, he might have mentioned something about the Eastern Aisles. Probably Le Half – that's his usual stop.'

'The Eastern Aisles,' Mortimer said, relishing the name as though it were a well buttered corn on the cob. 'I see. My good man, do you know of anyone who would – for an appropriate fee, of course – take me to Le Half?'

The innkeeper considered for a moment. 'Captain Kirque might do it,' he said eventually. 'I mean, he's not too fussy about where he puts in, as long as the money's right.'

'Oh, the money will be "right", I can assure you of that.'

'Well, you'll find him about two hundred yards further on down the quay, opposite Bob Klingon's Bar & Grill. His ship's called the *Enterprise*.'

Mortimer bowed ever so slightly and raised his hat. 'I am eternally grateful. I feel sure your business will enjoy continued success. Have a nice day now, won't you?'

Mortimer turned and strolled slowly out of the bar. The few customers that were there, all of whom had been listening to the conversation in a detached, whistley sort of way, breathed an audible sigh of relief.

'Nasty piece of work,' observed Captain Huck.

'Very,' agreed the innkeeper. 'I don't trust that quiet, soft spoken type. You never know what the fick they're going to do next.'

What Mortimer did in fact do next, was press twenty round notes into the hand of Captain Jaimz T. Kirque, in return for the promise of swift passage to Le Half and the Eastern Aisles.

6

Kicking gamely for the surface and fighting its way through shoals of electrified guppies, Reg's conscious mind burst screaming into the day. The shaft of sunlight lasering through the cabin porthole was a needle-sharp cadmium yellow finger, cruelly poking him in the one eye he had thus far dared to open. The inside of his mouth appeared to have turned into damp cardboard overnight, and he was convinced his brain was wearing a hair shirt. Tongues of internal flame radiated from his abdomen out along his limbs, and it felt as if someone had removed his eyeballs whilst he was asleep and replaced them with peeled grapes that had been rolled in sand.

He sat up slowly, his very bones weeping in protest, and gazed around in dull, crapulent stupefaction. Where the hell was he, and why did he feel as if he'd been badly beaten with a bag of bananas?

He cringed, as someone rapped lightly on the cabin door.

'Come in,' he croaked, and the effort made him wince.

The door opened slowly and the crumpled figure of Jeannette appeared, wearing only her long black sweater and a pair of knickers. Her hair looked as if something had recently attempted to construct a nest in it. The tone of her skin was grey beneath the remains of the previous day's make-up, and behind her steel rimmed glasses her eyes were tiny and bloodshot. Only her bare legs, which were perfectly pale and perfectly shaped, retained any semblance of attractiveness.

'Oh, it's you,' he said, extricating himself painfully from the straps of his rucksack.

'Er, yes. I think it is, anyway. How do *you* feel?'

'Bloody dreadful.'

'So do I.'

'What happened to us?'

Jeannette shook her head slowly, and winced. 'I think we got drunk with Captain Tanyick.'

'Oh God, now I remember. We're on his ship, aren't we?'

'I suppose so. But I don't remember getting here.'

'I don't remember much myself, but I've got a feeling the Captain fell off the gangplank.'

'Oh yes! He did.'

At that moment they were interrupted by what sounded like someone kicking the door. Jeannette opened it and stood back, and the acne-riddled young deckhand whom they'd met the night before sidled in sheepishly, bearing a silver tray. On it were two steaming mugs of black coffee and a plate piled high with thick slices of grilled ham and four fried eggs. Reg and Jeannette eyed the food cautiously, aware that in their present state, by popular belief they were supposed to clutch their stomachs and heave. Contemplating the fried eggs carefully, however, both experienced a definite lack of desire to do either of these things. In fact, what they felt was not nausea, but a peculiarly profound hunger, exploding the myth that people with a hangover inevitably feel sick.

The lad, who by an unkind stroke of synchronicity was named Etna, placed the tray on a small table by the side of the bed.

'Cap'n Tanyick always says starve a fever, feed a hangover,' he announced.

'How very sensible of him,' said Reg.

'The washroom's at the end of the corridor,' Etna told them, and scratching his bottom fiercely, gangled out and shut the door.

'I hope he didn't cook it,' Jeannette said.

Half an hour later, having eaten and washed (with real soap), Reg and Jeannette felt restored enough to make their way above and join Captain Tanyick on the bridge. The Captain was in an expansive mood, largely due to the fact that he was still completely pissed.

'Ah, Reg! And my dear Jeannette!' he exclaimed, thrusting a large hip flask towards them. 'Good morning! Have a drink!'

They both shook their heads, albeit gingerly. 'A little early for me,' Reg said.

'Yes,' agreed Jeannette, 'perhaps in another year or so.'

Captain Tanyick laughed and took a mighty swig.

'We're making good time,' he informed them. 'If the wind stays with us we should be across in two days.'

Reg was surprised. 'I thought it'd take longer than that.'

'Oh no,' the Captain assured him. 'As long as we don't get becalmed in the Ass-Whores, we should be in Le Half by tomorrow evening.'

'Oh, well, that's all right then. Only I don't suppose there's much to do aboard a ship like this.'

'There is if you're the Captain,' Tanyick pointed out.

'Ah, yes, I suppose so,' said Reg, feeling a little silly.

After a delightful lunch of soup, roast back-yaardvark and boiled potatils, Reg and Jeannette went below deck for 'a bit of a lie down', as Jeannette put it. Splendid though it was, the heavy meal on top of all that fresh sea air had made them both rather drowsy.

They reached Reg's cabin and he opened the door and stepped inside.

'Give me a knock if you wake up first,' he said, and Jeannette nodded. Reg started to close the door.

'Reg,' Jeannette said, and something in her voice made him pause.

'What is it?'

'D'you think we're ever going to get home, Reg? I mean, *really*?'

Reg was silent for a few moments, then he sighed, walked across the cabin and sat down on the bed. Jeannette followed him inside and sat down next to him.

'You don't, do you?'

Reg took a deep breath. 'I really don't know, Jeannette. I mean, according to Mahatma, this Roopert of Murdok is supposed to be to wizards what Bernard

Manning is to fat ignorant comedians, but has he ever sent anyone from one dimension to another before? Because that sounds like one hell of a conjuring trick to me.'

'But we *got* here easily enough.'

'I know. I just have a hunch that getting back's going to be a lot harder.'

Jeannette sighed a shaky sigh. 'I'm scared, Reg,' she said.

'Don't be scared,' he told her, and automatically put his arm around her. Although it was an ostensibly platonic gesture, the sudden physical contact had an immediate (if involuntary) effect, and Reg felt himself flush slightly.

'I'll look after you,' he said, placing the arm that wasn't around Jeannette across his lap.

Jeannette turned to look at him. 'Will you, Reg?'

'Of course I will. I mean, I'm no hero or anything, but I'll do my best.'

Jeannette smiled gratefully, then leaned forward and kissed him on the cheek. Reg smiled in return. Jeannette leaned forward and kissed him again, though this time it landed a little closer to his mouth. Reg leaned forward, and their lips brushed against each other. Then they both leaned forward simultaneously, and their lips met in a hard, wet, surprisingly passionate kiss. The kiss continued for quite some time, and Reg found his hands wandering to all kinds of interesting places. More to the point, he was acutely aware that Jeannette's hands were doing the same.

Slowly, their lips still locked, they fell back onto the bed.

There was a click, a bump and a scrape, and Reg suddenly found himself flying through the air.

'It was never like this before,' he thought madly, before landing in a heap in the corner of the cabin. Bruised but not broken, he scrambled to his knees and opened his mouth, with every intention of saying 'What the hell?' in a very loud and indignant voice. In the event, what actually came out was 'Wha . . .?'

The reason for this was a very sharp sword, the point of which was currently pressed lightly against the tip of his nose. At the other end of the sword, the end with the handle that is, was a large ugly man with one eye and a tea towel wrapped around his head. At least, Reg *assumed* he had one eye, since the other was hidden by a black leather patch. The man peered down at him with a sneer that was so disparaging it made Reg want to poke his other eye out.

'Who, er, who, who are you?' he stammered instead.

The man reeled in exaggerated astonishment.

'Who am I, you ask? Who *am I*? Who *am I*?'

'Er, well, yes.'

'Ha! I'm only the nastiest, meanest, most famous body stockist on Urth! I am—'

'Body stockist?'

'What?'

'You said body stockist.'

'Yes?'

'What's a body stockist?'

'Oh, it's another name for slave trader.'

'Ah.'

'Where was I?'

'Nastiest, meanest ... in other words up your ars.'

'Oh yes. The nastiest, meanest body stockist on Urth! I am the feared, the despised, the one and only, Black Nidger'

'Nidger?'

'Yes. Yunno, short for Nigel?'

'Oh, right.'

'Yes. So anyway, that's who I am.'

Reg nodded thoughtfully. 'I see.'

There was an embarrassing silence.

'Erm,' said Reg eventually, 'what is it you actually want, then?'

'What do I want? Ha!' The slaver issued a stentorian cackle. 'The girl, of course, what else?'

Jeannette instinctively reached for the little bottle around her neck, but it wasn't there.

Reg stared aghast at the one-eyed pirate. 'But, but, you can't have her!'

Black Nidge smiled almost kindly. 'My dear boy, surely you don't mean to try and stop me? For be assured, it will not be easy with your head and your body on different sides of the cabin.'

Reg peered at the cold steel blade in front of his face.

'Well, when you put it like that.'

'Very wise, my boy.'

Reg took a deep breath, then blurted: 'But you'll have to take me, too!'

'What?'

'That's right,' Jeannette chipped in. 'If he doesn't go, neither do I!'

'But—'

'I mean it,' she added. 'I'll die rather than leave him behind!'

Reg wasn't sure just how serious a threat that was, but it gave him a warm, glowing feeling all the same, and in a different situation he would doubtless have blushed and grinned sheepishly.

Black Nidge peered down at Reg. 'All right boy, stand up! Let's have a look at you!'

Reg did as he was told, squirming uncomfortably under the slaver's appraising gaze.

'Hmm, not bad,' Nidge said. 'A bit skinny, but healthy enough. You never know, some rich old widow might take a fancy to you. More money than sense, half of 'em.'

'You mean you'll take me too?' Reg said, wondering why in the world he should be sounding so pleased about the prospect of being abducted by the nastiest, meanest body stockist on Urth.

'I'll take anything I can make a few quad out of,' Black Nidge said. 'Now come on, up on deck – and no funny business!'

'What about our stuff?' Reg asked, indicating his rucksack. Black Nidge clicked his fingers and a huge bearded man with an ugly scar across his cheek appeared from the passage outside.

'Colin, gather their belongings and bring them with you.'

Colin nodded and picked up the rucksack, as Black Nidge prodded Reg and Jeannette out of the cabin, along the corridor and up onto the deck.

The first thing they saw when they got there was Black Nidge's ship, tethered alongside the *Iceberg*, a row of nasty looking cannons protruding from its side like so many lengths of sawn-off drainpipe. The second thing they saw was Captain Tanyick and his crew, huddled in a corner and guarded by two men with primitive looking pistols. The Captain looked at them helplessly.

'I'm sorry,' he said. 'We had to stop, or they'd have blown us out of the water.'

'That's okay,' Jeannette said. 'It's not your fault.'

'Less of the chatter!' commanded Black Nidge. 'You're being abducted, not going on a bloody cruise!'

Jeannette humphed indignantly.

'Right,' said Black Nidge, addressing Captain Tanyick. 'Anyone else on board?'

The Captain shook his head. 'No one.'

'No big-breasted blonde women hiding in store cupboards anywhere?'

'Nope.'

'No healthy young children with strong white teeth?'

'Not today.'

'A tall young man with dark hair and a lithe, slender body, perhaps?'

''Fraid not.'

'Hmm, pity. Well, no matter, the wench will bring a pretty pinny. Come! We sail for Le Half!'

With Colin leading the way, Reg and Jeannette tottered carefully across the gangplank connecting the two ships, Reg uttering a series of little yelps as Black Nidge poked him in the small of the back with the tip of his sword. Once aboard the *Golden Swine* (as Nidge's ship was called), they were manhandled below deck by two burly yet oddly effeminate youths, who shoved them along a dingy passage and into a small, sparsely furnished cabin. The door slammed behind them and they heard the sound of a heavy key being turned on the other side of it.

They gazed around at their new accommodation. On the outer wall was a tiny porthole, and below that was a large tin bucket, the function of which Reg dared not speculate on. Against the wall on the left was a crude, two-tier bunk bed, and the only other furniture consisted of two wooden chairs and a small table.

Reg took a huge breath and let it out in a long, horse-like raspberry.

'Well,' he said, slumping down into one of the chairs, 'what the hell do we do now?'

Jeannette slumped down onto the remaining chair. 'God knows – only I have a feeling He doesn't preside over this particular world.'

'I have a feeling you're right.'

Jeannette glanced around the cabin, searching for ideas.

'I don't suppose we could fit through the porthole?'

Reg shook his head. 'Not a chance. Besides, I think I'd rather be on a slave trader's ship than splashing about in the middle of the ocean.'

'Good point,' conceded Jeannette. 'What about the door?'

'What about it? You heard them lock it.'

'True.'

Jeannette glanced around again, but it was obvious that there was no other way out.

'So it looks as if we're trapped,' she concluded.

Reg nodded. 'That would seem to be about the size of it.'

They swayed slightly as the ship turned into the wind, and they could sense the forward motion as additional sails were unfurled. Reg got up and went to the porthole. Through the thick dusty glass he could see the *Iceberg* growing smaller in their wake, and on her deck, he thought he could just make out the figure of Captain Tanyick, issuing orders and holding something to his lips.

'Oh well,' he said, 'so much for the *Iceberg*.'

'At least it didn't hit one,' Jeannette pointed out.

'Touché,' said Reg, and sat down again.

At that moment they heard the sound of the key turning in the lock, and with a wizened creak, the cabin door swung open revealing the tall muscular figure of

Colin. With a swagger and a 'Hah!', he tossed their rucksacks into the middle of the floor.

'You carry some strange belongings,' he said, with what he hoped was a piratical sneer, 'and by the way, the deckhands congratulate you on your sandwich fillings.'

With an unpleasant ya-boo-sucks sort of cackle, he slammed the door and locked it, and they could hear him chuckling to himself as he made his way along the passage.

'Oh well,' Reg said, 'at least we got these back.'

'Yes. I wonder . . .'

'What?'

'I took the bottle of invisible potion off before I went to sleep last night. I wonder if they found it.'

'Well,' said Reg, 'I think it's about time we took a look at the contents of these damned things anyway. God knows what Mahatma put in them.'

Thankful for something to do, they began to pull objects out of the rucksacks, examining them curiously as they did so. They were amused to discover that the Tupperware boxes once again contained sandwiches, and had they not eaten so recently, they would have taken great delight in scoffing them. Other surprises included several items of warm clothing, a book called *A Traveller's Guide to the Eastern Aisles*, two neatly folded pieces of canvas with the word 'Shelter' printed on them, two small leather purses filled with what appeared to be circular bank notes, and a length of rope.

Rummaging through assorted items of make-up, several hairbrushes, a can of 'Impulse' and a veritable plethora of Sainsbury's till receipts, Jeannette finally found what she was looking for.

'Da daa!' she said, and held it up triumphantly.

'The invisible potion!' exclaimed Reg, somewhat unnecessarily.

'Exactly. Now all we need is a plan.'

'A plan?'

'Yes. An escape plan.'

'Oh, right. Mmm, yes, that's a good idea.'

'What is?'

'The escape plan.'

'What escape plan?'

'Well, there isn't one yet.'

'Oh.'

'What I mean is, the escape plan idea is a good idea.'

'Oh, I see.'

'Yes. All we need now is a plan.'

'Right.'

There was a lengthy pause as Reg and Jeannette mulled over the possible alternatives.

Suddenly Reg leapt from his chair. 'Of course! It's so simple!'

'What is?'

'The escape plan! I mean, now that we've got the potion, all we have to do is wait till we reach this Le Half place, make ourselves invisible, and then when they come to fetch us we sneak out of the cabin and off the ship.'

Jeannette jumped up and clapped her hands. 'Reg, you're a genius!' she announced, and flung her arms around his neck. She was, however, diplomatic enough not to mention the fact that the very same plan had occurred to her several minutes earlier. After all, Reg was supposed to be looking after her, and it seemed kinder to let him come up with the plan for himself.

They stood for a moment in triumphant silence, their arms around each other.

Slowly, their lips met.

Tentatively, their hands wandered.

Quietly, they moved to the bed.

Annoyingly, the door opened.

'What d'you think this is, the bloody Love Boat?' yelled Colin.

Reg and Jeannette pulled away from each other, flushed and embarrassed.

'Sorry,' said Reg, 'we were just—'

'I know what you were bloody doing, I'm not stupid! Well, not completely, anyway. So we'll have less of it, or you'll have Black Nidge himself to deal with.'

'Sorry,' Reg said again.

'Anyway, here's some bread and water for you.'

Reg and Jeannette smirked.

'And no more canoodling, d'you hear?'

'We promise,' Jeannette told him.

Colin grunted, then slammed the door and locked it.

The hours passed slowly.

Reg lay on the lower bunk and twiddled his thumbs. Then he got up and stood by the porthole, watching the interminable waves as they leapt and crashed and foamed and eddied. When he got bored with that, he sat on one of the chairs and carved his name on the table top with his switchblade. Then he lay down on his bunk again.

Jeannette sat on the top bunk, her legs swinging, and read *A Traveller's Guide to the Eastern Aisles*.

'Did you know the first settlers on the Eastern Aisles were convicts,' she asked, 'deported from the Western Aisles by the Bittish Government?'

'Bittish?'

'That's what it says.'

'How odd.'

'It also says the Eastern Aisles is now a "thriving, independent country with a lively cultural heritage and an exciting, vibrant social life".'

'Sounds wonderful,' said Reg, without enthusiasm.

Jeannette turned the page.

'Oh, this might be useful.'

'What's that?'

'A list of things to avoid when visiting the Eastern Aisles.'

'Really? Like what?'

Jeannette scanned the list.

' "One, avoid deprived inner city areas after midnight; two, avoid Sharwood Forest if possible – the inhabitants can be hostile; three, avoid the Rodney

Marshes and in particular the Luanda Lovelace Quicksands (where men have been known to get sucked to their death); four, avoid the drinking water in Costa Fortuna (Note: it may be advisable to avoid Costa Fortuna altogether)". Oh, this one sounds interesting. "Eight, avoid the native Cherry Key Tribe: see page ninety-one for further information".'

Jeannette flicked through the book to page ninety-one, then read aloud: ' "The native Cherry Key Tribe, originally led by the infamous warrior known as Geranium, are the only remaining indigenous inhabitants of the Eastern Aisles. They have a strong cultural tradition which spans many hundreds of years, and are said to be able to foretell the future, forecast the weather and predict the winner of the three-thirty at Old Haven. They have an unbridled hatred of the white settlers, who massacred two-thirds of the tribe when they arrived in the Eastern Aisles over two hundred years ago".'

'It looks as if white men are the same all over the universe,' Reg observed.

Jeannette closed the book and lay back on the bed.

'Why are people so horrid to each other, Reg?' she asked.

'I don't know,' he admitted. 'It's just human nature, I suppose.'

'Yes, but *we're* human, and *we're* not horrid to people.'

'No, but everybody's made differently. That's what

makes the world go round – even this one, it would seem.'

'I thought it was love that made the world go round.'

'That too. I mean, it's everything I suppose. Love, hate, hope, fear. It's all part of life's rich tapestry.'

Reg paused in thought for a moment. 'What a crock of shit,' he said at last. '*Money* makes the world go round, and anyone who says different is either broke or lying.'

'Probably both,' said Jeannette, and sighed.

There was a long silence, broken only by the low hiss of the waves and the creaking of the wooden ship.

The silence continued, an event which caused it to become even longer.

Eventually someone snored.*

* * *

A small two-masted vessel pulled up alongside the *Iceberg*.

Peering over the rail of his ship, Captain Tanyick espied a tall, cadaverous gentleman in a long black coat and a black fedora standing on the bow below him. Had the captain been from Earth as opposed to Urth, he might well have remarked on the man's uncanny resemblance to the Munster family's butler.

* For those who need to know, it was Reg.

'Good day to you,' the man called. 'Captain Tanyick, I presume.'

The captain nodded and touched his cap. 'Aye, that's me.'

'Allow me to introduce myself. My name is Mortimer.'

'Mortimer, eh? Yes, well, there you go then.'

'I believe, Captain, that you have two passengers on board.'

Captain Tanyick sighed and shook his head. 'Nope.'

'I beg your pardon?'

'I said, nope.'

'You mean you *don't* have two passengers on board?'

'That's right.'

'But I was told most assuredly that you did.'

'I did.'

'You did?'

'That's right.'

'But then, surely Captain, you still do.'

'Nope.'

The face of the man named Mortimer took on an additional quality of malevolence, and his eyes narrowed to two black pinpoints.

'Captain Tanyick, are you telling me that your passengers simply ... got off, out here in the middle of the ocean?'

'Nope.'

Mortimer sighed dangerously. 'Then what *are* you telling me, Captain?'

'They got *took* off.'

'*Took* off?'

'That's right.'

'Am I to understand that they were abducted, forcibly, from your ship?'

'You are, sir. Abducted from right under me very nose.'

'I see. How exceedingly irritating.'

'You can say that again. They hadn't paid me!'

'And by whom, may I ask, were they abducted?'

'Black Nidge.'

'Black Nidge?'

'Aye. The slave trader.'

'Ah, indeed?'

Mortimer thought for a moment.

'And where do you suppose, Captain, he would be likely to take them?'

'Who knows? There's markets all over the Eastern Aisles. If he wanted to sell 'em quick, mind, Le Half's the nearest.'

'I see. So your guess would be Le Half?'

'I reckon so.'

'Very well, then, I must proceed there with all haste.'

'Aye, you'd best. If he's already sold 'em, you'll never find 'em. The slave racket's not exactly legal, you know, so nobody'll tell you nothin'. They'll just disappear off the face of the Urth. It'll be like looking for—'

'Yes, yes, thank you, Captain, I do appreciate the urgency of my mission.'

'Oh, right, okay then.'

Mortimer raised his hat briefly.

'I am grateful for your help, Captain Tanyick. I must say, however, to lose one passenger may be regarded as a misfortune; to lose both looks like carelessness. Have a nice day now, won't you?'

Mortimer turned to the captain of the *Enterprise*. 'We will proceed as planned.'

'All right, Mr Soo Loo,' said Captain Kirque, 'set a course for Le Half. Wind factor 9, if you please.'

Mr Soo Loo responded with a nod and a knowing smile. 'Aye aye, Cap'n.'

Slowly the small ship pulled away from the *Iceberg*, and moved off in the direction of Le Half. Captain Tanyick watched it go thoughtfully. He had no idea who Mortimer was, but he couldn't help wondering if Reg and Jeannette might not be better off where they were than in the clutches of the evil looking man in the black hat. He could only speculate on what Mortimer wanted them for, but in Captain Tanyick's experience, people who looked like that either intended to subject you to a slow painful death or present you with a tax demand.

The captain sighed and turned to his crew.

'All right, full speed ahead for New Fork,' he commanded. 'We're going home.'

7

'I can see land!' Reg declared excitedly. 'It must be the Eastern Aisles!'

Jeannette jumped off her bunk and ran to the porthole. Through the dingy glass she could just make out an indistinct coastline, some few miles distant. Lights twinkled in the gathering dusk, and the tantalising strip of land – once described by an Arbleenian statesman as 'the most dangerous place outside Hilda the Head's* bedroom' – looked both thrilling and terrifying. Shimmering behind what was obviously the port of Le Half, mist-shrouded hills could be seen, and beyond them, distant bluish mountains loomed towards the purpling sky.

Jeannette experienced a surge of quiet excitement. 'It looks terribly romantic,' she sighed.

'It's also got a reputation for being terribly dangerous,' Reg pointed out.

'Oh, don't be a spoilsport, Reg. We'll be all right if we're careful.' She dangled the little bottle of green potion in front of him. 'We've got this, remember?'

'Speaking of which,' said Reg, 'we'd better get our rucksacks on and get ready to do our disappearing act.'

They duly strapped their luggage to their backs, and

---

* A reference to Hilda Meyer Sukitoff, a notorious Arbleenian prostitute famed for her oral dexterity.

Reg pressed his ear against the door, listening for the approach of footsteps, whilst through the porthole Jeannette watched the ship draw slowly into Le Half.

Some ten minutes later Reg heard the sound of heavy leather boots descending the wooden steps at the end of the passage.

'Jeannette!' he hissed. 'Quick! Somebody's coming!'

Jeannette bounded quietly across the cabin to where Reg was pressed against the wall behind the door. She unscrewed the silver cap of the little bottle, and carefully allowed a drop to fall onto the back of Reg's outstretched hand. She poured a drop onto the back of her own hand, and grinning at each other nervously, they rubbed the potion in and waited.

The footsteps outside the door grew louder. Reg and Jeannette stared at each other in mounting horror, neither, so far, displaying any signs whatsoever of becoming anything other than distinctly visible.

They jumped as they heard the sound of the key being turned in the lock.

'Why isn't it working?' hissed Reg.

Jeannette spread her hands in desperate nescience. 'How should I know?'

The lock clicked loudly, and with its customary wizened creak, the door swung open.

'All right you two—' said the voice of Colin, and stopped. The momentary silence which followed positively reeked of puzzlement, as Colin's less than adequate brain attempted to compute the significance of the signals it was receiving. He took a couple of paces into the cabin and peered around.

Reg and Jeannette, huddled together behind the door, were convinced that at any moment he would hear the deafening roar of their beating hearts, and the game would be up. In the event, it was not their combined cardiovascular activity which caused Colin to turn around, but the latter's sudden realization that he had so far neglected to look in the single most obvious hiding place – to wit, behind the door. Slowly, like a rhino that has just been insulted, Colin turned and stared at them. Reg and Jeannette grinned back at him sheepishly.

Then a very peculiar thing happened. Colin turned round again, scanned the cabin once more, planted his hands on his hips and said, 'Now where the hell have those two gone?'

Reg and Jeannette gazed at each other in astonishment. The same idea occurred to them simultaneously, but this was patently not the time to discuss it. Reg took Jeannette's hand, and with an instinctive animal stealth they were not even aware they possessed, they crept around the door, out of the cabin and along the passage.

Emerging through a trap door in the ship's deck, Reg's invisible head peered around at the bustle of a newly docked ship being unloaded. The air was thick with the cries of stevedores, and Black Nidge himself strode up and down the deck, hurling orders at small gangs of reptobates, who were loading a number of

rope nets with canvas bales of illegal smelling substances. Reg was convinced he caught a distinct whiff
of cannabis, but there was so much spice and perfume
around, it was hard to tell. To the left he spotted a
wide gangplank leading to the dockside, down which
were plodding a procession of reptobates with sacks
over their shoulders.

Reg scrambled through the trap door, pulling Jeannette behind him, and they crept over to the rail near
the top of the gangplank. (Just why they were creeping
is unclear, since it was perfectly obvious that not a soul
could see them.)

Suddenly a gap appeared, as one of the reptobates
struggled to lift a heavy sack, and they leapt onto the
gangplank and tottered down it to the relative safety
of the dockside.

'Now what?' whispered Jeannette.

'Now I think we just run like hell,' Reg said, and
still clutching Jeannette tightly by the hand, he set off
in the direction of what looked like the main part of
town. Unfortunately, at the same moment Jeannette
took off in the opposite direction, almost pulling Reg's
arm out of its socket and giving herself whiplash in the
process. They both immediately turned around to
follow the other, collided, and landed in a heap on the
cobbles. Picking themselves up and brushing dust and
cotton fluff from their invisible clothes (a sight which
caused a loitering stevedore to head immediately for the
nearest bar), they finally set off in the same direction.

Aboard the *Golden Swine*, Colin emerged through

the deck hatch with an odd, quizzical expression on his face. He was shaking his head slowly and muttering to himself. Black Nidge, currently engaged in thrashing one of the reptobates with a cat o'ten tails, spotted him and stopped mid-lash.

'Colin!' he yelled, 'where the hell are my bodies?'

Colin looked up, and stared at Black Nidge as if he'd never seen him before.

'What?'

'My bodies! The girl and her mate! Where are they?'

'Ah. Yes. Erm, you're not going to like this, Nigel.'

'What the devil are you talking about, you moron?'

'Your bodies.'

'What about them?'

'Well, they've erm, they've gone.'

'Gone?'

'Yes.'

'Gone where?'

'Well, I don't know. The door was locked, the porthole doesn't open and there's no other way out. But they've gone.'

Black Nidge crimsoned, and a silent rage welled inside him. He purpled, and his rage exploded in a deafening, sonorous roar. Finally, his face turned a hideous shade of black, and seizing Colin as though he were no heavier than a sack of feathers, he threw him over the side of the ship.

It might have been kinder to throw him over the side that wasn't up against the dock, but that was Black Nidge all over. Not to mention Colin.

*

Reg and Jeannette clattered noisily along the quayside, leaving bemused dockworkers staring suspiciously at each other in their wake. Skittering around a likely looking corner, Reg dragged Jeannette up a cobbled street and along a series of alleyways, before passing through a small stone arch which brought them out in the middle of a rather pleasant, paved courtyard. They gazed around in a silence punctuated only by their own wheezing, trying to decide which of several arched doorways looked the most likely to lead to safety.

'What about this one?' Reg said, pointing.

Jeannette looked doubtful, but nodded. 'It's as good as any, I suppose.'

Tentatively they crossed the courtyard and peered through the doorway, which gave onto a narrow, winding passage.

'What d'you think?' Reg asked.

Jeannette shrugged. 'Nothing ventured, nothing gained.'

Reg nodded. 'That's what my father said just before he lost two hundred quid at the Doncaster races.'

Slowly, and with scalp-prickling apprehension about what they would find around the next turn, they set off down the passage. At first their progress was facilitated by the light from the doorway, but as they turned corner after heart-stopping corner, the darkness closed in around them like a black candy-floss blanket. Finally, they were feeling their way along the tunnel in pitch blackness, and the very air, it seemed, had assumed a fleshy, tangible aspect.

'I don't like this, Reg,' Jeannette confessed, and her voice sounded thick and flat.

'Don't worry,' Reg assured her, trying hard to keep the wobble out of his own voice. 'Just keep hold of my hand and we'll be okay.'

As they trudged on through the inky darkness the ground under their feet became softer and more yielding, as if the cobbles had suddenly turned into grass. It had the springy, resilient quality of a well tended lawn, and Jeannette fancied that it even smelled like grass.

'What are we walking on?' she wondered aloud.

'I dread to think,' Reg admitted, 'but it's not cobbles any more.'

'I wish I knew where we were going.'

'So do I. I feel like Alice in Wonderland. I keep expecting a white rabbit to run past any minute.'

'Reg,' Jeannette said, her voice still dull and hollow, 'is it me, or is it getting darker?'

'How can it get any darker than impenetrable blackness?'

'Well I – oh! I've got my eyes shut.'

'To be honest, I don't think it makes any difference.'

They felt their way along in silence for almost another two minutes.

Suddenly, Reg stopped.

'Jeannette!' he hissed. 'Have you got your eyes open?'

'No,' she told him.

'Well open them.'

Jeannette did so, then let out a whoop of excitement. 'Ooh! Reg, is that light?'

They peered ahead to a faint pinprick of – not light, but not dark either, which twinkled tantalisingly in the distance.

'It *must* be,' Reg decided. 'I mean, this passage has got to end somewhere, and I can't see them going to all the trouble of building it just to have it end in a blank stone wall.'

'You never know,' Jeannette pointed out. 'There are some weird people on this planet.'

'Well, there's only one way to find out,' Reg decided, and began to feel his way cautiously towards the pin-prick of non-dark. As they approached whatever it was, it got noticeably larger, and this they took to be a good sign. Gradually the thing began to take shape, and the closer they got, the more it began to resemble daylight pouring through an open doorway.

'I think we've made it,' whispered Reg, a note of excitement in his voice.

'Yes, but to where?' Jeannette wondered.

By now they no longer had to feel their way along, as the darkness scattered in disarray and fled before the superior forces of daylight. They looked down, and were relieved to discover that it was indeed grass upon which they were walking – thick, lush, magnificently green grass of the kind normally seen only on the covers of magazines with names like *Perfect Lawns*.

At last, they stumbled through the doorway and peered around, blinking and bewildered. As their eyes grew accustomed to the light, they were delighted to find themselves in the middle of the most beautiful garden they had ever seen. The sun was shining brilliantly (an occurrence rendered somewhat curious by the fact that when they had entered the passage it had been dusk), and the ground was covered in the same thick grass as in the tunnel. Everywhere there were luscious green trees filled, not just with blossom, but succulent red fruit as well. In a silence of wonder, Reg and Jeannette strolled towards the sound of running water, and discovered a wide silver stream rushing happily over a collection of beautiful multi-coloured pebbles.

'It's gorgeous,' breathed Jeannette, drinking in the musky fragrance of the fruit blossom.

'It's certainly a cracking garden,' admitted Reg. 'I wonder whose it is?'

Jeannette pirouetted daintily, crushing a delicate blue flower in the process. 'I can't see a house or anything.'

'There are no houses here,' said a sibilant reedy voice from above them. They jumped, looked at each other, then up at the tree next to them. At first they could see nothing, then gradually an odd, serpent-like head appeared from within the foliage. It winked at them, and its long forked tongue flicked out lazily at a passing bee. It missed.

'How do you do?' it hissed, and slithered a little further along its branch.

'Erm, erm . . .' said Reg, patently unused to conversing with reptiles, 'erm, fine, fine. How er, how are you?'

'Oh, sso sso, you know.'

'Erm, you're not dangerous are you?' Jeannette wondered.

'No. I may have been oncce, I ssuppose, but I'm far too old now.'

'Ah.'

'Positively ancient, in fact. I've been here ssincce the dawn of time, you know.'

'Really? Well, er, good heavens.'

'Don't talk to me about Hevvan,' hissed the serpent, and tossed its head indignantly.

'How come you can er, talk then?' asked Reg. 'I mean, do *all* snakes talk in this world?'

'Oh, by no means,' answered the serpent, 'although you'd be ssurprised jusst how many thingss *can* talk. Mosst of them choose not to, of coursse, becausse ninety-nine per cent of the time it'ss a complete wasste of breath. I mysself learned to do it ssimply to passs the time. It getss awfully boring sslithering about and eating hamssters all day.'

Jeannette shuddered. 'Does no one else live here then?'

'No, not a ssoul. There *wass* a young couple, oh, musst be hundredss of yearss ago now, but they left. Alan and Edith I sseem to remember they were called.'

'What happened?' asked Jeannette.

'Well, to cut a long sstory short, Alan got banished, then Edith got bored and buggered off with one of the bricklayers who wass employed to build the wall around the garden.'

'Sounds oddly familiar,' commented Reg.

The serpent looked wistful. 'I ssuppose a lot of it wass my fault, if the truth be known. I mean, they were really quite happy pranccing about in the altogether, ssplashing in the sstream and living on vegetables from the allotment. Then I went and talked Edith into eating an apple from the Tree of Nullidge. I know I shouldn't have done it, but between you and me, the poor girl looked deccidedly anorexic. Sso I thought to mysself "Ooh, yess, a nice juiccy apple will do her the world of good". Of coursse, everything went to pieccies after that. They both noticed that they weren't quite . . . *built* the ssame, if you get my drift, and took to sspending a lot of time behind the magnolia bushes over in the corner. Naturally, Goat cottoned on to what wass happening and booted Alan out, and thingss have never been the ssame ssince.'

'It's the Garden of Eden!' declared Jeannette, visibly thrilled.

'The Garden of Nede, actually,' said the serpent.

'But that's Eden backwards.'

'Is it? Oh well, if you ssay sso.'

'We have a similar story in our own world,' Reg explained.

'Thiss may be a ssilly question,' the serpent said cautiously, 'but what exactly do you mean by your "own world"?'

'Oh, well, we're not actually from Urth. We come from another dimension . . . I think.'

'Indeed? Yess, well, I ssuppose that ssort of thing

happenss all the time nowadayss. I haven't been outsside the garden for ccenturies, you ssee.'

'Ah. So you wouldn't happen to have heard of a
Roopert of Murdok then?'

The serpent shook its scaly head sadly. 'Ssorry, 'fraid
not. Get me on fruit and young people in fig leaves
and I'm a veritable mine of information. Not too hot
on what goess on outsside the garden, though, that'ss
the problem.'

'Do you never get any visitors, then?' Jeannette
asked. 'From outside, I mean.'

'Oh, perhapss one every hundred years or sso I ssuppose. There is a gate, you ssee, but unfortunately it'ss
only visible from *insside* the garden. The only other
way in is through a long dark passage built by the
Thaumaturgical and Ssagaciouss Bricklaying Corporation, but the entrance to that only existss for one
hour every sseven years. Needless to ssay, crowd control is not one of my problemss.'

'What about the wall?' Jeannette persisted. 'Don't
you ever get people climbing over it?'

The serpent shook his head again. 'You don't climb
over wallss built by wizardss.'

'Why not?'

'I'm not absolutely sure, but I think it'ss ssomething
to do with gramaryeic radiation. You don't even *look*
at a wizard wall, let alone try to climb over it.'

Reg turned to Jeannette. 'Well, there's one good
thing about it. We seem to have stumbled into about
the safest place on the whole of the Eastern Aisles.'

Jeannette nodded. 'It seems ironic that the Garden of Eden—'

'Nede,' corrected the serpent.

'—should be situated smack bang in the middle of what, by all accounts, is the most uncivilized city on Urth.'

'Oh, I don't know,' said Reg. 'It is the home of original sin, after all.'

Jeannette shrugged. Annoyingly, Reg had a point.

At that moment, with a silence born of a million years' practice, the sun winked out and plunged the garden into darkness. Jeannette cried out, and had it been a little less tight, Reg might well have jumped out of his skin.

'My God! What's happened?' he said instead.

'Oh, don't worry,' the serpent assured them, 'it'ss just night. Don't you get it in your world?'

'Well, yes, but it happens rather more gradually than that.'

'Ah, yess, well, there's no fiddling about with dawn, or dussk, or anything like that here. Jusst goes sstraight from day to night and back again. Mind you, at leasst you know where you sstand. No waiting for the ssun to come up, or worrying about fading light.'

'Pity they can't hold Test matches here,' commented Reg.

'Actually,' said Jeannette, poking the soft grass with the toe of her shoe, 'since it *is* dark, perhaps we ought to spend the night here.'

'Oh, by all means,' offered the serpent. 'You're more than welcome, I assure you.'

'What if it rains?' Reg said.

'It never rains here,' the serpent told him.

'Never?'

'Not ssince the dawn of time.'

'How come the grass and the trees are so healthy then?'

The serpent gave as creditable an impression of a shrug as it is perhaps possible for a limbless reptile to give. 'Who knows?' he said. 'Goat movess in myssteriouss ways, his wonders to perform.'

'Well,' said Reg, considering, 'I suppose it wouldn't be a bad idea to get some sleep, then make an early start in the morning.'

Jeannette wandered over to a nearby tree, and using her rucksack as a pillow, lay down beneath it.

'This grass is wonderfully comfortable,' she said, bending her legs at the knees, 'and it's still warm from the sun.'

Something stirred in the region of Reg's groin (it was his penis to be exact), as Jeannette's skirt rode up to reveal a pair of shapely thighs encased in black nylon.

'Ahem. Comfortable then, is it? Well I'll er, I'll come and join you, then.'

He strolled nonchalantly over to the tree, divested himself of his jacket and rucksack and lay down next to Jeannette. They both sighed.

'Yess, well, I'll be off looking for hamssters then,' said the serpent tactfully. 'Ssleep tight both of you.'

Some twenty minutes later, Reg and Jeannette were startled by a frantic rustling sound in the grass nearby. Suddenly the serpent's head appeared a few feet away.

'Erm, I'd rather you didn't do that if you don't mind,' he said, somewhat testily. 'That's what sstarted all the trouble in the firsst placce.'

'Ah. Sorry,' said Reg, a little breathlessly.

Jeannette groaned.

*   *   *

Mortimer swept past the crumpled body on the quay-side and stomped purposefully up the gangplank of the *Golden Swine*, scattering startled reptobates before him. Striding onto the deck he stood and peered around, his sunken eyes exuding something which, no matter how much you played about with it, could never be described as benevolence. Gervase, the chief deckhand, sidled up to him nervously.

'Are you being ser—, I mean, can I help you at all?' he enquired.

Mortimer turned and surveyed this small effeminate young man in the leather trousers and knee-high boots, and sniffed disdainfully.

'It is possible,' he allowed. 'I am looking for the man known as Black Nidge.'

'Ah, yes. Well I'm afraid Nigel isn't feeling very well at the moment. In fact, he's having a little lie-down in his cabin.'

Mortimer sniffed again. 'Nevertheless, I would still like to see him.'

'I'm afraid he gave strict instructions that he wasn't to be disturbed.'

'It is very important,' Mortimer said slowly, fixing Gervase with menacing gaze number seven, which, to date, had never failed to get results. Nor did it now, and Gervase's air of polite efficiency dissipated like so much cigarette smoke. He pulled a lavender-scented handkerchief from his waistcoat pocket and mopped his brow.

'Erm, well, all right then,' he said. 'If you'll follow me, I'll show you to his cabin. But I feel it's only fair to warn you that he'll probably be in a dreadful mood.'

'His mood is of no interest to me,' said Mortimer dismissively. 'It is information I require.'

'Yes, well, if you'll walk this way.'

Keeping a firm grip on his gait, Mortimer followed Gervase across the deck to the hatch, then down the wooden steps and along the passage to an ornate mahogany door at the far end. Gervase hesitated for a moment, then, having glanced at Mortimer and decided that waking up Black Nidge might well be the lesser of two evils, he knocked on the door.

'Who is it?' came a thunderous voice from inside.

'Erm, it's Gervase, Nigel.'

'Ah, Gervase,' said the voice, its tone noticeably

softer. 'Come in, dear boy, I could do with cheering up. And I can't think of anything nicer than one of your exquisite—'

'Excuse me, Nigel,' said Gervase quickly, 'but there's someone here to see you.'

'What? Who?'

Gervase glanced enquiringly at Mortimer.

'The name is Mortimer,' the latter informed him.

'It's a Mr Mortimer.'

'What does he want?'

'What do you want?'

'Information.'

'He wants information.'

'What kind of information?'

'What kind of information?'

'It concerns two young people, who I have reason to believe were abducted from the *Iceberg*.'

'It's about the two bodies, Nigel.'

From the other side of the door there came a grunt and the sound of muffled footsteps. The door swung open suddenly and the crimson face of Black Nidge appeared, his one exposed eye clenched in a suspicious squint.

'What about my bodies?' he demanded of Mortimer. 'Do you know where they are?'

Mortimer blinked. 'I was rather hoping you could supply *me* with that particular information.'

'That I can't.'

'But I was led to believe that it was you yourself who abducted them from Captain Tanyick's ship.'

'So I did. And I'd have got a pretty pinny for the girl at Le Half Market, I can tell you.'

'So where are they now?'

'Disappeared, mate, that's the top and bottom of it.'

'You mean you let them escape?'

'You can call it that if you like, but I'm buggered if I know how they did it. They were in a locked cabin with a porthole that doesn't open and no other way out, but I'll be a juggler's armpit if by the time we docked they hadn't gone.'

'How very peculiar,' said Mortimer thoughtfully. 'It has all the trappings of a Martha Konan Boyle story. You're quite certain there's no other means of exit from the cabin?'

'Positive. If you ask me, there's magic at work here. Mind you, if that's the case I'm probably better off without 'em.'

Mortimer nodded understandingly. 'Well,' he said, treating Nidge to the briefest of smiles, 'thank you for your help, meagre though it turned out to be. I shall leave you to your repose.'

Raising his hat little more than a millimetre, Mortimer turned on his heel and glided back down the passage. As Gervase turned to follow him a strong hand grasped him by the shoulder and pulled him into the cabin. The door closed quietly.

8

The man known as Baron von Fothemoni loaded the last of several small brown paper packages onto the back of his waggon and licked his fingers. He was a tall, spare sort of figure, around forty years old with a lean, tanned face. His black hair was long and thick, scraped back from his forehead and tied in a ponytail, and on his well manicured fingers he wore several expensive rings. There was also a large gold ring in his left ear, and anyone passing him in a street on Earth might well have mistaken him for a highly paid American session musician. He crossed the small cobbled courtyard and passed through a low doorway into his house.

From the outside, the building looked like hundreds of other houses in the bustling port of Le Half, built of local stone, with small leaded windows and a sagging stone-flagged roof. The interior, however, was quite a different story, and about as far removed from the inside of most of Le Half's dwellings as it was possible to get (without actually going anywhere, that is).

The spacious living room was beautifully designed, built on two levels and dotted – but dotted thoughtfully – with exotic pieces of furniture and rare ornaments from all over the Aisles. Lush Porschean rugs were scattered over the polished wooden floor, and works by some of the greatest artists on Urth hung on the pale green rag-rolled walls. The master bedroom upstairs was a pulsating beacon in the history of erotic interior design, and the bathroom, with its sunken jacuzzi and mirrored ceiling, was a symphony in Con-Menara Marble.

Closing the back door behind him, the Baron strode across his living room to the front window, pulled aside the exquisite lace curtain and peered out.

'Damn,' he said under his breath, 'damn, damn.'

This was going to delay his departure. He would have to wait until things had quietened down before he could leave, and if that cost him a sale, someone – it didn't matter who – would suffer. He let the curtain drop, crossed the room and flopped down onto a huge Plainsfolk-skin cushion. He lit a hand-rolled cigarette and blew out a cloud of exotic-smelling smoke. He supposed he oughtn't to complain. After all, the people in the streets were simply trying to get the law changed, and their ultimate success in that enterprise would most certainly be to his own advantage.

The Baron turned to thoughts of his coming journey across the Eastern Aisles, and experienced a pang – albeit a faint one – of apprehension. The trip would be perilous, he knew, but then it always was – and the Baron was no stranger to the concept of sudden and violent death. He had come close to it before on a number of occasions, but had always managed to charm (or kill) his way out of it. Besides, the trip was necessary. The Sihkstiz Tribe over in the Glassed-on-Berry Mountains would be running low on supplies by now, and if he didn't show up they would simply go and buy from his arch rival, Count Toofer-Thesho, and that could cost the Baron very dearly indeed.

*   *   *

Reg and Jeannette awoke suddenly, as the sun burst into life like an electric lightbulb, bathing the Garden of Nede in a brilliant, clear radiance.

'Good morning,' said the serpent, who was currently reclining on a branch directly above them. 'You sslept well, I hope.'

'Like a log,' said Jeannette, rubbing her eyes.

'But logs don't ssleep,' the serpent pointed out.

'Oh yes, I forgot.'

Reg sat up. 'What does he mean, logs don't sleep?'

'Let's not get into it,' Jeannette said climbing to her feet. 'It's a bit complicated.'

'I ssuppose you'll be leaving now,' said the serpent.

'Well,' Reg admitted, 'we really ought to get going. We've still got to find this Roopert chap we told you about.'

'Oh well, it'ss been nicce talking to you anyway. I ssuppose ssomeone else will pop through the tunnel in another hundred years or sso.'

'Why don't you have a little holiday?' suggested Jeannette. 'You know, go out and meet a few people.'

'Alass, I cannot leave the garden. Frankly, I wouldn't want to anyway. I'd be ssomebody's handbag before you could ssay Robert Robinsson.'

'Oh well, it's been nice meeting you.'

'The feeling'ss mutual, I'm sure. By the way, if you're thirssty the sstream is perfectly ssafe to drink from – and there'ss always appless if you're feeling a bit peckish.'

'Weell...' said Reg, thinking of the effect the garden's apples had on the original female occupant.

'Thanks,' Jeannette put in, 'but we've got provisions with us. We'll probably stop for a bite later on.'

'As you please,' said the serpent. 'I'll bid you fare-well, then. I'm off to catch breakfasst.'

So saying, he slithered down the tree and rustled off through the lush green grass.

'Nice sort of chap – I mean snake, or whatever,' commented Reg.

'Yes, but he must get awfully bored living here by himself.'

'I suppose he's used to it after all this time.'

Jeannette nodded. 'I can't help feeling sorry for him, though.'

Reg, who was finding it difficult to feel sentimental about a limbless reptile with a serious speech impedi-ment, glanced around the perimeter wall. 'Ah, that must be the gate over there,' he said, pointing.

Hitching their rucksacks onto their backs, Reg and Jeannette strolled across the garden to where a small, green wooden gate was set into the high stone wall. Half expecting it to be locked, Reg pressed down the brass latch and breathed a little sigh of relief when the gate swung open. With a last wistful glance at the

beautiful garden, they stepped through it to find themselves in a deserted cobbled street. As Reg closed the
gate behind them he was a little startled by the way it
suddenly disappeared from view, as though it had never
been there at all. As they gazed at it, the very wall
itself seemed to become vague and indistinct, and they
both experienced a strong urge to avert their eyes
from it.

'I can see what the snake meant about wizard walls,'
said Reg, turning away.

'Me too,' said Jeannette, and shuddered.

Almost directly opposite them on the other side of
the street was a narrow cobbled alleyway.

'Shall we try down there?' suggested Reg.

'Why?'

'Well, why not? When I have no idea which is the
right direction, I tend to pick the nearest route and
follow it till I find somebody to ask.'

There was a certain amount of logic in this, Jeannette had to admit, so they crossed the street and
started down the alley.

As they proceeded along it, closed in on either side
by high windowless walls, they became aware of a
strange and somehow unpleasant noise in the distance.
For some reason it reminded Reg of a football match.
As they got closer to what was obviously the end of
the alley, the sound coalesced into a kind of strident
phonic multi-ululation. By the time they got to within
a few yards of the opening, they were able to identify
the sound quite clearly as that caused by a lot of people

running around and shouting very loudly.

'I'm not sure that I like the sound of that,' commented Reg.

As they turned cautiously into the wide street at the end of the alley they were almost swept away by a tide of around two hundred people, clattering across the cobbles and waving banners and placards. They were closely followed by a hundred or so men in smart green uniforms, who were obviously the cream of Le Half's considerable police force. Everyone seemed to be shouting at once, and as they retreated, the mob hurled bricks and bottles (and anything else they could lay their hands on) at the advancing police. In turn, the police lashed out with their batons at anyone foolish enough to come within hitting distance, including each other.

Ducking below the trajectory of a stream of miscellaneous missiles, Reg and Jeannette managed to find a convenient doorway, into which they pressed themselves as closely as possible, (cursing their bulky rucksacks). The mob swept past them, some of the younger ones pausing occasionally to smash a window or overturn a delivery cart.

'I wish we'd stayed in the garden,' hissed Jeannette.

Reg nodded vehemently and pressed himself harder against the door. 'So do I.'

There was a soft click, and suddenly the door swung open, causing Reg and Jeannette to tumble untidily onto the opulent living room floor of the man known as Baron von Fothemoni. The Baron leapt up from his cushion and with a practised flourish, drew a short, lethal-looking sword from beneath his cloak.

'What's the meaning of this?' he demanded.

'Ah, I'm terribly sorry,' said Reg, struggling to his feet. 'We were hiding from the mob and the door just suddenly sort of popped open.'

Jeannette nodded in agreement. 'That's right. We weren't trying to break in or anything.'

The Baron regarded them shrewdly, and after a few seconds lowered his sword.

'Yes, well,' he said, sliding the weapon into a jewel-studded sheath, 'I suppose I should have bolted it, with all that going on outside.'

He strode across the room, closed the door and slid two heavy bolts into place.

'My name is Baron von Fothemoni,' he said, extending a hand.

Reg shook it. 'Pleased to meet you, Baron. I'm Reg, and this is Jeannette.'

The Baron looked them up and down curiously, intrigued by Reg's faded Levis. 'You are obviously not from these parts.'

'No, we're not.'

'You are students perhaps, touring The Aisles?'

'Er, no,' Reg said. 'Actually, it's rather a long story.'

The Baron indicated a velvet-covered chaise longue. 'Pray, sit down and tell me about it. You intrigue me.'

'Oh, well, thanks,' said Reg, as he and Jeannette divested themselves of their rucksacks, 'although I'm not sure you're going to believe it.'

The Baron sighed. 'I have travelled far in my life and seen many things, and have realized that very little is impossible.'

'Well,' said Reg, taking a deep breath, 'it all began a few days ago . . .'

The Baron listened in silent fascination as Reg (with a little interjectory help from Jeannette) went on to describe their arrival on Urth, their adventures on the *Golden Swine* and their mission to find The Omnipotent Roopert of Murdok, who they hoped would be able to send them back to their own dimension. When Reg finally stopped speaking, the Baron sat back and shook his head in wonder.

'Incredible,' he said. 'Absolutely incredible. I have heard talk of Charring Crossers before, but I never hoped to be lucky enough to meet two of them in person. And such charming ones, too,' he added, smiling pointedly at Jeannette. Unable to help herself, she gave him the satisfaction of seeing her blush.

'So tell me, where does this Roopert of Murdok live?'

Jeannette took Mahatma's scrap of paper from the pocket of her rucksack and read out the address.

The Baron nodded. 'Near the village of Ailar-Tsua, yes, I have heard of it. In fact, I am going in that direction myself as I have some deliveries to make. Perhaps I could offer you a lift.'

'Oh, I say,' said Reg, 'that would be awfully helpful.'

'It would be my pleasure,' said the Baron, smiling at Jeannette again. 'After all, I have room on my waggon, and I know the ways of the road.'

'Well that would be great, wouldn't it, Jenn?'

'Er, yes, yes it would,' said Jeannette, still not certain that she entirely trusted this charming man in the long velvet cloak. He was certainly very polite, and really quite handsome, but there was definitely something about him that made her squirm. Unlike a nuclear attack button or a nipple, it wasn't anything she could put her finger on, but she felt sure that if he ever touched her she would either scream or throw up. (In the event, it turned out to be the former.)

'That's settled then,' said the Baron, clapping his hands. 'We travel together to Ailar-Tsua.'

'When were you actually thinking of leaving?' Reg enquired.

'As soon as possible, my friend. Indeed, I would have left already had it not been for the Pill Tax riots.'

'The what?'

'Pill Tax riots. It's a little complicated, but the local council in Le Half are trying to stamp out drug abuse (as they call it), and have imposed a Pill Tax on the town's population. Every time someone takes a pill they must pay the council five shellings. Nice idea, of course, but badly thought out, since the tax also includes harmless pain killers and pills prescribed by doctors.'

'How silly,' agreed Reg. 'No wonder the people are rioting.'

The Baron climbed off his cushion, crossed over to the window and peered out.

'It seems quiet now,' he observed. 'The police have probably chased them down to the dockyard. There will be some sore heads tonight.'

The Baron turned and gestured for them to follow.

'Come. We shall depart whilst the coast is clear.'

He led them out of the house and into the cobbled courtyard at the back, where a covered, horse-drawn waggon stood waiting. The Baron climbed up onto the front of it and took the reins.

'There are wooden seats in the back,' he told them. 'Not very luxurious I'm afraid, but better than walking, I think you'll agree.'

'We'll be fine,' Reg assured him, and throwing the rucksacks into the back, he gave Jeannette a peg up over the tailgate and climbed in behind her. They settled down on the two benches and grinned at each other. The Baron peered over his shoulder, smiled and nodded.

'Very cosy,' he said. 'If you are sitting comfortably, we will begin.'

'Hi ho Silver!' said Reg, cracking an imaginary whip, and Jeannette smiled rather unconvincingly.

Within ten minutes of leaving the Baron's courtyard, the streets of Le Half became noticeably narrower and shabbier, and before long, open countryside could be glimpsed through the gaps between the houses. Green fields stretched away into the distance, dotted here and there with copses of peculiar looking trees.

'You know,' said the Baron, speaking over his shoulder, 'it's really rather lucky that you stumbled into my house the way you did. The Eastern Aisles can be somewhat dangerous if you don't know the territory.'

'Well it's very kind of you to give us a lift like this,' Reg said.

'Think nothing of it.'

Reg gazed with curiosity at the small brown packages stacked along the sides of the waggon.

'By the way,' he said, 'what exactly are you delivering?'

Jeannette, who had been watching the Baron for some time now, could have sworn that he stiffened in his seat. There was a pause.

'Sugar,' said the Baron after a few seconds. 'Yes, it's er, not easy to come by in some of the wilder parts, so people pay me to deliver it.'

'Ah, right,' said Reg, with the credulity of the thoroughly naive. Jeannette's suspicions, on the other hand, were aroused still further by the obvious uncertainty in the Baron's voice. 'If that's sugar,' she thought, 'I'm Arthur Scargill's cat!'

For the next few hours they continued along what was now little more than a dusty track, surrounded by rolling hills and occasionally passing through dark, leafy wooded areas. Isolated settlements, consisting of a few cottages, an inn and a general store, came and went, and at one point Reg spotted what looked like an English castle lurking secretively amongst the trees of one of the forests.

'How long is it likely to take to get to this Ailar-Tsua place?' Reg enquired presently.

'If we stop at night, around four days.'

'Oh. And *will* we be stopping at night?'

'I think Hercules would appreciate it.'

'Hercules?'

The Baron turned and smiled at Reg. 'My horse,' he said simply.

'Oh, yes, of course. I never thought of that.'

'We should reach the edge of Sharwood Forest shortly before nightfall, and will make camp there.'

'Ah. Is it, er, safe? I mean, you know, not dangerous?'

'As safe as anywhere else, my friend. Deep inside the forest there are . . . things, but they rarely venture as far as the forest edge. Most of them are incurable agoraphobics.'

'What sort of "things" do you mean?' Jeannette wanted to know.

The Baron shrugged. 'The inhabitants of the forest are many. Some are almost human, others take the form of animals, but almost all are entirely wild. Even the trees themselves have been known to attack people, or so it is rumoured.'

Reg frowned. 'Do we actually have to go *through* the forest?'

'It is not imperative, but going around it would add perhaps another two days' ride to our journey.'

'I see. And you've er, you've been through it before, have you?'

'Many times.'

'And so far you've always got through unscathed?'

The Baron smiled to himself. 'Let us just say that so far, I have always got through.'

'Ah, right, yes.'

Reg nodded thoughtfully, and Jeannette couldn't help smiling. He really wasn't the hero type, this man that she now knew she was falling in love with, but you had to give him ten out of ten for effort. She remembered that day in Reg's cabin on the *Iceberg*, when he had told her not to worry because he would look after her, and although she knew it was no more than reckless bravado, she felt sure that he'd meant it with all of his heart. She looked at him now, chewing anxiously on one of his fingernails, and felt a wave of affection break on the beach of her breast.

Apart from passing a bearded man in sandals riding a donkey in the opposite direction, the rest of the day passed uneventfully, and as their shadow on the road ahead slowly lengthened, Sharwood Forest marched into sight on the distant horizon. It really was magnificent, and as they got closer, Reg realized the futility of attempting to bypass it. As far as the eye could see, thick green foliage danced and billowed in the breeze, and even from this distance, Jeannette fancied she could almost hear the leaves rustling.

Within half an hour they had reached the edge of the forest, and the sight of this sheer wall of trees stretching into the distance on either side was quite spectacular. There was also, Reg noticed, a faint smell of curry.

'It's really something, isn't it?' said the Baron, climbing down from the waggon and tethering Hercules to a tree at the side of the track. Reg and Jeannette threw out their rucksacks and jumped down onto the road, then gazed up at the forest canopy way above them.

'It certainly is,' agreed Reg. 'What kind of trees are they?'

'Arborundum Spicealicus,' the Baron told him, 'better known as Vinderlew sycamores. Unique to this particular area, as a matter of fact.'

They walked between the trees and a little way into the forest, and were surprised at how dark it was inside. The smell of curry was stronger here, too.

'I wouldn't fancy travelling through it at night,' admitted Reg.

'It's not much better during the day,' the Baron told him reassuringly.

A few yards further on Baron von Fothemoni indicated a small grassy clearing by the side of the track.

'This is where I usually make camp,' he said. 'It's far enough in to give shelter, but close enough to the edge to be safe.'

Reg surveyed the little clearing, in the centre of which were the remains of a small camp fire. The long grass had been trampled flat, and several plastic wrappers fluttered in what little breeze had managed to find its way between the trees.

'Oh well, we're not the first ones to camp here,' he observed.

'The spot is well used by travellers,' the Baron informed him.

Reg stepped into the clearing, selected a comfortable

looking patch of grass and set his rucksack down. He opened it, peered inside and rummaged about for several seconds. Finally, he pulled out the folded piece of canvas marked 'Shelter'. He turned it over and spent several more seconds studying the detailed instructions on the back. Although incredibly complicated and written in pidgin English, Reg at last narrowed the directions down to a small piece of string tucked into one of the corners. This he located, and tugged sharply. He leapt backwards, as the canvas suddenly launched into a series of noisy convulsions, the end result of which was an exceedingly creditable one-man tent.

'I say, that's a bloody useful gadget,' Reg said, walking carefully around the triangular construction. 'Certainly beats farting about with all those guy ropes and pegs.'

Choosing a spot a few feet from Reg's tent, Jeannette erected her own shelter, giving a little whoop of delight as it 'popped' itself into shape. Then they both helped the Baron to put up his large and rather luxurious bivouac, which looked a little like the kind of thing a medieval jouster might have got changed in. From a trunk built into the floor of the waggon he brought cushions and embroidered sheets, along with a small wooden bedside cabinet.

'Even on the road,' he explained, 'I see no reason to abandon entirely the comforts of home.'

Reg and Jeannette collected a quantity of dry leaves and branches from beneath the surrounding trees (along with some wild poppadoms they found growing there), and the Baron, obviously skilled in such matters, created a blazing camp fire on the remains of the previous one.

With shafts of moonlight streaming through the gaps in the forest canopy, the three travellers sat in the glow of the fire and ate a cosy, companionable supper. Afterwards, the Baron lit one of his exotic smelling cigarettes and reclined on his cushion, watching the smoke twist lazily in the slight breeze. The evening was warm, and the aroma of the camp fire and the Baron's cigarette, together with the distinctive smells of the forest, began to have a soporific effect on Reg. He yawned.

'Well this is very pleasant,' he said, 'very pleasant indeed. I shall sit here and relax for a bit longer, then I think I'll hit the sack.'

'What sack is that?' asked the Baron, peering about him curiously.

'Oh, it's just a figure of speech. It means go to bed.'

'Ah, indeed?' The Baron seemed to think of something. 'Before you do, you must have a nightcap with me.'

He got up and went into his tent, emerging a few seconds later with two small leather-bound flasks and three tiny silver goblets. From the smaller of the two flasks, he filled a goblet and handed it to Reg.

'You must savour that, my friend,' he said. 'It's very special.'

From the other flask he filled the two remaining goblets and handed one to Jeannette.

'Am I not allowed to have what Reg is having?' she asked, somewhat sulkily.

The Baron looked shocked. 'But of course, my dear. I merely thought that this particular liqueur might prove more appealing to the female palate.'

'Why are *you* drinking it then?'

'Alas, I am only allowed the other on very special occasions. Doctor's orders, you know.'

'Oh,' said Jeannette, unconvinced, 'I see.'

The Baron raised his goblet. 'To a safe and fruitful journey,' he said.

Reg and Jeannette raised their own goblets and repeated the Baron's toast then, following his example, threw back their drinks in one. Reg winced, as the liquid burned its way down his throat bringing tears to his eyes, then smiled involuntarily as a warm glow spread up from his abdomen and into his brain. The sensation was not unlike drinking several tequila slammers one after the other.

'By George, that hits the spot,' he declared.

'Potent, isn't it?' agreed the Baron.

Jeannette thought that her own drink tasted a little like egg flip, though it did produce a rather nice glowing sensation in the pit of her stomach.

After a few more minutes of pleasant conversation it became obvious that Reg was having difficulty keeping his eyes open, the major clue to which was the fact that they were shut. Jeannette nudged him.

He sat up and peered around in alarm. 'What?

What's happened?'

'You were dozing off,' Jeannette explained.

'Was I?'

'Either that, or you're the only person I know who snores when they're awake.'

'Oh, yes, well, I suppose I'd better go to bed then.'

Looking like a man of eighty, Reg struggled to his feet and stood there grinning and swaying.

'Well, it's been a very pleasant evening,' he said, 'and I'd like to thank you, Baron, for your hostipality.'

'It's been my pleasure,' said the Baron with a wry smile.

'Good night, then. See you in the norming,' said Reg, and tottered off to his tent. Feigning a yawn of her own, Jeanette got up and stretched. Although she wasn't particularly tired, there was no way she was going to sit there alone with the Baron. She wasn't at all sure why, but she found herself shuddering slightly every time their eyes met.

'Well, I think I'll follow Reg's example,' she said. 'Good night.'

'Oh, but Jeannette,' said the Baron in his most seductive tones, 'stay and talk awhile, please. The night is still young.'

'Yes, well, I'd like to, but I'm very tired. It's been a long day.'

'But—'

'Good night, Baron.'

Before words of further protest had even formed in the Baron's mind, Jeannette was inside her tent and securing the flaps. The Baron sat back and sighed. Ah well, no matter. The girl would succumb in time, of that he was certain. No woman had ever been able to resist his charms for long, particularly after drinking his special 'liqueur'. He had never failed yet, and he did not intend to let the opportunity of having his way with a Charring Crosser slip by. This really would be a prestigious notch on the bedpost.

Lying awake in her tent, Jeannette began to experience some rather peculiar – though not unpleasant – sensations. Her nipples ached in a strangely erotic kind of way, and she was aware of warm, happy, tingling feelings creeping about in areas they had no business to be in. It was at this point that she began to wonder if the Baron's liqueur had contained some potent form of aphrodisiac. Either that, or she had just discovered that sleeping in a tent in the middle of a forest made her horny (although she'd never noticed it when she was in the Girl Guides).

Ten minutes later the sensations had not subsided. If anything, they were more intense, and Jeannette finally decided she couldn't stand it any longer. She didn't care how tired Reg was, she needed a man. Now.

She untied the tent flaps and crawled on her hands and knees to Reg's tent. He hadn't bothered to fasten it, and Jeannette slipped inside to find him sprawled on the canvas groundsheet like a dead body. This impression was heightened by the fact that – unusually for Reg – he wasn't snoring. Jeannette lay down next to him, and worming her hand inside his shirt, began to tickle his belly. He failed to respond. She whispered something in his ear, but still he failed to respond. She whispered something stronger, the normal reaction to which would have been galvanization, but Reg remained every bit as inert as a cloud of krypton. Jeannette got a bit cross at this point, and poked him savagely in the ribs. When this also failed to elicit a response, the first inklings of doubt began to sidle through the half open doors of Jeannette's mind. Something was wrong. Okay, so Reg was tired, but no matter how knackered you were, if someone poked you in the ribs you woke up. She clambered to her knees, and grabbing Reg by the shoulders, shook him violently. Nothing, not even a grunt. In desperation she slapped him hard across the face, but like particularly viscous taffy, Reg refused to stir.

Consumed by panic, she crawled out through the flaps and ran over to the Baron's tent. Pushing her way through the unfastened opening, she dropped to her knees by the side of the Baron's bed of cushions.

'Baron, quick!' she pleaded. 'It's Reg! I can't wake him up! I think he might be . . . might be . . . dead!'

The Baron sat up and smiled unpleasantly. 'So, my little potion has taken effect then?'

Jeannette stared at him, her eyes wide with horror. 'You mean . . . that drink! You, you *poisoned* him!'

'My dear Jeannette, that is too harsh a word. I simply wanted him out of the picture so that you and I could be alone together.'

'You bastard!'

'I do love a girl with spirit,' said the Baron, and in a sudden swift movement, he grabbed Jeannette by the shoulders, threw her onto the cushions and forced himself on top of her.

Jeannette's screams echoed through the vast, dark forest.

* * *

Mad Rolf Hilter paced the length of his private study in a state of considerable agitation, pausing only briefly to gaze through the huge picture window which looked out over Birchingley Gardens. He turned and paced the other way, his pale skin glistening under a sheen of cold sweat and strands of black hair hanging lank and greasy over one eye. His hands were clasped behind his back, and he stared intently at the floor as if expecting to receive inspiration from the expensive oriental carpet that covered it. The large and rather pallid looking man who had for the last half hour been sitting in one of the carved wooden chairs at the side of the room, looked on apprehensively.

'Gobbles!' exploded Rolf suddenly. 'I want Gobbles!'

Herman jumped up from his chair and clicked his heels together. 'At once, Mine Fury, I will summon him immediately.'

He trotted to the door at the other end of the room,

opened it and poked his head into the corridor. 'Summon Herr Gobbles!' he bellowed. A few moments later a second, more distant voice repeated the command, followed by a third and then a fourth. Less than a minute after that the sound of running, leather-soled boots could be heard, growing steadily louder as their owner approached the conference room. At last Herr Gobbles burst through the door, breathless and panting, and executed a brief Nasti salute.

'You summoned me, Mine Fury,' he gasped.

Hilter, who by this time was slumped disconsolately on a leather chaise longue in the corner, looked up in surprise.

'What?' he snapped.

'You er, you summoned me.'

'Did I?'

'Erm, I believe so, yes.'

'Oh. What for?'

'Forgive me, Mine Fury, but I have no idea.'

'What do you mean, you have no idea?'

'Well, I . . .'

At this point, Herman emitted an embarrassed cough. 'Ahem. I believe, Mine Fury, that you intended to enquire about the progress of the search for the two Charring Crossers.'

'Of course I did!' yelled Hilter. 'I know that! I just fail to understand why Herr Gobbles was not aware of it.'

Gobbles shuffled uncomfortably. 'Forgive me, Mine Fury, a brief lapse of concentration. It will not happen again, I assure you.'

Hilter nodded curtly. 'I'm glad to hear it. Now then, what news of the two aliens?'

'Well, Mine Fury, I am informed by—'

'Stop! Don't mention his name! Remember, walls have mouths.'

'Of course, Mine Fury, forgive me. I am informed by your chief of secret police—'

'Let us simply refer to him as the man in the black hat, shall we, Gobbles?'

'As you wish, Mine Fury. I am informed by the er, man in the black hat, that the two Charring Crossers have made their way across the Big Water to the Eastern Aisles. He has followed them to Le Half, and is at this very moment, or so I am given to understand, making enquiries as to their whereabouts.'

'You mean he still hasn't found them?'

'They appear to be proving surprisingly elusive, Mine Fury.'

'But it's been almost a week!'

'I believe the next two or three days will see them apprehended, Mine Fury.'

'I should damn well hope so! I want those two Charring Crossers found!'

'I understand, Mine Fury.'

'No you don't! You don't even *begin* to understand, you mini-minded dolt! The future of the whole planet hangs in the balance, and everything depends on finding the two aliens. If we are to invade Poh Land in September, we need weapons, and we need them now!

We must find out how the aliens got here, then compile a shopping list to take with us to their world. We must have rifles and artillery and machine guns and exploding rockets – oh! and lots and lots of armoured cars, we mustn't forget those.'

Gobbles whipped out a notebook and scribbled in it, muttering 'armoured cars' under his breath as he did so.

'The point is, Gobbles, we have the will and we have the manpower – all we require now is the firepower.'

'I will acquaint the man in the black hat with the urgency of his mission, Mine Fury,'

'Do so, Gobbles, for if he fails me this time, I shall have his guts for suspenders.'

Gobbles clicked his heels.

'Not that I ever *wear* suspenders,' added Hilter quickly.

'Of course not, Mine Fury.'

'Good Hevvans, no. I wouldn't be seen dead in them.'

'Quite so, Mine Fury.'

'I mean, that time you walked into my room without knocking, I was just trying on a pair of Eva's. Just to see what they felt like, you understand.'

'Of course, Mine Fury.'

'Simply an exercise in idle curiosity.'

'As, no doubt, were the stilettos, Mine Fury.'

'That's right! Of course, yes, the stilettos. I mean, one can't try on stockings and suspenders without stilettos, can one?'

'Absolutely not, Mine Fury.'

'It just wouldn't feel the same.'

'I'm sure it wouldn't, Mine Fury.'

'And a good heel does so improve the turn of one's ankle.'

'How true, Mine Fair – er, Fury.'

'Ahem. Yes, well, anyway, about these aliens.'

'Yes, Mine Fury.'

'You will instruct Herr – I mean, the man in the black hat, to redouble his efforts to find them, and impress upon him that time is of the essence. I mean to march on Parriz before next spring, and if the Nasti flag isn't flying from the Awful Tower by the time the apple trees blossom, heads will roll.'

Gobbles snapped out a brisk salute and clicked his heels. 'I will make contact with him immediately, Mine Fury, and inform him of your wishes,' he barked, then spun around smartly and marched out of the room.

Hilter watched him depart, then returned to his chaise longue, took out a white silk handkerchief and mopped his brow.

'I must have those two Charring Crossers, Herman,' he said wistfully, 'I really must. It may be another hundred years before an opportunity such as this one comes along again. It is a sign from Goat, Herman, you see that, don't you? When all seemed lost, He has provided us with exactly what we need – the opportunity to purchase arms from another world. Are you not gratified to know that Goat is on our side, Herman?'

'Oh indeed, Mine Fury, absolutely so.'

The crazed would-be dictator rolled up his trouser

leg. 'By the way,' he said absently, 'have you any nail varnish? I seem to have got a ladder.'

* * *

Mortimer swept through the streets of Le Half with single-minded determination. Although ostensibly a stranger to the town, he walked with the purposeful stride of a man who knows exactly where he is going, the main reason for which was the fact that he knew exactly where he was going.

In fact, Mortimer's destination was a small tavern on Mevagissy Street, known locally as Ugly Dick's, the proprietor of which less than salubrious establishment was the unfortunately yet aptly named Dick Hedd. The peculiar pertinence of this name stemmed directly from the landlord's rather unusual nose, which was almost exactly the same shape, size and texture as a flaccid penis. Whilst understandably sensitive about this peculiar deformity, Dick had over the years learned to live with the fact that his face looked as if it should be wearing underpants, and was aware that a good deal of extra custom was generated by his curiously proportioned snout.

Mortimer pushed open the door of Ugly Dick's and stepped into a room filled with smoke, beer fumes and profanity. The bar was crowded, as it usually was, populated by assorted criminals, racketeers and general ne'er-do-wells. He edged through to the counter and caught Dick's eye. (The reader will note that the temptation at this point to throw in a quip concerning prosthetics, has sensibly been resisted.)

'Mr Mortimer!' said Dick, cheerfully but cautiously. 'Haven't seen you in here for a moon or two.'

'I am no longer in the Service,' Mortimer told him, 'although I still have occasion now and then to call upon old contacts.'

The landlord nodded. 'You'll be after Willie Singer, then.'

'I had hoped to find him here, yes.'

'You're in luck, Mr Mortimer. He's in his usual corner by the fire exit.'

Mortimer raised his hat slightly and smiled, then turned and made his way across the crowded room to a secluded booth in the corner. Sitting at a table there was a small, weaselly man with long greasy hair and gold teeth. His skin was sallow, his face drawn and emaciated, and if he wasn't on some form of powerful drug, he probably should have been. As Mortimer slid into the seat opposite him, he looked up from his drink, startled.

'Hello again, Willie,' said Mortimer quietly.

Willie glanced around nervously to make sure no one was watching, then, having satisfied himself that no one was, he turned to Mortimer and grinned.

'Hello Mr Mortimer. Gave me quite a start you did. I heard you'd left the Service.'

'You heard correctly, my friend. However, I am now in the service of . . . someone else.'

'Ah. Same line of work?'

'Not as such, no, though there are occasional similarities.'

'Hmmm. So er, what can I do for you?'

'I need some information.'

'What kind of information?'

'It concerns two Charring Crossers.'

'What? Did you say Charring Crossers?'

'I did.'

'You mean people from another world?'

'Correct.'

'Crikey! So all those old wives' tales are true, then?'

'The phenomenon of interdimensional travel has
been documented, yes.'

'Well fancy that. I never really believed it, you
know.'

'Yes, well, the truth is often stranger than fiction.
The point is, I need to find these two people rather
urgently. I believe they passed through Le Half some hours
ago, and I need to know in which direction they went.'

'You'd better give me a description of them then.'

'One is a young man, tallish, a little on the skinny
side. He has shoulder-length blonde hair and is wearing
a corded jacket and blue work trousers. The other is a
young girl; pretty thing, so I've heard – though she
wears eye-glasses. She's dressed all in black.'

'And you say they passed through here several hours
ago?'

'As far as I can ascertain, yes.'

'It might take a while. There was some trouble here

earlier. Pill Tax riots and stuff. Streets were full of cloppers, so most of my . . . "associates" have been keeping a low profile.'

'I understand. I will wait here until you return.'

Willie slid out from his seat and stood up.

'And Willie,' Mortimer added, 'don't let me down, will you?'

Willie winced inwardly and shook his head. 'I'll do my best, Mr Mortimer.'

Glancing around the room once more, Willie slipped behind a nearby curtain and out through the fire exit. Mortimer sat back, closed his eyes and waited.

Running like a ferret through the backstreets and alleyways of Le Half, Willie Singer made his way to the shabby, rundown area known as the Scarab Quarter.[1]

---

[1] The name 'Scarab' originally derived from the fact that the area was infested with a large and particularly unpleasant species of dung-beetle, which over the years had become immune to every form of pesticide known to man. The preferred method of extermination, therefore, was to drop a brick on them, since the idea of crushing one underfoot was simply unthinkable. It is also perhaps interesting to note that the beetles were locally referred to as 'brick-teasers', owing to their annoying habit of pretending to be unaware that a brick was about to be dropped, then scuttling six inches to the left a split second before the brick landed. This epithet should not be confused with the term 'prick-teaser', which has nothing to do with either insects or bricks. (Usually).

Skidding to a halt outside a small and dilapidated red-brick warehouse, he glanced around cautiously then rapped lightly on the door. Almost immediately, a small panel slid back and a pair of menacing and suspicious eyes peered out.

'Oh, it's you,' said the owner of the eyes, and the panel slid shut. There was the sound of bolts being slid back and chains being unfastened, and the door finally swung open slightly with an unhappy creak. Willie slipped through the narrow gap, and the door slammed shut behind him. He followed the doorman (who was known to his friends as 'Ron the Bugger') through a large dusty room filled with wooden packing cases, to a small partitioned area in the corner which served as an office.

'Enter!' said a voice in response to Ron's knock. Willie opened the door, and was not in the least bit surprised to find four men sitting round a packing case playing cards. A nasty looking youth lolled on the edge of a desk by the wall, smoking a hand-rolled cigarette.

Mac the Fife, so named owing to his habit of playing a small tin flute while kicking people to death, turned and regarded Willie in some surprise. 'Hello, Singer,' he said. 'What brings you here?'

'Mr Mortimer's looking for someone,' explained Willie, a little breathlessly.

'Mortimer? I thought he'd quit the Service.'

'He has. He's working for someone else now.'

'Oh. Who's he after, then?'

'A young girl and a bloke. Reckons they're Charring Crossers.'

'Billocks. There's no such thing.'

'That's what I thought. But if Mr Mortimer says they're Charring Crossers, then Charring Crossers is what they are.'

'Got a description, then?'

'The bloke's thin with blonde hair. The girl's dark, a bit of a looker apparently. Oh, and she wears eye-glasses.'

Mac the Fife shook his head slowly. 'Can't say I've seen 'em around.' He glanced enquiringly at the other three, who shook their heads.

'I seen 'em,' said the nasty looking youth by the desk. They all turned to look at him.

'What're you talking about, Nipper?' asked Mac.

'I seen them two people. On the road back from Passiondale.'

'When?'

'This morning. I saw a waggon comin', so I hid behind some bushes, an' when I looked out I saw it was the Baron.'

'Baron von Fothemoni?'

'Yeah, 'im. An' there were two people in the back – a bloke wi' long blonde 'air an' a bird wi' eye-glasses on.'

'Is this one of your fairy stories?'

'No, it's true, I swear!'

Mac turned to Willie. 'Sounds like them all right.'

Willie nodded. 'And they were heading towards Passiondale, you say?'

Nipper nodded enthusiastically. 'S'right. In the Baron's waggon.'

'Thanks, lad. You might just've saved my balls.'

As Willie slid back into his seat in the corner of Ugly Dick's, Mortimer opened his eyes and gazed at him levelly. Willie nodded slightly, and his thin lips curled into what could almost have been described as a smile.

'I take it you have some news for me?' Mortimer said.

Willie nodded again, still trying to catch his breath. 'They were seen on the road out to Passiondale. It seems they've hitched a lift with Baron von Fothemoni.'

'The Baron? Now that *is* interesting.'

'That's what *I* thought.'

'Either von Fothemoni has turned over a new leaf, or he's up to something. I've never known him do anyone a favour without wanting something in return. I wonder what.'

Willie shrugged. 'Maybe they offered him money.'

Mortimer shook his head. 'I doubt if they could afford the kind of money the Baron would require.'

Willie shrugged again.

'Well, no matter,' said Mortimer, and stood up. He reached into his pocket and pulled out a worn Plainsfolk-skin wallet. From it he took a fifty-round note which he laid on the table in front of Willie. 'Thank you, Willie. You have done me a great favour.'

'No problem, Mr Mortimer,' said Willie, sliding the note off the table and into his pocket. 'Always glad to be of service.'

Mortimer touched the brim of his hat, then made his way through the crowded bar and out onto the street. He set off in the direction of Harry Honder's Motor-Horse Hire Shop, a menacing yet somehow worried expression on his face. The introduction of the Baron into the picture was an unexpected development, and it was one he didn't like. It wasn't that he was afraid of him – Mortimer knew how to deal with people like the Baron – but he *was* afraid of what the Baron might do to the two Charring Crossers. The Baron could be an extremely charming man, but that very fact made him an exceedingly dangerous one, too.

9

Jeannette struggled furiously, kicking her legs and bucking for all she was worth, but the Baron was simply too strong for her. He pressed down on her mercilessly, clutching her left arm in a vice-like grip whilst his other hand sought a way through her clothes. Jeannette pummelled him repeatedly with her free hand, which was roughly as effective as trying to down an elephant with a pea-shooter. She could feel something long and hard pressing against her stomach, which she fervently hoped was the Baron's sword (although she vigorously renewed her efforts in the screaming department just in case). She felt a warm slimy hand slide up the inside of her sweater, where it touched bare flesh, and she froze.

At that moment there was an odd swishing noise and the Baron's body also went stiff. He straightened his arms, slowly raised himself up and looked down at her with an expression of complete surprise.

'Erm,' he said, and slumped lifelessly on top of her. Jeannette wriggled and squirmed and managed to prise herself out from beneath him, then crawled away into the corner of the tent and huddled, shaking with terror. She stared back at the motionless body of the Baron, and was a little perplexed to see a perfectly ordinary feather-tipped arrow protruding from between his shoulder blades. There was a dark stain on his cloak where the arrow had entered his body, and Jeannette shuddered (although she was already shaking so much that you'd never have noticed).

A figure materialized suddenly at the entrance to the tent, whose appearance so surprised Jeannette that she forgot all about being terrified and immediately stopped shaking. The figure was dressed in a beautiful lincoln green silk blouse and a green mini skirt, and wore green tights, green boots and a green beret.

'Nice outfit,' Jeannette found herself thinking. 'I must remember that one.'

'Are you all right?' asked the figure, in a surprisingly masculine voice.

'Erm, well, yes, I think so.'

'Ah, good. I hope I didn't misinterpret the situation, by the way. I assumed he was trying to rape you.'

'Yes, yes he was.'

'Oh good. Only I had this sudden moment of doubt just after I'd let the arrow go. I mean, you know how it is, some people just happen to be noisy in the sack – I am myself – and I began to wonder if maybe he was your husband or something and you were screaming in ecstasy.'

'Oh no, I was terrified. He was just someone who gave us a lift from Le Half on his waggon, then when we stopped for the night he poisoned my friend and attacked me.'

'Ah, well, that's all right then. My name's Robyn Hudd, by the way.' Ms Hudd strode across the tent and helped Jeannette to her feet. 'I live here in the

forest with my Merry Women. We rob the rich, you
know.'

'And I suppose you give all the money to the poor.'

'Why would we do a silly thing like that?'

'Well, because . . . oh, never mind.'

'What's your name, pretty one?'

'Jeannette,' said Jeannette, trying not to blush.

Robyn shook her briskly by the hand. 'Pleased to
meet you.'

At that moment two more women appeared at the
door of the tent, supporting a bleary looking Reg
between them. Jeannette let out a shriek, rushed over
and flung her arms around him, almost knocking him
down in the process.

'Ah, good,' said Robyn. 'Well done, Little Joan.'

The large, stockily built woman known as Little
Joan grinned and held up a small bottle. 'We gave him
some of Friar Nora's brandy and it seemed to revive
him.'

'Excellent.'

Robyn gazed around the tent and caught sight of
the Baron's body sprawled across the cushions.'

'Who was this guy, anyway?' she asked.

'His name is – *was* – Baron von Fothemoni,' Jeannette told her, still clinging onto Reg, who merely grinned and swayed.

Robyn gasped. 'My Goat! I don't believe it! I've
actually got the bastrad at last!'

'You mean you *knew* him?'

'You could say that,' admitted Robyn. 'He was a

notorious drug runner. Supplied herrocane to half the major dealers on the Eastern Aisles. He passed through the forest regularly, but we've never been able to catch him – until now.'

'But why did you want him? I mean, with all due respect, you don't exactly work on the right side of the law yourselves.'

'We're thieves, I admit that, but we don't hold with drugs. Or rape. The Baron was a bastrad and we wanted him dead.'

Jeannette nodded. 'Well, I'd say you've achieved your objective.'

'Now if only we could get our hands on Viscount Toofer Thesho – he supplies the other fifty percent – we'd have the whole drug problem cracked.'

'You seem very passionate about it,' observed Jeannette.

A hard, narrow-eyed look passed over Robyn's face. 'My younger sister died of a herrocane overdose two years ago,' she said quietly. 'She was seduced by that bastrad over there,' she added, pointing to the Baron, 'and he turned her into an addict. When she died, I swore I would get revenge, and at last I have fulfilled my promise. Now my dear sister can rest in peace.'

'Yes, well, I think I'd better take Reg back to his tent,' said Jeannette, feeling a little embarrassed. 'I think he needs rest.'

Robyn nodded. 'You'd both better get some rest. This must all have been very traumatic for you.'

'I've had better nights,' Jeannette admitted.

Supporting Reg, who was still grinning and swaying like an idiot, Jeannette staggered across the clearing to his shelter, manoeuvred him inside and wrapped him in his blanket. He continued to grin, and had he not been lying on the floor, would doubtless have continued to sway as well. Jeannette kissed him lightly on the lips and lay down next to him. Suddenly she felt exhausted. The previous day's journey and her struggle with the Baron had inevitably taken their toll, and no sooner had she closed her eyes, than slumber came to claim her.

She awoke next morning to the sound of Reg snoring loudly, and she would never have believed such a dreadful noise could be so comforting. She raised herself on one elbow and watched him for a while. His long serious face somehow looked terribly pleased with itself, and she wondered what it was he was dreaming about. She glanced down the length of his blanket and noticed a definite bulge half way along it. She grinned.

'Wake up, sleepy head,' she said, shaking him gently. 'I don't see why you should have all the fun.'

'Hnneurgh,' said Reg, as his eyes popped open, 'werbuss?'

'It's me, the *real* Jeannette.'

He turned to look at her and his face broke into a grin. Then he winced and screwed his eyes shut. 'Shit! What was I drinking last night?'

'Don't you remember?'

'Well, I remember a campfire, and that Baron geezer, and some little silver goblets, and then . . . nothing.

And I've just had the weirdest dream, about Robin Hood being a woman in green stockings and suspenders.'

Jeannette tried to conceal her disappointment.

'Really? Well I hope you enjoyed yourself.'

The attempt was not particularly successful.

'What?'

'Nothing. Come on, you'd better get up and I'll tell you all about it.'

Jeannette crawled out of the tent and stood up, and was a little surprised to find that the Baron's elaborate bivouac had completely disappeared. Reg emerged behind her and stood blinking in the filtered sunlight.

'Oh. It looks as if the Baron's abandoned us,' he said.

'You really don't remember a thing, do you?'

'Nope. Whatever he gave me to drink, it certainly blew my head off. I've got one hell of a hangover.'

At that moment, Robyn and several of her Merry Women appeared through the trees and Reg, utterly confused and not a little startled, stepped back a pace.

'Good morning,' Robyn said cheerfully.

'My God! It's the woman of my dream,' Reg said.

'I say, steady on,' said Robyn. 'I thought you and Jeannette were erm . . .'

'He means he dreamed about you this morning,' Jeannette told her.

'Oh, I see. Well, I suppose that's understandable.'

Reg looked at Jeannette. Then he looked at Robyn. Then he looked at Jeannette again.

'Could someone possibly tell me what's going on?' he asked. Jeannette led him over to a convenient fallen tree and proceeded to describe the events of the previous night. As she did so, Reg threw in the occasional exclamation such as, 'Sleeping potion?', and 'Tried to what?', and 'I thought he was delivering sugar.' When she'd finished he shook his head.

'Well, the absolute bastard!' he declared. 'And he seemed like such a friendly chap. Good job you happened to be passing,' he added, glancing at Robyn.

'All in a day's work,' said Robyn modestly.

'Jeannette glanced around the clearing. 'What did you do with the Baron's, with his, I mean where . . .?'

'We disposed of him.'

Reg nodded knowingly. 'Buried him in an unmarked grave, eh?'

'Actually, no. His waggon was loaded with drugs, so we wrapped him up in his tent, threw him on the back of the waggon and put a Zappo to it.'

'Zappo?'

Robyn whipped out a small brass petrol lighter, flipped open the lid and lit it.

'Best lighters on Urth,' she told them. 'Guaranteed for life.' She clicked the lid shut and slipped it back in her pocket.

'You mean you cremated him?' said Jeannette, shuddering at the thought.

'The bastrad didn't deserve a decent burial,' Robyn said, and spat on the ground.

'What about the horse?' Jeannette wanted to know, 'You didn't . . .?'

'No, of course not. We set him free.'

'Oh well,' sighed Reg, 'I suppose that means we're on foot again.'

'Where are you headed?' Robyn enquired.

'We're looking for the Omnipotent Roopert of Murdok,' Jeannette told her. 'He lives near a village called Ailar Tsua.'

'Ah, then you still have some way to go. We can offer you safe passage through the forest, at least.'

'Oh, well, that's jolly decent of you,' said Reg. 'I believe it's quite dangerous.'

'It can be,' said Robyn airily, 'if you don't know your way around.'

Having eventually worked out how to re-fold the canvas shelters, Reg and Jeannette breakfasted on bacon sandwiches and hot coffee from the magic Tupperware, and some time later the little party set off into the depths of the forest. As they moved away from the clearing a dull green gloom closed in around them, punctuated occasionally by the odd shaft of sunlight which had been tenacious enough to pierce the forest canopy. On each side of the track the impenetrable tangle of trees and undergrowth stretched away into darkness, and Jeannette was thankful that they had Robyn to guide them. It occurred to her that getting lost in the middle of all that would be a little like trying to find your way out of Manchester's Arndale Centre.

They stopped around lunchtime and had a bite to

eat, then set out again at a brisk pace, having been advised by Robyn that they needed to reach the other side before nightfall.

'Why's that then?' asked Reg.

'Well,' said Robyn, 'there are things that live in the heart of the forest which only come out at night, and it would be better to avoid them if possible.'

'What kind of "things"?' Reg wanted to know.

'Don't ask,' said Robyn.

Some time later, as they were passing through a particularly dense part of the forest, Jeannette thought she caught sight of something watching them from the undergrowth at the side of the track. It was only a fleeting glimpse, but in her mind's eye she had the impression of a face – a large, oddly familiar looking face covered with fur. She slowed down and peered hard at the undergrowth, but all she could see was – well, undergrowth. She shook her head, as if that would dislodge the image, and walked on.

A few minutes later it happened again. It was nothing definite, and certainly not something she could describe with any degree of accuracy – just this fleeting image of a large furry face, peering at them through the dense green foliage.

A moment later, an acorn bounced off the back of Reg's head.

'Ouch!' he said, and turned in surprise. 'What the hell was that?'

Robyn stopped and looked at him enquiringly. 'What?'

'Something just – ouch! it did it again.'

Jeannette jumped as an acorn bounced off her chest.

Within seconds the air seemed to be full of them, and it was a little like being caught in a large and rather violent wooden hail storm.

'Come on,' shouted Robyn, 'we'd better run for a while.'

As she turned to follow Robyn, Jeannette thought she caught sight of something out of the corner of her eye, but it was something so utterly ridiculous and unexpected that she immediately decided she must have been mistaken. She quickly revised this decision, however, when it occurred to her that in a world inhabited by such curiosities as leather people and talking snakes, it would be rash to dismiss the improbable out of hand. She looked again, and was strangely relieved to discover that what she thought she had seen was what she really had seen, and nodding to herself in a satisfied manner, she trotted off after the others.

A few hundred yards further on Robyn stopped, and leaning against a tree to catch her breath, waited for the others to catch up. They arrived one by one, panting and wheezing in the dank forest air.

'Sorry about that,' said Robyn when they were all together again. 'It happens occasionally.'

'What', asked Reg, somewhat breathlessly, 'the hell was it?'

'Squirrels,' said Robyn simply.

Reg stared. 'Did you say . . . squirrels?'

'That's right, squirrels.'

'You mean those little furry rodents with bushy tails who run around in trees?'

'Well, no, not exactly. These are rather large squirrels.'

'Oh really?' said Reg, his voice imbued with the kind of lilting tone which indicates that the speaker suspects he is having the piss taken out of him. 'And how large is that, then?'

'Oh, around four foot five on average, I'd say.'

Reg nodded matter of factly. 'Four foot five, eh?'

'About that, yes.'

'And these four foot five squirrels were throwing acorns at us, right?'

'Yes. They're not dangerous or anything, but they don't like humans, so they throw the acorns at us to make us go away.'

'But squirrels are supposed to *eat* acorns, not throw them at people!'

'Yes, well, the squirrels here found something they liked better than acorns.'

'Oh? And what was that?'

'The leaves of the wild madras plant. That's why they've grown so big over the years.'

Reg snorted. 'This is ridiculous! I don't believe a word of it.'

'I do,' said Jeannette. 'I saw one.'

Reg turned and stared at her. 'What?'

'I saw one. Back there in the bushes. It looked just like an ordinary squirrel – apart from the fact that it was nearly as tall as me.'

Reg stood in silence for a few moments. He looked back down the track and shook his head. Then he looked at Jeannette and shook his head a second time. Finally he looked at Robyn and her Merry Women.

'Anybody got any Jack Daniels?' he asked.

For the next few hours they trudged along the forest track, the soft earth and layers of dead leaves cushioning their footsteps. On several occasions Reg and Jeannette thought they heard sounds coming from the undergrowth – strange rustling, sighing, groaning sounds – and they both tried very hard to ignore them.

At one point they struck up a conversation with a couple of the Merry Women, and were only partially surprised to learn that Robyn lived in constant fear of capture by someone called Nerys of Shottingham, who had offered a reward of five hundred rounds for her, dead or alive. According to Little Joan, the reward meant little to the people of Shottingham, whose own pockets it had come from in the first place via a number of ludicrous levies imposed by the Nerys administration. The latest of these was the Beard Tax, which seemed particularly unfair coming – as it did – so closely on the heels of a ban on the import of razors.

Some time later they were attacked by a gang of trees.

* * *

Mortimer rattled and roared along the dirt track

towards Sharwood Forest on one of Harry Honder's hired motor-horses, his long black coat billowing out behind him in the slipstream. He was hunched forward over the handlebars, his face set in a determined grimace against the oncoming wind, the brim of his hat flapping madly. (The question of how he managed to keep the latter on his head without the aid of elastic bands or safety pins would have kept Paul Daniels baffled for several years, and might even have caused him to shut up for a while.)

As the forest hove into view on the distant horizon, Mortimer revved the motor-horse harder still, kicking up a shower of dirt from the back wheel. The gears groaned and the engine rattled, and one or two of the cycle's less essential components dropped off.

Twenty minutes later Mortimer reached the edge of the forest itself, where he discovered the charred remains of what looked as if it had once been a waggon. All that was left was a large patch of blackened ash, a number of nuts, bolts and strips of metal, and the iron hoops which had bound the waggon's four wheels. In the middle of this mess was a rather ominous looking lump.

Propping the motor-horse against a tree, Mortimer walked over to examine the ashes more closely. From his coat pocket he took a telescopic stick, which he extended and used to probe the charred remains. The lump in the middle looked to Mortimer suspiciously like a body, and as he poked it with his stick, what had once been the Baron's tent crumbled away like the brittle charcoal it had become, revealing a black and melted face which stared up at him accusingly.

Mortimer regarded the face impassively. Identification was impossible, and he only hoped this was not one of the two Charring Crossers who were the object of his mission. He had a sneaking suspicion that the girl might well have been the sole reason for the Baron's interest in the two of them, and if that was the case, it would have been necessary for him to dispose of the male. Young attractive females were the Baron's one weakness, and he would have thought nothing of murdering the girl's companion to get what he wanted.

Mortimer suddenly sniffed, as a familiar odour drifted up from the ashes. The smell was distorted by the effects of fire and smoke, but to Mortimer's experienced nostrils, it was unmistakable. Hexodramyl Cocalidexadrine – better known as Herrocane, or 'Happy Charlie'.

From a silver cigarette case Mortimer took a long, slender cheroot, and lit it. He inhaled deeply, and letting the smoke drift from his mouth in a white curling ribbon, began to ponder. Now why would the Baron go and destroy thousands of rounds' worth of his own grade A Herrocane? It simply didn't make sense. Granted, the Baron needed to get rid of Reg before he could get his hooks into Jeannette, but would he have been desperate enough to destroy his whole stock in the process? Mortimer didn't think so. Was it possible that this was not the Charring Crosser's body after all? Could it, by any chance, be that of the Baron himself?

Mortimer threw the cheroot onto the ashes, crossed the track and climbed back onto the motor-horse. He kicked the engine to life and roared off into the dark depths of the forest, the noise of the machine becoming strangely dull and flat as the trees closed in around it.

For half an hour Mortimer skidded and bounced along the uneven forest trail, and so absorbed was he in his own thoughts that he completely failed to notice the length of cord stretched tightly between two trees up ahead. As his body connected with it at chest height he was thrown violently backwards, whilst the bike continued on its riderless way until stopped by an inconveniently positioned tree. The front wheel crumpled under the impact, and the engine gave one final metallic death rattle, before phutt-phutting into silence. Mortimer landed heavily on his back, rolled over and came to rest in a crouching position, his arms stretched out in front of him and a small pearl-handled revolver in his hands. (Anyone who saw this would have concluded that he had been watching a little too much 'Starsky and Hutch' recently.) He turned and trained his pistol on the undergrowth to his right, just in time to catch a glimpse of two figures dressed in green retreating rapidly into the denser foliage.

'Just a couple of Robyn's Merry Maidens,' he thought to himself, and fired a resounding warning shot over their heads.

His deep, dark eyes peered around cautiously, his ears alert to the slightest of sounds, but apart from the chirrup of bird life high up in the forest canopy, there was a dull dead silence. Mortimer stood up and slid the revolver back under his coat and into its leather holster, then wandered over to examine the crippled motor-horse. Even if he'd had tools and spare parts with him – which he hadn't – the machine was patently beyond repair, and he kicked the back wheel in frustration. This was going to slow him down considerably. His only consolation was the pile of ashes several miles back along the track, because it meant that the two Charring Crossers were now on foot as well.

With a grunt, Mortimer set off along the path, and such was the look of malevolent frustration on his face that even the squirrels decided to leave him alone.

10

Trees are not generally regarded as sentient organisms.

This is not only the case on Earth, but also applies to the majority of the inhabited worlds which exist within the dimensional layers of the omniverse. The reason for this is not difficult to identify, and stems largely from the fact that trees don't actually do a lot. They are certainly not renowned for being competent jugglers, for example, or becoming involved in fund-raising activities for registered charities. This observation is misleading, however, since the fact that an object is inanimate does not automatically preclude sentience. In fact, trees are a highly intelligent species of wood being, and the fact that the majority of them prefer to lead a stationary life, grow old gracefully and die, is based entirely on their awareness of the futility of ever attempting to actually achieve anything. In the final analysis, we achieve nothing – certainly nothing that matters in terms of the whole Universal Picture, at any rate. Trees inherently know this, which is why they prefer, on the whole, not to get involved. Occasionally, however, a tree will get a tad pissed off with standing around providing oxygen for people who will eventually come along with an axe (or petrol-powered chain saw), chop them down and turn them into attractive Scandinavian furniture, and will decide to do something about it.

In Sharwood Forest there are a number of very old and rather beautiful oak trees, and it was one of these that first decided to uproot itself and attempt to start a revolution. For the next few years the tree spent its days wandering the forest and trying to persuade other trees to join it, in the hope that one day, the forest could uproot itself as one and bugger off to somewhere a bit more pleasant. The tree had met with minimal success thus far, however, and the little band of oaks it had managed to recruit had taken to lumbering around the forest like a gang of drunken lager louts, looking for people to attack. It was during the course of one of these aimless sorties that they stumbled upon Robyn Hudd's little travelling party.

The first thing Reg knew about it was when a branch suddenly swept through the air from nowhere and knocked him off his feet. As he tried to get up, the branch swept back in the opposite direction and knocked him down again. One of the Merry Women was knocked over when a tree simply ran into her, and she quickly scrambled to the relative safety of the undergrowth.

'Killer oaks!' yelled Robyn, as she realized what was happening. 'Run for it!'

'Killer what?' said Reg, and the branch hit him on the head again, the result of which was a severe dizzy spell which left him floundering helplessly in a pile of dead leaves. The attacking tree loomed over him, preparing itself for the fatal moment when it would crash down on top of him.

Jeannette, who was far more in tune with the complex vibrations generated by the forces of nature than she knew, regarded the trees with interest.

'Excuse me,' she said to an advancing oak, 'but why do you want to kill us?'

The oak stopped, mid lumber, and regarded her in that curiously impassive way that only trees and nightclub bouncers can. Its leaves rustled indecisively as it shuffled from one root to the other.

'I can sense that you want to kill us,' Jeannette pressed on, 'I'd just like to know what your reasons are.'

The other trees stopped what they were doing (which mostly consisted of trying to fall on Robyn and her Merry Women) and turned towards Jeannette. The tree in front of her shuffled uncomfortably, and from deep within its trunk came a hollow, booming vibration which almost, but not quite, resembled the voice of Orson Welles.

'Erm,' it said, 'what exactly do you mean?'

'Well,' said Jeannette patiently, 'you want to kill us, right?'

'Er, right.'

'Okay. What I want to know is, why?'

'Well,' said the tree, rather petulantly, 'you seem to take great delight in killing *us*.'

'True, we chop down trees,' admitted Jeannette, 'although I think the word "delight" is a little misplaced.'

'All right, so you don't enjoy it, but you still kill us.'

'Yes, but—'

'And what's more,' the tree went on, 'you don't even have the decency to let us rot with dignity. Oh no, you have to go and turn us into things like tables, and chairs, and . . .' the tree shuddered . . . 'and toilet seats.'

'But that's *why* we chop you down – because wood is one of the most useful and versatile materials known to man. We don't just do it for the hell of it. Besides which, most people don't realize that trees can think, or that they have feelings.'

'Don't they?'

'Of course not. *I* didn't know until a few days ago.'

'Really?'

'Hadn't a clue.'

'Well, okay, but what difference does it make whether people know or not?'

'All the difference in the world,' Jeannette assured it. 'For a start, they wouldn't go chopping you down willy nilly if they knew you had feelings.'

'Wouldn't they?'

'Certainly not.'

'How do you know?'

Good question, Reg thought to himself, but said nothing.

'I just know, that's all. Where I come from people think trees are just inanimate lumps of wood, but they've still set up a worldwide Save the Trees campaign.'

'Really?'

'Really. They've finally realized how important trees

are to the environment and the balance of nature, and they're trying to stop people chopping them down.'

'Good thing, too,' said the tree, rustling its leaves in approval.

'People have come to understand that trees are far more valuable alive than they are dead. They're even re-cycling paper now so that they don't have to use up more wood.'

'So what are they making furniture out of?'

'Oh, furniture isn't important. You can make furniture out of anything – metal, plastic, laminates, all kinds of things. The important thing is that we save the trees, because by doing that we're actually saving ourselves.'

'So what you're saying,' ventured the oak, 'is that we trees are just as important as people.'

'If you want to put it like that, yes,' agreed Jeannette, 'because if there weren't any trees, there's a fair chance there wouldn't be any people either.'

'Why's that then?'

'Because trees are a vital part of the global ecosystem, providing oxygen to feed the ozone layer, sanctuary for a multitude of wildlife and all kinds of other things we can't do without. Wise up, guys, you're actually heroes!'

'Are we?'

'Of course you are.'

The tree looked abashed (or as abashed as it is possible for a deciduous oak to look). 'I never thought of it like that,' it admitted.

'The point is,' Jeannette went on, 'rather than running around the forest like a bunch of football hooligans, wouldn't you be far better off using your time to organize a campaign to educate people?'

The tree cocked its trunk. 'How d'you mean?'

'Well, let them know that you have feelings, and that you don't like being chopped down. March on the towns and cities and express your views to the people. Let them know how vital you are to their existence. It's got to be more productive than going around *killing* everyone you meet.'

The trees swayed and rustled their leaves as they considered the merits of this unusual idea.

'Well,' said the spokestree at last, 'I suppose it *might* work.'

'Give it a try,' urged Jeannette. 'What've you got to lose?'

The tree rustled. 'And you really think people would stop chopping us down if we talked to them?'

'It'd certainly make them think twice.'

The tree pondered for a few moments, then seemed to make up its mind. 'All right,' it said firmly, 'we'll give it a go. Like you said, what've we got to lose? If people won't listen, we'll simply go back to knocking them over and falling on them.'

'Good for you,' said Jeannette.

'Well, er, we'll be on our way then,' said Robyn tentatively. 'If you don't mind, that is.'

'No, no,' said the tree, waving a dismissive branch. 'You toddle off. We have things to arrange. We must prepare a speech for the people. Something concise, I think, but informative; not too sentimental, yet appealing to the heart. Come, my oaks, we have much to do.'

So saying, the trees lumbered slowly off into the forest, leaving a trail of fallen leaves in their wake. Robyn stared after them in astonishment.

'Brilliant!' she said. 'I never thought of talking to them.'

Reg clambered to his feet, rubbing gingerly at a lump on the top of his head.

'Well I've heard of talking the hind leg off a donkey,' he said, 'but talking a tree out of killing you really takes the biscuit.'

Thankfully there were no further encounters with the inhabitants of the forest, and by dusk, a large expanse of open countryside could be glimpsed through the trees up ahead.

'There's a deserted cottage about half a mile further on,' Robyn told them as they approached the forest edge. 'I'd advise you to spend the night there. Then if you set out early enough, you should reach Passiondale by tomorrow evening.'

'What's Passiondale?' asked Reg.

'The next village. There's a market and some shops – oh, and quite a nice little inn.'

'Ooh,' said Jeannette with feeling, 'you mean real beds?'

'Very comfortable ones, so I've heard.'

'Well that sounds splendid,' said Reg, grinning at the thought of a cosy bar with a roaring fire and home-cooked pub grub.

'Well,' said Robyn, smiling warmly, 'we'll be off then. We've had word that a wealthy merchant is passing through the forest tomorrow morning with an escort of Nerys's guards. We must go and plan a little reception party for them.'

'Well, good luck,' offered Reg, 'and thanks for everything.'

'Yes,' agreed Jeannette, 'thanks a million. If you hadn't turned up when you did . . . well, I shudder to think.'

'Oh, it was nothing,' said Robyn, failing magnificently to look modest, 'a mere bagatelle.'

'Well thanks anyway.'

Robyn raised her hand as if about to slap her thigh, then seemed to stop herself. 'Good luck, then,' she said instead. 'I hope you find this Roopert fellow, and everything works out all right.'

She turned to leave, then thought of something and turned back again.

'By the way,' she added, 'make sure you keep to the track as you approach Passiondale. And when you get there, try not to get involved in any arguments.'

'Okay,' said Reg, and with a friendly wave, he and Jeannette turned and started along the track. A few seconds later it occurred to Reg that it might be a good idea to ask the reason for this parting advice, but by the time he'd turned around again Robyn and her cohorts had already melted back into the forest.

'Oh well,' he said, and trotted off after Jeannette.

It took them another fifteen minutes to reach the cottage Robyn had mentioned, which turned out to be a tumbledown stone dwelling with a thatched roof, set back a few yards to the left of the track. The whole place exuded an air of uninhabitedness, and looked not so much neglected as conscientiously ignored. Jeannette regarded the little house doubtfully, and its single window peered back at her like an unblinking dark eye.

'It's not exactly the Ritz, is it?' she commented.

'No,' admitted Reg, 'but it's a hell of a sight cheaper.'

He walked up to the cottage, pushed open the door and peered inside.

'Actually, it looks quite cosy. There's even some straw to sleep on.'

Jeannette shrugged. 'Oh well. I suppose it saves having to pack the tents up tomorrow morning.'

Besides the straw there was a rickety chair and a plain wooden table, on top of which was a bottle with a candle stuck in the neck. Judging by the layers of wax which covered the sides of the bottle, they were by no means the first travellers to have spent the night here. Another door led into a tiny kitchen, which housed a stone sink and a number of disappointingly empty cupboards.

Having explored what little there was to explore,

Reg took off his rucksack, pulled his blanket from it
and spread it out over the straw. Using his backpack
as a pillow, he settled down on the makeshift bed and
sighed.

'I don't know about you, but I'm knackered,' he
announced.

Jeannette flopped down next to him. 'Join the club.'

'I haven't done this much walking since I got lost
for three days in the Lake District.'

'How did you manage that?'

'I dropped my map in a lake.'

Jeannette chuckled, and snuggled closer to him.

Even through his clothes, Reg could feel the warmth
of her body next to his, and automatically his brain
began sending out signals to warn the appropriate bits
of his anatomy of impending activity. Blood rushed
madly around inside his arteries, bumping into itself
and apologizing.

'Reg,' said Jeannette quietly.

'Yes?'

She paused. 'Nothing. It doesn't matter.'

'Oh.'

There was a short silence.

'Only . . .' Jeannette began again.

'Only what?'

'Well, there's something I've been wanting to say to
you for a few days now.'

'Is there?'

'Yes.'

'Oh.'

'Mmm.'

'Er, what is it?'

'Well, the truth is, Reg . . .' Jeannette paused again. 'There's someone standing at the table making a sandwich.'

This wasn't quite what Reg had expected. 'Ah. I see. And you've been wanting to tell me this for a few days now?'

'No, Reg, I mean there really *is* someone standing at the table.'

Reg's eyes popped open and he stared across the room towards the table, where a figure was indeed standing, apparently engaged in the act of making a sandwich. He was dressed in knickerbockers and a primitive shapeless overcoat, and his hair was long and badly kempt.

Reg sat up and coughed. 'Erm, excuse me, can I help you at all?'

The figure turned around in obvious surprise, and Reg was a little perplexed to realize that, although the intruder was now standing directly in front of the table, he could still see the bottle with the candle in it behind him.

'Do I take it that you are addressing me, sir?' asked the figure, in a voice that was at once quiet and yet filled the room.

'Er, yes, that's right,' Reg confirmed. 'I just wondered what you were doing here.'

'Did you now? Well that is easily answered, my friend. I *live* here.'

'Oh. I see. Only we were told this place was deserted.'

'And so it is.'

'Ah.' Bewilderment's grip on Reg's exhausted brain was getting tighter by the minute. 'But didn't you just say that you lived here?'

'Forgive me,' said the figure with a slight bow, 'but the word "live" is probably a little misleading. The fact is, I *used* to live here, although now I suppose you could say that I merely *reside* here. I'm actually dead, you see.'

Reg did what he always did when he was thoroughly confused, and blinked rapidly several times.

'I beg your pardon, but did you say "dead"?'

'That's right,' replied the figure, 'dead as a doornail.'

'Ah.' Reg nodded.

'Erm, I don't mean to nit-pick,' said Jeannette, 'but dead people don't usually stand around making sandwiches.'

'Oh, you'd be surprised what dead people get up to. Take my old uncle Albert, for example. Spends all his afterlife playing strip poker with a bunch of dead waitresses. Point is, of course, the living can't usually *see* what the dead are doing. Which reminds me, how is it that *you* can see me?'

Reg and Jeannette glanced at each other, then turned back to the ghost.

'I've no idea,' admitted Jeannette.

'You're not dead yourselves by any chance, are you?'

'No,' said Reg. 'At least, I don't think so.'

'But we are from another dimension,' added Jeannette.

'Ah, there you are then, that explains it.'

'Does it?' said Reg, blinking again.

'Of course. If you're not in your own dimension, it stands to reason you'll be able to see things that other people can't. Like hedgehogs.'

'You mean other people can't see hedgehogs?'

'No, I mean that hedgehogs can see things that other animals can't.'

'Can they?'

'Certainly. Why d'you think they've evolved possibly the most effective form of natural defence of any species on the planet?'

'You mean the spikes?'

'No, I mean the smell.'

'That's skunks, isn't it?'

The ghost shrugged. 'Skunks, hedgehogs, whatever. What I'm saying is, the reason you can see me is because you're from another dimension.'

'Oh, well, if you say so,' said Reg.

'I don't mean to pry,' said Jeannette, 'but why were you making a sandwich? I mean, I wouldn't have thought dead people needed to eat.'

'We don't,' admitted the ghost. 'In fact, we *can't*. Food has a habit of going straight through us. The thing is, when you've died of starvation, the idea of spending the rest of your afterlife making succulent beef sandwiches has a certain ironic appeal.'

'Ah.'

'I wasn't the only one who starved, mind you. The Great Potatil Famine of 1845 wiped out whole towns and villages, so there tends to be quite an obsession with food over here.'

'Over where?'

'On the other side.'

'Ah. Right.'

'Some ghosts like to haunt kitchens, others hang around in bakeries or butchers' shops. Me, I do sandwiches.'

'I suppose one has to make a crust somehow,' said Reg, and chuckled feebly.

'Incidentally,' said Jeannette, 'do you mind if we spend the night here? I mean, with it being your house and everything.'

The ghost gestured magnanimously. 'Not at all, my dear, you make yourselves at home. I think I'll go out for a bit of a float. Pop over to Passiondale perhaps, and find a few chains to rattle.'

'Visit a few of the old haunts, eh?' said Reg, and chuckled again.

'That's right,' said the ghost matter of factly. 'I like to keep my hand in, so to speak. It's ages since I gave a drunk a good fright, and I do so enjoy that. It's terribly amusing, because no one ever believes them, of course.'

The knickerbockered spirit pulled an ethereal fob watch from its pocket and consulted it.

'Ah well. Can't stand around here chatting all night. Places to go, people to scare. Sleep well, both of you.'

The ghost picked up his loaf, and with a cheery wave, floated through the wall and disappeared.

Reg turned to Jeannette. 'Did we really see that?'

'See what?'

'A ghost with a loaf under its arm disappearing through the wall.'

'Yes, I think so.'

'Oh.'

'Why?'

Reg shrugged. 'Just checking.'

There was a short silence.'

Outside the cottage the night creatures roamed the land in search of food, their crimson eyes floating through the darkness like burning cigarette ends. Inside the cottage the silence was eventually broken by the sound of someone snoring. (For those who need to know, it was Reg again).*

* It is acknowledged that some readers may find this a somewhat tame ending to an otherwise fairly exciting chapter. It must be stressed, however, that the author can only depict events as they actually occurred, and to let his personal imagination run riot would be to deny his audience an accurate portrayal of what really happened. If by falling asleep Reg and Jeannette are guilty of slowing down the pace of what has thus far been rather a thrilling little tale, it must be remembered that they've been doing an awful lot of walking just recently, and are consequently very tired.†

† Swallow that, and you'll swallow anything.³

³ As the bishop said . . . oh, forget it.

Life on Urth

*   *   *

For the last eighty years the people of Passiondale have led unusual and somewhat violent lives.

It all began back in 1914, when Lord Ferdinand Francis, who was then Lord of the Manor, attended a cocktail party given by Sir Hubert Principal, a local mill owner who also happened to employ fifty per cent of the village's workforce. The two most powerful (and rich) men in the area, Lord Francis and Sir Hubert were much revered by the people of Passiondale (from whose emotional and hot-headed nature the name of the village was, incidentally, derived), and were afforded the kind of distant yet devout adulation normally reserved for members of the Royal Family or TV weatherpersons.

On the occasion of the aforementioned cocktail party, however, Sir Hubert, who had always been partial to a glass or three of Courvoisimartin brandy, became rather potvaliant. In fact, according to eye-witness reports he was seen to 'stagger not imperceptibly and fart not a little.' Bunny, Sir Hubert's large and exceedingly diplomatic wife, always dreaded these grand social gatherings, since her husband would invariably get as pissed as a bladdertail,* then proceed to wander around the room insulting anybody silly

* A rare Urth species of goldfish which live in bowls filled with Green Chartreuse.

enough to listen to him. It was Bunny's function on such occasions to steer Sir Hubert away from trouble, and make sure he didn't insult anyone that mattered.

Disastrously, on the night of the cocktail party Bunny found herself pinned into a corner by an earnest young man who was describing to her the merits of a revolutionary new type of window, which was apparently made up of two panes of glass and was absolutely guaranteed to prevent draughts and eliminate condensation. Consequently Sir Hubert had been left to his own drunken devices, and was having a rare old time tottering around the room and being rude to people. Finally, inevitably, fate saw fit (and probably had a good giggle over it, too) to steer him into the path of Lord Francis, and there followed an historic exchange.

'Ah, Sir Hubert,' said Lord Francis, 'splendid bash.'

'D'you think so?' enquired Sir Hubert, swaying noticeably. 'Seems rather dull to me.'

'Not at all, not at all. Positively stimulating.'

'Oh well, I suppose if you like this sort of thing . . .'

'Oh, indeed yes. Terribly jolly, dashed good fun.'

'Strikes me they're nothing but a bunch of freeloaders.'

'What? Who?'

'This lot,' hissed Sir Hubert, swinging his drink around to indicate the gathering at large (and spilling a good deal of it in the process).

'I say, steady on old boy, you did invite them you know.'

'Bunny's idea. Wouldn't give 'em house room if I

had me own way. All they do is eat my food and drink my booze, and I'm perfectly capable of doing that on my own.'

'Yes, well, no use crying over spilt milk, as they say. They're here now, so you might as well enjoy yourself.'

'Pah!' said Sir Hubert, and took a slug of brandy.

Lord Francis reached out absently and plucked the last tuner fish vol-au-vent from a plate on the buffet table.

'What's that?' snapped Sir Hubert, just as Lord Francis was about to take a bite out of it. He paused, then peered at the little pastry cup in his hand.

'What's what?'

'That. In your hand.'

Lord Francis waggled the hors d'oeuvre. 'You mean this?'

'Yes, that.'

'Why, it's a tuner fish vol-au-vent, unless I miss my guess.'

'And what are you going to do with it?'

'Well, frankly, old boy, I was going to scoff the little blighter.'

Sir Hubert shook his head and tut tutted. 'Ah well, it's your funeral I suppose,' he said.

Lord Francis blinked. 'I'm sorry?'

'Just don't come running to me when you keel over clutching your chest.'

'Keel over?'

'Have you any idea how many calories there are in puff pastry?'

'Well, no I—'

'No, of course you haven't, or you wouldn't be planning to eat the thing.'

'Yes, but I—'

'Hundreds, that's how many, absolutely hundreds. Put at least another inch on the old waistline, that will.'

'Never! An inch?'

'At least. And you're not exactly skinny as it is. That extra inch could well be the straw that breaks the camel's back.'

'Camel? What camel?'

Sir Hubert patted his chest. 'Ticker, old boy. Too much weight puts a tremendous strain on the heart.'

'Does it?'

'Take my word for it. Ever heard of cholesterol?'

'Er, no.'

'Neither have I, but I'll lay odds that little vol-au-vent is positively dripping with the stuff.'

Lord Francis peered at the pastry nervously.

Sir Hubert shrugged. 'It's entirely up to you, of course, but personally I wouldn't touch puff pastry with a barge pole. Not unless I wanted to drop dead in the street the following week, that is.'

Lord Francis looked at his host, then back at the apparently odious vol-au-vent. 'Cholesterol, you say?'

'Practically the main ingredient.'

'And it's bad for the heart?'

'Burns holes in it so I've heard.'

Lord Francis grinned sheepishly at his host. 'Yes, well, er, come to think of it, I hate tuner fish.'

Very carefully, as if it might go off at any minute, Lord Francis placed the hors d'oeuvre back on the empty plate. Quick as a flash, Sir Hubert snatched it up again and popped it in his mouth.

Lord Francis stared aghast at Sir Hubert's bulging grinning cheeks, and an unfamiliar emotion began to seep through the pores of his being. It oozed into his bloodstream like sewage, trickled through the corrugations of his brain like acid and gathered at last in an icy pool around his heart. It was an emotion which Lord Francis hitherto had little use for, but it welled inside him now like a rain-swollen river, bursting at the banks and sweeping away everything in its path. It was possibly the single most difficult human emotion to control, and its name was Rage.

Unable to stop himself, Lord Francis lashed out and dealt his host a resounding slap across the cheek, causing gobbets of vol-au-vent to fly in several directions. Sir Hubert coughed and spluttered and barely managed to stop himself from choking.

'What the—?' he began, but Lord Francis's booming voice cut him dead.

'You, sir, are a fat, selfish pig!' he bellowed, causing every head in the room to turn in his direction. 'And an ignorant one at that!' he added. Pausing only to collect his bewildered spouse, Lord Francis strode out of the room, leaving astonished guests staring in his wake.

'Well bugger you, then, too,' said Sir Hubert, and tossed off the last of his brandy.

Over the days that followed the village was split down the middle by this sudden enmity between the two great men. The half of the village that worked for Sir Hubert naturally took the side of their employer, whilst the half of the village who benefited from Lord Francis's magnanimous nature not surprisingly fell in with their benefactor. Passions ran high, tempers flared, and scuffles broke out in the street. At the end of a week of increasing tension, one of Sir Hubert's supporters was murdered, and the following night a gang of Principalities burst into the local inn and savagely belaboured a group of Franciscans who were playing dominoes. Two of them later died of their injuries, and several hours after that, a state of civil war was declared.

The two opposing sides rapidly armed themselves, and at either end of a huge poppy field adjoining the village, long, deep trenches were dug, protected by earth mounds and coils of barbed wire. The men of the village settled into their defensive positions for a protracted war, and gradually a dull, monotonous pattern began to emerge. Every few months, one side or the other would go 'over the top' and try to capture and secure a few feet of no man's land. After a short and futile firefight, during which several of the advancing force would inevitably be wounded, the soldiers would retreat back to their trench and the injured would be stretchered to the village to be looked after by their wives/girlfriends/mothers.

As months turned into years and the prospect of peace became ever less likely, the women of the village began to experience an increasing sense of frustration – in more ways than one. Finally, they agreed amongst themselves to send a delegation down into the trenches with what seemed to them to be a practical solution to the problem. The proposal was quite simply this: that the men should spend their days in the trenches as usual, but at five thirty every evening they should return to their homes and get stuck into all those odd jobs (and other things) which had not been touched since the beginning of the war. They should also, the women decided, have weekends off. This struck the menfolk as a jolly splendid idea, and consequently, at five thirty the following evening the soldiers laid down their arms and trudged back to the village, duly returning to the trenches at nine a.m. the next morning.

All of this had taken place more than seventy years ago, and although Lord Francis and Sir Hubert were now long dead, the sons and grandsons of the original soldiers still spent their days crouched in the trenches and their evenings ministering to the needs of their wives. Although officially at war every day from nine o'clock, after five thirty an unofficial truce would be declared, and the two opposing sides would meet for a teatime drink at the local inn and argue over the vol-au-vent incident: why did it happen? Who was to blame? Could Lord Francis have avoided it by taking a different route around the party? By this time so inured were they to the idea of war, that it simply never occurred to them to let bygones be bygones and make peace.

And thus did the people of Passiondale live their lives.

11

As Reg and Jeannette approached the village of Passiondale some twenty-four hours after leaving Robyn
at the edge of Sharwood Forest, they were a little
startled to hear what sounded like intermittent gunfire
coming from a large field to their left. Though somewhat unnerved to hear rifle shots in what appeared to
be fairly close proximity, they couldn't help noticing
that there was a certain desultoriness about them, as if
whoever was firing was doing so merely out of force
of habit.

Jeannette glanced searchingly at Reg, who shrugged.

'Might be poachers,' he suggested.

'Or a hunting party.'

'Could be.'

Reg stood on tiptoe and peered in the direction of
the gunshots.

'Perhaps I ought to go and have a look,' he said
without enthusiasm.

'Remember what Robyn said,' Jeannette reminded
him. 'We're supposed to keep to the track as we
approach the village.'

Reg attempted to hide his relief by looking disappointed.

'True,' he conceded. 'I suppose we'd better do as
we're told.'

So Reg and Jeannette did as they were told and

kept to the track, and within five minutes they were wandering along Passiondale's picturesque main street. The buildings on either side of it were quaint, stone-built, one-storey cottages, some with thatched roofs and others sporting attractive red tiles. There were several shops in between the houses including a bakery, a grocer's store and a shop with a number of peculiar looking carcasses hanging in the window. Further on the street widened into a kind of cobbled village square, where a number of surprisingly elderly barrow boys were busy packing away their wares. One of them caught sight of Jeannette as she passed and called out cheerily.

'Fancy some juicy plumscrotes before I pack up, love? Only ten pinnies a bag, and picked fresh this morning!'

'I don't like the sound of those,' muttered Reg.

'Not today, thanks,' Jeannette called back.

'Come on, love, they'll be past their best by tomorrow. I'll only have to throw 'em away.'

'Thanks anyway, but no.'

'Five pinnies, then. Come on, love, I can't do better than that now, can I?'

'No thank you,' said Jeannette firmly, 'I really don't want any.'

'Well fick you, then,' said the trader and stuck two fingers up.

'Just like being back home, isn't it?' observed Reg.

A little further on they came to a large two-storey building, over the door of which hung a painted sign proclaiming it to be 'The Poppy Inn'. Below it was a smaller sign which read:

'WHY NOT POP INTO THE POPPY FOR A PECK
AND A PINT OF PIPPIN'S PREMIUM PECULIAR?'

Reg read this with interest. 'I wonder what Pippin's Premium Peculiar is?' he wondered.

'Well, this is probably the inn that Robyn told us about, so why don't we go in and find out?'

'An excellent plan, my dear Jeannette,' said Reg, and headed for the door.

The inn's interior was almost exactly as Reg had pictured it, with huge oak beams, a stone-flagged floor and a roaring log fire. The bar was simply a long wooden counter, behind which was a large mirror surrounded by wooden shelves and rows of interesting looking bottles. The Poppy's landlady, who was very fat and very pink, beamed at them jovially as they walked in.

'Hello there, m'dears,' she chirped. 'What can I do for you?'

'Well,' said Reg, 'we were wondering if we could have a room for the night.'

'Of course you can, m'dears. Is it a double you want?'

Reg glanced at Jeannette, who looked down at her shoes.

'Erm, yes, yes a double would be fine.'

'With a shower?'

'Ooh, yes please,' said Jeannette, immediately losing all interest in her footwear.

Reg nodded. 'Yes, that sounds perfect.'

'Splendid. That'll be fifteen rounds fifty.'

A group of old men standing at the other end of the bar suddenly fell victim to a fit of coughing and spluttering, and the landlady shot them a cautionary glance. Oblivious as ever, Reg took the wallet from his rucksack and counted out sixteen of the circular bank notes, which he placed on the counter. The landlady duly deposited these in a wooden cash box behind the bar, and handed Reg a large silver coin to the value of fifty pinnies.

'There you go, m'dear,' she said cheerfully. 'You can have room number seven. Up the stairs, turn left and it's at the end of the corridor. You'll find the key in the door.'

Reg and Jeannette thanked her politely, then made their way up to room number seven.

The room itself was quite delightful, and looked like the kind of bedroom one might find in the pages of *Beautiful Homes* magazine – comfortable and chintzy, yet painfully tasteful. A peculiar Heath Robinson-esque piece of equipment (which they took to be the shower) was discreetly concealed behind a floral curtain in a corner alcove.

Despite the doubtful appearance of the plumbing, the shower turned out to be highly efficient, and half an hour later Reg and Jeannette were considerably cleaner and much refreshed. It was mutually agreed

that food should be next on the list of essential require-
ments, and Reg felt strongly that this ought to be
accompanied by at least one pint (if not two or three)
of Pippin's Premium Peculiar.

An hour after that Reg and Jeannette could be found
sitting in satisfied silence by the log fire, replete and
replenished following the consumption of two huge
mouth-watering steaks, the origins of which they had
agreed it best not to speculate on. In front of Jeannette
was a half empty glass of what had turned out to be
a delicious fruit wine, and in front of Reg was all that
was left of his second pint of Pippin's Premium Peculiar.

Reg sighed. 'Those steaks really did melt in the
mouth, didn't they?'

'They certainly did.'

'I wonder what animal—'

'Reg, I thought we agreed not to discuss it.'

'Sorry, I forgot.' Reg sighed again. 'What's the wine
like?'

'Lovely. Tastes like strawberries and cream. How's
the beer?'

'Excellent. Sort of a cross between Guinness and
best bitter with a hint of banana.'

'Sounds disgusting.'

'It's not, I can assure you.'

At that moment the door to the bar opened and a
group of young men entered noisily and lined themselves up in front of the counter. They were all dressed
in what appeared to be some kind of military uniform,
although all were badly faded, and the knees and

elbows of some had been repaired with patches in a variety of floral patterns. The men ordered drinks and then sat down around a long table next to Reg and Jeannette. A few moments later the door opened again and another group of young men walked in. They too were dressed in ragged uniforms, though of a slightly different style and colour, and after ordering drinks, they sat down at another table on the opposite side of the room.

Though at a loss to understand why so small a village should require so apparently large a military presence, Reg decided that it probably wasn't important and determined therefore to ignore it. He finished off his pint.

'Yes, please,' said Jeannette, as he stood up and delved in his pocket for change.

'Same again?'

Jeannette nodded, emptied her glass and handed it to him.

As Reg stood at the bar waiting for the drinks, the soldiers began to chatter amongst themselves, and Jeannette, who was not noted for her lack of curiosity, began not being able to help overhearing. What she heard confused and puzzled her, because unless she'd got completely the wrong end of the stick, it sounded very much as if the two groups of men were at war with each other. That in itself was bad enough, but if Jeannette had heard what she thought she had heard, the cause of the fighting was nothing more nor less than a humble vol-au-vent. By the time Reg returned with the drinks, Jeannette was positively bristling with curiosity.

'What's up?' he asked, as he settled down next to her.

'It's incredible,' she said.

'What is?'

'This village.'

'Why's that?'

'Because it's at war with itself.'

'Really? Oh well, better leave them to it. Remember what Robyn said about not getting involved in any arguments.'

'Yes, but Reg, d'you know what they're fighting over?'

'No, what?'

'A vol-au-vent.'

Reg paused in the act of raising his pint and stared. 'A what?'

'A vol-au-vent. You know, a little puff pastry case—'

'Yes, I know what a vol-au-vent is. I was just having a little trouble getting my head around the idea of anyone going to war over one.'

'I'm not surprised. Isn't it just the most ludicrous thing you've ever heard?'

'Actually, no. I once heard someone say that Terry Wogan was a good interviewer.'

'Seriously though, Reg, it's ridiculous!'

'Well, yes, but there's nothing you can—'

'And from what I can gather, this thing with the vol-au-vent happened over seventy years ago!'

'Yes, but there's probably more to it than that, Jeannette, so I think it'd be better if you didn't—'

'Excuse me please,' said Jeannette in a very loud voice.

'—get involved,' finished Reg lamely.

The soldiers on the next table fell silent and all eyes turned towards Jeannette. She flushed slightly, but pressed on regardless.

'I'm sorry to interrupt you, and I apologize for listening in on your conversation, but am I right in thinking that you people are at war with each other?'

The men nodded.

'For over seventy years now,' said one of them, with something disturbingly akin to pride.

'And that it's something to do with a vol-au-vent?'

'It wasn't just any old vol-au-vent,' said the soldier defensively, 'it was a tuner fish vol-au-vent.'

'And it was the last one on the plate,' added the young soldier sitting next to him.

Jeannette sat back and shook her head in wonder. 'Have you any idea', she enquired, 'how incredibly silly and futile that is?'

Reg groaned, picked up his pint and knocked half of it back in one. He had a feeling it was going to be a long night.

Within seconds, Jeannette and the two groups of soldiers were locked in fierce debate, and Reg began to feel a little like a Wimbledon umpire at a doubles match. He sat back and listened and tried to make sense of the numerous arguments flying back and forth across the net, but after two and a half pints of Pippin's Premium Peculiar, this was no easy task.

In fact, Reg's views on armed conflict were by no means as unimpeachable as Jeannette's, but he had to admit, the concept of allowing a small pastry cup filled with fish sauce to foment a bloody, seventy-year war, did seem a little ludicrous.

'It's the principal of the thing,' the first soldier was saying. 'That's what's important.'

'What principal?' demanded Jeannette. 'What possible principal can there be in a vol-au-vent?'

'It's not the vol-au-vent that matters, it's the fact that Sir Hubert stole it.'

'Look,' said Jeannette, her hands becoming more and more gesticulatory, 'personally I don't believe anything is worth going to war over – although some causes are more justified than others – but I can't think of anything *less* worthy of a war than a vol-au-vent!'

'But Sir Hubert—'

'I know, I know, Sir Hubert stole it, but so what? Lord Francis could've had a mushroom one instead.'

'Lord Francis didn't like mushroom vol-au-vents.'

'Well he could've had some bread and pâté then, it doesn't really matter. The point is, what you're doing is completely futile. I mean, what do you hope to achieve at the end of it?'

The soldier shrugged. 'Victory,' he said simply.

'Fine. And what do you get for that? What's the prize for winning?'

'Well, there's no actual prize, as such. Our reward would be the knowledge that we'd defeated the enemy.'

'Right, most of whom are your next door neighbours, yes?'

'Er, yes.'

'So how do you think you could ever live in peace again, after one side's won and the other side's lost?'

'Well, it wouldn't be easy . . .'

'It'd be impossible! The village would be split down the middle for ever. The resentment would be simply unbearable.'

'Well, we'd just have to learn to live with it.'

'Like the Serbs and the Croats, I suppose?'

'Pardon?'

'Never mind. The point I'm trying to make is, even if one side does eventually win – and by the sounds of it that in itself is unlikely – nobody's going to be any better off.'

'Not exactly better off, no . . .'

'So if nobody's going to be any better off, what's the point in carrying on fighting? Why not just make peace, and let bygones be bygones?'

'Well it's the principal of the thing,' the soldier insisted, 'that's what's important.'

The minutes ticked by, the argument raged on, and eventually Reg's glass became empty again. Not fully conscious of what he was doing, he rose to his feet and floated gently to the bar.

'Another pippin of Premium's pint Peculiar,' he said,

and the old men at the end of the bar snickered into their tiny glasses.

Some time later – he wasn't sure how long – Reg mentioned to Jeannette that he thought he'd better go to bed as he was feeling rather tired. Jeannette nodded vaguely and patted him on the knee, before resuming her argument with the soldiers.

'Are you sure you'll be all right on your own?' mumbled Reg, hardly aware that he was already half way up the stairs.

'B'cos'll stay if you want to me,' he burbled, as he lurched into the bedroom.

'I've to got look aft'you,' he drawled, and the bed floated up slowly to meet him.

Consequently, some two hours later, Reg was completely oblivious to the sounds of rejoicing which floated in from the street through the half open bedroom window. He was also oblivious to the robust male voices drifting from the lounge downstairs, joined in the hearty rendition of some ancient song celebrating peace, love and someone called Joan Lemmon. He was equally oblivious to the lights which flickered behind the curtains, as the villagers took to the streets in force, forming a torchlight procession which wound inexorably towards the town hall.

Moments later Jeannette burst into the room in a state of considerable excitement. She leapt onto the bed and started shaking Reg furiously by the shoulders, his response to which was to gurgle and mumble something about green stockings.

'Reg! Reg! Wake up!' she hissed in his ear. 'I've done it! I've stopped the war!'

'Gofsu,' said Reg.

'Reg! Do you realize what it means? Nearly eighty years they've been at war with each other, and I've ended it! They're on their way right this minute to tell the Mayor they want to declare peace!'

'Nnfayaa,' Reg replied.

Jeannette gazed down at the inanimate lump that was Reg, and the excitement gradually drained from her body like dirty water from a bathtub, her sense of achievement all but snuffed out by the forefinger and thumb of Reg's unresponsiveness.

'Reeeg,' she said, in a coy, pleading sort of way, 'please wake up. I'm too excited to sleep.'

She drew her finger gently down Reg's nose and let it rest lightly on his lips.

'We've got this beautiful bed all to ourselves, Reggie. The door's locked, there's no one to disturb us, we can do anything we want.'

Reg swatted her finger from his lips and grunted.

She bent forward and whispered something incredibly filthy in his ear, to which Reg responded with a loud and reverberant snore.

'Piss head!' hissed Jeannette, and she slumped down next to him, contemplating without relish the long sleepless night ahead.

And fell asleep.

*   *   *

Mortimer peered up at the sign above him.

'WHY NOT POP INTO THE POPPY FOR A PECK
AND A PINT OF PIPPIN'S PREMIUM PECULIAR?'

He turned and gazed back along the main street of
Passiondale, and nodded to himself in a satisfied
manner. Yes, if the two Charring Crossers had passed
through the village, they would almost certainly have
stayed at the inn. With luck – although that was something which seemed to have rather forsaken him over
the last few days – they would still be here.

He pushed open the door and stepped into the bar.
The landlady's friendly smile froze on her face like
rigor mortis as she took in this tall dark stranger with
the hooked nose and evil, hooded eyes. He walked over
to the counter, raised his hat by a millimetre and a
half, and treated her to a view of his yellow, uneven
teeth. To the landlady they looked unpleasantly like
tombstones, and she had to make a conscious effort
not to squeal and duck behind the counter.

'Good morning to you,' said Mortimer in his dry,
lispy voice. 'A pleasant day is it not?'

'Er, yes, yes, very pleasant,' agreed the landlady,
nodding vigorously and looking everywhere except at
Mortimer. The group of old men at the end of the bar
shuffled uncomfortably and gazed into their tiny glasses
of Pip (as Premium Peculiar was affectionately known).
One of them started to whistle aimlessly, then thought
better of it.

'May I trouble you for a glass of oakapple juice?' Mortimer enquired.

'Of course, yes, oakapple juice,' muttered the landlady, and she waddled over to the rows of bottles behind the bar, selected the appropriate one and blew a film of thick dust from its surface.

'With ice?'

'Thank you, no,' Mortimer told her. 'I find its dilutory quality has an unfavourable effect on the flavour.'

The landlady nodded and opened her mouth, but found herself unable to procure the appropriate words with which to fill it. Instead, she poured out the drink and pushed it across the polished bartop towards Mortimer, who in turn slid a coin in the opposite direction. The landlady, still unable to look him in the eyes, shook her head and held up a podgy, soap-raddled hand.

'No no, that's all right, sir, it's on the house.'

Mortimer smiled his vile smile and raised a single eyebrow. 'How very kind of you,' he murmured, and picking up the drink, despatched two-thirds of it without apparently swallowing.

'By the way,' he went on, placing his glass carefully on the bartop, 'I'm looking for two friends of mine. I was wondering if they might have stayed here recently.'

'Friends?' repeated the landlady, as if the concept of Mortimer having friends was unthinkable – even acquaintances seemed an unlikely idea.

'That is correct,' Mortimer assured her, and went on to describe Reg and Jeannette.

The landlady shuffled uncomfortably in her sheepskin slippers. 'Eye-glasses you say? Yes, yes I know who you mean. Nice young couple they are. I even gave them my best room.'

'Ah. They are not, by any chance, still here?' Mortimer ventured, hope peeping at him timidly from behind a bottle.

'They set out this morning along the road to Ailar Tsua,' the landlady told him, and anyone watching closely might well have seen his shoulders sag very slightly.

'Very grateful we are to the young lady, too,' the landlady went on cheerfully. 'She stopped the war, you know.'

'Indeed? How very irresponsible of her.'

'Oh, I wouldn't say that.'

Just then the door into the bar swung open with a contented creak and two young men strolled in, their faces lit by carefree smiles. They nodded amiably at Mortimer and approached the bar.

'Two glasses of Pip please, Bet,' said the taller of the two.

'Thought we'd celebrate our first day of peace,' said the other.

'I still can't believe it,' the tall one went on. 'This is the first weekday since I was seventeen years old that I haven't spent in the trenches.'

'I know,' replied the other. 'My father was there, and *his* father before him. Both got wounded, too. In fact, my grandfather got wounded four times! Funny thing, but he always seemed to get it in the foot.'

'Wasn't your grandfather the one they called "Hop-palong Yeller"?'

'That's right!' agreed the smaller man. He looked thoughtful for a moment, then added, 'Funny name really.'

'Excuse me, gentlemen,' Mortimer said, unable to contain himself any longer, 'I wonder if I could ask you a question?'

'Certainly,' said the tall one. 'It's a free country.'

'Quite,' Mortimer said with an ironic smile. 'The point is, I was just wondering what the young men of the village will do for work, now that the war is over.'

The two men looked at each other.

'Well,' said the tall one, 'there's the munitions factory.'

'I don't think so,' Mortimer said quietly. 'Apart from the fact that the factory already has a more than adequate workforce comprised of women, you forget that it will shortly be closing down.'

'Closing down? Why?'

'Because now that there is no longer a war, there is no longer a demand for munitions. Ipso facto, no factory. Not only are *you* out of work, gentlemen, but your wives will shortly be out of work, too.'

A worried wrinkle crawled across the brow of the taller of the two men.

'Well,' he ventured, 'they could turn it back into a woollen mill.'

Mortimer shook his head. 'Far too costly. The price of the machinery alone would bankrupt the village.

Besides which, nobody has any sheep any more. All the shepherds went to war, remember?'

'Well all right, we could become farmers again.'

'I'm afraid you have neglected the land for too long. It would take years to reclaim it and make it suitable for crop growth.'

'Well in that case we could . . . we could . . . erm . . .'

Mortimer shook his head slowly. 'Let's face it, gentlemen, for the last seventy years the whole of Passiondale's economy has been geared to the war effort, i.e. the manufacture of munitions, ordnance and spare parts. The fact is, if there is no war, there are no jobs. If you have no jobs, you have no money. If you have no money, you can't buy food. And if you can't buy food . . .'

The two young men stared at each other, horror creeping across their faces in shades of pale green. The tall one turned back to Mortimer.

'So what you're saying is, unless we go back to war . . .'

'Your families will starve,' Mortimer finished.

A cold silence descended on the room as its occupants distilled the essence of Mortimer's words, and concluded finally, tragically, irresistibly, that he was right.

The two young men glanced at each other in panic. 'The Mayor!' they said in unison, and bolted out through the front door.

Mortimer turned to the landlady, who gaped at him speechlessly.

'That's the trouble with the young of today,' he said. 'They have no grasp of economics.'

He raised his hat and strolled out of the inn, and no one moved for almost five minutes.

12

Somebody once said 'the best things in life are free'. Just *why* they said it is hard to fathom, since it is, of course, arrant nonsense. You can be assured that anything worth doing, having or seeing is paid for in full one way or another, whether financially, emotionally or with one's life. Alcohol, on the other hand, has never been free, although the consumption of it has long been one of the most popular pastimes known to man (not to mention woman). The point about drinking is that one embarks upon it with one's eyes open, fully aware of the potential strain – not only on one's pocket, but also on one's mental and physical wellbeing. If you set out with the intention of drinking ten pints of strong German lager, you know full well that it's going to cost you the equivalent of a small private jet and several million brain cells, and this knowledge does have a somewhat restraining influence. At the very least, forewarned is forearmed.

Unfortunately, Reg was not so lucky, and as his fourth pint of Pippin's Premium Peculiar slipped nectar-like down his gullet, he was blissfully unaware of the fact that he was drinking a lethal concoction brewed from malt, hops, sugar and the puréed bladder of the gutficker lizard. The following morning, however, this blissful ignorance was replaced by a positively rabid crapulence, the like of which he had experienced only once before, after drinking Bacardi spiked with lighter fuel (a topping wheeze perpetrated by a rugby-playing acquaintance of his). Even now, two days after leaving Passiondale and the soldiers at the Poppy Inn, Reg still had the Hiroshima of hangovers.

'I wonder if they have aspirin on Urth,' he mused, as he and Jeannette trudged along the dusty track towards the village of Ailar Tsua.

'I wouldn't be at all surprised,' Jeannette admitted, 'although I can't say I've noticed an abundance of Boots stores along the way.'

'I wouldn't mind if it stayed in one place,' complained Reg, 'but it keeps moving about.'

'What does?'

'My hangover. One minute it's a headache, the next minute it's stomach ache, and five minutes later it's backache. It was even earache at one point.'

'I have no sympathy,' Jeannette said primly. 'It serves you right for drinking all that beer.'

Reg nodded gloomily. 'I know. I just wish I knew what the hell they brewed it with.'

It was at this point that they first noticed a horse and cart on the track up ahead. It was roughly half a mile away and travelling fast, and they regarded it with some trepidation. Almost unconsciously, Jeannette moved a little closer to Reg.

'Friend or foe, I wonder?' she whispered (somewhat unnecessarily since the cart was still several hundred yards away).

'Dunno,' Reg admitted. 'Pity he's going in the opposite direction, though. We could've hitched a lift.'

'Remember what happened the last time we got a lift?' Jeannette reminded him rather testily.

'Ah, yes, well, perhaps not then.'

They continued in silence for the next few minutes, peering nervously at the horse and cart as it approached them in a cloud of dry, yellow, Eastern Aisle dust. The driver, they could now see, was an elderly man with a bald head and a wispy grey beard. A long wooden pipe dangled from his mouth, and pinpoints of sunlight glinted off a small pair of spectacles perched like a seagull on the end of his nose. He certainly didn't *look* dangerous.

Moments later the waggon rumbled to a halt a few yards in front of them. The driver took the pipe out of his mouth and squinted at them through his tiny spectacles.

'Hello there,' said Reg, trying to sound friendly and casual, and failing miserably.

'Yes, yes, hello,' said the driver. 'Reg and Jeannette, isn't it?'

Reg and Jeannette stared in silent astonishment, not certain that they had heard the old man correctly, but certain that they had.

'Erm, wu, yes...' mumbled Reg. 'But, but, how...?'

'My name's Testic,' the old man informed them, as if this explained everything.

'But how did you know our names?' asked Jeannette.

'Ah yes, well you see, the Omnipotent Roopert sent me. He's expecting you.'

'Is he?'

'Certainly.'

'But, I mean, how does he know about us?'

'The Omnipotent Roopert knows everything. He sees everything and hears everything. That's why they call him omnipotent.'

'Oh, I see,' said Jeannette, who didn't really.

'Come on then,' Testic said, beckoning them with a long bony finger, 'hop aboard. We'll be there in half an hour. I think cook's putting a spot of lunch together.'

The mention of lunch seemed to bring them to their senses, and they trotted over to the waggon and threw their rucksacks in the back. Jeannette experienced a momentary pang of uncertainty as she remembered the Baron's seemingly innocent offer of a lift, but, she concluded, even Reg should be able to deal with a spindly old geezer like this one. The heck, if it came to that, she could probably deal with him herself – he had to be eighty if he was a day. As they clambered in the old man turned the waggon around, and moments later they were trundling down the track at a brisk old pace.

A few miles further on the ground rose steeply, and as they rattled over the crest of the hill the village of Ailar Tsua unfolded below them, nestling in the cleavage of a lush green valley. Beyond the village was another, larger hill, and on the top of this stood an imposing gothic tower built from impossibly huge blocks of what looked like black granite. It twinkled and sparkled in the sunlight, and its very nigritude seemed to radiate light.

'Murdok Hill,' Testic told them proudly, 'and that's the Tower of Power.'

'Is that where the Omnipotent Roopert lives?' Jeannette asked.

'Certainly is. One of the oldest buildings on Urth, that is. No one knows who built it, or why, but there's magic in it, that's for sure. You can tell just by looking at it.'

'It's certainly very impressive,' Reg admitted.

The waggon rolled down the hill and past the village, then began the winding ascent to the Tower of Power. As they approached it, blue electric sparks seemed to cannon off its surface, and the air around them adopted a heavy, purple attitude, as if it was about to thunder.

'You can feel it, can't you?' said Testic. 'The magic, I mean.'

'Actually, yes, you can,' agreed Jeannette.

'Either that, or it's going to rain,' said Reg.

After parking the waggon in a small stable behind the main building Testic led them around the tower towards a massive mahogany door, attractively adorned with the kind of olde worlde black metal studs available at most B & Q superstores. Despite the fact that it weighed the equivalent of a small motor car, the door swung open easily, and Reg and Jeannette followed

Testic into the Tower of Power's huge reception hall. Once inside, one had the impression that the building was not merely an inanimate pile of giant stones, but a living thing, and the air seemed to hum in a high, glassy register that one felt rather than heard.

The reception hall itself was vast, and like the *Tardis*, the tower seemed somehow bigger on the inside than it looked from the outside. Testic guided them across the polished wooden floor towards a door in the far wall, through which was another impossibly vast room. This one was obviously a banqueting hall, and in it was the biggest dining table Jeannette had ever seen – that, and rather a lot of newspapers. Thousands of newspapers, to be precise. In fact, the walls of the room were lined with huge bundles of them, tied with string and stacked four or five high, making it look a little like the warehouse of a large branch of W. H. Smith's.

Sitting at the far end of the table with his head buried in a creased and rather grubby looking tabloid was an old man, who bore a remarkable and uncanny resemblance to Wilfred Hyde White. As Testic ushered Reg and Jeannette through the door, the old man looked up, then bounded to his feet in a flurry of arms and legs. He hurried the length of the room (with remarkable alacrity for someone so old) and beaming delightedly, thrust a bony hand towards Reg.

'You got here, then? Splendid, splendid, so glad to see you at last!'

Reg shook the proffered hand and smiled bemusedly. 'Er, well, it's very nice to meet you.'

The old man turned to Jeannette. 'Delightful, simply delightful,' he said approvingly. 'But then I've always had a weakness for girls who wear glasses.'

Not for the first time during her stay on Urth, Jeannette blushed.

'Are you er, the er, the Omnipotent Roopert of Murdok, then?' asked Reg somewhat tentatively. This kindly old man with the white hair, who looked as if he had too many arms and legs, wasn't quite what he'd been expecting. He wasn't at all sure just what he *had* expected, but it certainly wasn't Wilfred Hyde White.

'I am the very same,' the old man told them. 'The villagers call me The Omnipotent One, but you can call me Roopert. Or Roop if you prefer. I quite like Roop.' He gestured vaguely in the direction of the table. 'Come, sit down. You must be weary after your journey and . . . whatsizname, the other thing, the one where you need food?'

'Hungry?' ventured Jeannette.

'Hungry, that's it! Yes indeed, you must be ravenous. Come, sit, and we'll talk and eat. Or is it eat and talk? I don't suppose it matters much really, does it?'

'I don't suppose it does,' agreed Reg, and slipping out of their rucksacks, they sat down at the far end of the table on either side of the old man. Moments later, Testic hobbled in pushing a brass coloured hostess trolley, from which he served a selection of delicious cold smoked meats accompanied by chunks of ripe melon and a variety of piquant sauces. As they ate, Reg and Jeannette described the events of the last few days, and Roopert listened in silent fascination. (Jeannette found it necessary to poke him with a fork at one point, since he appeared to have dozed off.)

Finally, as their story wound inexorably to the present, Roopert sat back in his chair with his hands beneath his chin and pressed together as if in prayer. He nodded to himself slowly and sighed.

'It is much as I read it. Your journey here, I mean. I've been following your story in The Newspapers, you see.'

Reg gaped. 'Newspapers? You mean we're famous?'

'Ah, not exactly, no.' The old man indicated the bundles of daily papers stacked around the walls. 'These are not ordinary newspapers, you see. They are what you might call – for want of a better phrase – my crystal ball.'

'You mean they contain news about the future?' guessed Jeannette.

'Occasionally, yes. More often than not it is news of the immediate present, but it keeps me abreast of the times, so to speak. One has to have one's finger on the pulse if one is going to call oneself omnipotent.'

'But where do they come from?'

'They arrive every morning through my letter box.'

'Oh, I see. So who delivers them?'

'No one delivers them.'

'I'm sorry?'

'They are not actually delivered, as such. They just sort of . . . arrive.'

'Oh. Well, who writes them then?'

'As far as I know, they're written by magic.'

Reg stared at the stacks of newspapers and tried to decide whether or not he was astonished. The problem was, they had encountered so many extraordinary things over the last week or so, it was becoming a little difficult to tell. Finally he decided that he probably *was* astonished, but had grown so accustomed to the sensation that he was no longer aware of it.

'Okay,' he said at last, 'so if you've been reading all about us in your magic newspapers, presumably you know why we're here.'

Roopert nodded. 'Because you wish to go back to your own world, and you have been advised that I am possibly the only man on Urth who can send you there.'

Reg banged the table with his fist. 'Exactly right!'

The mage shook his head sadly. 'Exactly wrong, I'm afraid.'

'I beg your pardon?'

'I said, "exactly wrong, I'm afraid".'

'Yes, I heard what you said, but what did you *mean*?'

Roopert shook his head again and looked uncomfortable. 'The fact is, my dears, I can't do it.'

An icy hand closed around Reg's heart, and Jeannette felt as if someone had just emptied a bowl of warm water into her stomach.

'Can't – do – what?' said Reg slowly.

'Well, I don't want to beat about the bush, no sense in that, beating about the bush I mean, always found it a pretty pointless exercise myself, much prefer to come straight to the point, get right to the heart of the matter, none of this shilly-shallying around—'

'Can't do what?' repeated Reg.

'Ah. Yes. Well that's the point, you see. I'm afraid I can't send you home. To your own world, I mean. Simply can't do it.'

The silence which followed this statement was one of the quietest in the long and soundless history of silences, and even the glassy hum of reverberating magic seemed to pause momentarily. You could've heard a pin drop. In fact, you would have heard if one of Jeannette's eyelashes had chosen that moment to fall out and land in her lap.

Roopert finally broke it by emitting a short, embarrassed cough.

'Sorry,' he said.

Reg suddenly exploded. 'But I thought you were the most powerful thaw, thaw—'

'Thaumaturgist.'

'—on Urth! You're supposed to see everything and hear everything! You're bloody omnipotent for Christ's sake!'

'All that is true,' conceded the wilted mage, 'but although I see everything and hear everything, alas, I cannot *do* everything. The fact is, I can do very little nowadays. There was a time when my powers were beyond compare and a legend throughout the Aisles, but over the years the tower has drained all but the most basic magic from my body.'

'The tower?'

'The Tower of Power. I had no idea when I bought it, but the tower feeds on magical energy. What you see around you is an illusion, a vast magical field generated by the building itself. In reality, the tower is no more than a crumbling stone spire with broken windows and holes in the roof. It has taken my power and used it to replenish itself. All that remain are my basic skills in telepathy and an entry in *Who's Who in Thaumaturgy Today*. Consequently, I'm afraid that sending people through the dimensional fabric of existence to a specific world at a specific point in its history is a little out of my league.'

Reg slumped back in his chair. 'That's it then. We're stuck here forever. Now my book will never get published.'

'I didn't know you'd written a book,' Jeannette said.

Reg looked at her glumly. 'Didn't I tell you? I'd just finished it when I got sucked out of my bathroom and ended up in *this* godforsaken place.'

'What's it called?'

'Urth. I thought you'd gathered that.'

'No, I mean the book.'

'Oh. *Figure of a Man, Bending*.'

Jeannette stared, her mouth open and her eyes wide behind the prescription lenses of her spectacles.

'Did you say, *Figure of a Man, Bending*?'

'Yes. Why?'

'Because that's the title of my last sculpture.'

'You're joking.'

'No I'm not. Before I ended up here I was going to create a life-size version of it and have it cast in bronze.'

'But that's ... incredible! The female character in my book is a sculptress, and she makes a model called "Figure of a Man, Bending"! That's where I got the title of the book from!'

'This is seriously weird. I mean, I've heard of coincidence, but this is ridiculous!'

'How very interesting,' Roopert said, nodding his head thoughtfully. 'Yes indeed. This.... *coincidence*, as you call it, might well have something to do with your being here.'

'Really?' said Reg and Jeannette together.

'Yes indeed.'

He paused for a moment in thought, then added, 'On the other hand, of course, it might not. It could be, as you say, simple coincidence.'

'In other words,' said Reg, 'we're still no nearer to getting home.'

Roopert shook his head slowly. 'All I can suggest is that you return to the point at which you first entered this world.'

'What?' A look of horror sprawled across Reg's face. 'You mean we've got to tramp all the way back to that silly little cowboy town on the other side of the ocean?'

'I take it you are referring to Bogwater Creek?'

'Yes!'

'If that is where you first arrived on Urth, then I'm afraid that is where your search must begin.'

'Search for what?'

'For the holes in the wall of the Universal Mainframe.'

'What holes?'

'The holes through which you passed when you entered this world, i.e. the points at which you each made the Charring Crossing.'

'But will they still be there?' asked Jeannette.

'Ah. Now that, my dear girl, is the million-doily question.'

'Doily?'

'Standard currency of the Northern Aisles.'

'Oh.'

Reg slumped in his chair and rolled his eyes. 'I don't believe this! It's taken us nearly two weeks to get here, we've been abducted, drugged, menaced by squirrels and attacked by trees, and now you're telling us we've got to go all the way back!'

The old wizard squirmed uncomfortably in his blue velvet robe.

'Sorry,' he said meekly.

Jeannette didn't know whether to laugh or cry. In the end she decided that neither would be particularly appropriate, and simply stared into space instead. Reg peered glumly at the empty plate in front of him, his elbows on the table and his head in his hands. The thought of walking all that way back, and the possible perils of such a journey, left him feeling bleak and depressed. And when (not to mention *if*) they got back to Bogwater Creek, there was no guarantee that the mysterious holes through which they had passed would still be in existence – and even if they were, how did they go about finding them?

'I could lend you a couple of horses,' Rupert suggested tentatively.

Reg's glare would have melted the wizard's hat had he been wearing one.

On the dusty cart track approximately a quarter of a mile from the Tower of Power a lone figure strode out briskly, his face a mask of quiet determination. He was exceptionally tall, thin and gaunt, with a large hooked nose and a narrow cruel mouth. Around his neck was a bootlace tie with a silver clasp and on his head he wore a soft black fedora. Perhaps the most startling aspect of the man's appearance, however, was his eyes. They were hooded, and appeared to be sunk deep into his skull, and were possibly the calmest and most calculating eyes on the whole of Urth. They were the kind of eyes one can look into for only the merest soupçon of a moment, before being forced to shift one's gaze to something less unpleasant (like someone having their bowels removed, for example). They were deadly, baleful, inhuman eyes. In fact, we're talking the kind of eyes that would merit a whole paragraph in Roget's Thesaurus under the heading *malevolent*.

In a few short minutes he would reach the crest of

the hill and begin the brief descent to the village of Ailar Tsua.

Reg stood up. 'Well that's that, then,' he said.

'That's what?' enquired Roopert.

'That's it. Business concluded. Meeting over. Time to go.'

'Go where?' asked Jeannette.

'Back to bloody Bogwater Creek. I mean, there's no point in hanging around here, is there? We might as well push off.'

'I won't hear of it,' objected Roopert. 'You must have dinner with me and spend the night here. I'm afraid I've been of very little help to you, so at least let me entertain you for an evening.'

Jeannette patted Roopert's wizened hand. 'Don't feel bad about it, Roop, it's not your fault. When Mahatma sent us to you he admitted it was a long shot.'

'That's right,' Reg agreed, 'don't blame yourself. It's just our bloody bad luck.'

'But surely you'll stay?'

Reg shook his head. 'Personally I'd rather make tracks. What about you, Jenn?'

'Well, the sooner we get back, the sooner we can start looking for these holes in the wall of the Universal thingummyjig.'

'If they're still there,' said Reg, slipping on his rucksack.

Jeannette wagged her finger. 'Think positive, that's what my mother always used to say. Mind you, this was the woman who refused to go to the doctor in case he found something wrong with her.'

Reg turned to Roopert. 'Well, thanks for the lunch. And don't worry about not being able to send us back. We'll find a way – somehow.'

Jeannette stood up and patted the old wizard's shoulder affectionately. 'Thanks for your help,' she said, and treated him to one of those smiles which seemed to light up the room.

'But I have done so little. And you have travelled so far.'

'Never mind, it's not your fault it was a wasted journey. If we blame anyone I suppose we should blame Mahatma, but he was only trying to help. I mean, how was *he* to know that you'd lost all your magical powers?'

The old man nodded. 'Then at least let Testic give you a lift as far as the river,' he suggested.

'That's okay,' said Reg, 'I think we'll nip down to the village and see if we can hire some kind of transport. Frankly, I've had it up to here with walking.'

Roopert sighed deeply. 'So be it. All I can do then, is wish you luck. I take it you have provisions enough for your journey?'

Reg patted his rucksack. 'Mahatma gave us everything we need.'

'Then Goat's speed, and may good fortune be your constant companion.'

Reg and Jeannette shook hands with the depleted

sorcerer, then walked a little glumly through the tower's huge reception hall to the big studded door.

'So much for being omnipotent,' muttered Roopert to himself. He stood up, wandered over to an ornately carved drinks cabinet and poured himself a stiff Arm 'n Yak.[1]

'I wonder if my magical powers would come back if I moved out of the tower,' he said to no one in particular. There was a low, ominous rumbling sound and the floor seemed to vibrate beneath his feet.

'Hmm. Perhaps not,' he decided, and threw his drink down in one.

Reg lifted the heavy iron catch and the huge front door swung open, a shaft of yellow sunlight sending the shadows scurrying into the corners of the gloomy reception hall. Jeannette let out an involuntary whimper. Silhouetted in the doorway was a tall, dark figure in a long black coat and a floppy fedora. Reg and Jeannette stared at him in uneasy silence, taking in the gaunt face, the hooked nose and those dreadful, baleful eyes. Reg slipped his hand into his pocket and clutched the handle of the switchblade tightly. The man regarded them for several seconds with an impassivity that was positively chilling.

[1] A type of brandy brewed in the Gorm Careless Mountains by goblins. The recipe has remained a secret for many hundreds of years, mainly because no one has ever had the nerve to ask what it is.

'Are, er, are you looking for the Omnipotent Roopert?' asked Jeannette, and her voice sounded high and thin.

'No,' said Mortimer, 'I am looking for *you*.'

'Us?'

'That is correct. You are, I believe, Jeannette and Reg.'

Reg gulped. 'Er, yes. How did you know?'

'I have been following you for some time,' Mortimer told them.

'Why?' asked Jeannette, with some justification.

'Because I have something for you.'

Mortimer's hand slid slowly into a pocket somewhere inside his coat, and Reg felt a cold sweat break out on the shiny, tanned skin of his forehead. The man had a gun in his pocket. Or maybe a long, curved dagger. Something nasty and lethal at any rate, of that Reg was certain. His heart beat like a drum in his chest as he remembered the promise he'd made to Jeannette. Don't worry, he had said, I'll look after you – but could he do it? Sure, he had the switchblade, and a nifty little piece of hardware it was too, but could he ever really use it? And even if he tried, Mortimer looked like the kind of guy who poured milk over switchblades and ate them for breakfast.

Slow as an arthritic tortoise towing an anvil, Mortimer's hand slid out from under his coat, but what was in it was definitely not what Reg had expected. Instead of a lethal looking knife or a small, pearl-handled revolver, there were two rather dog-eared and grubby white envelopes. On the front of one was clearly printed the name 'Reginald Bethel'; the other was addressed to 'Jeannette Higginbottom'. They stared at them silently for several seconds, their thoughts racing around inside their heads and giggling, as if engaged in a boisterous game of tag.

'What are they?' asked Jeannette at last.

'You'd better open them,' advised Mortimer. 'I was sent merely to deliver them and then accompany you back.'

'Back where?'

'I believe the address is inside.'

Reg and Jeannette reached out tentatively and took an envelope each. Reg tore his open with hands that seemed determined to be as unsteady as they possibly could, and pulled out an expensive looking folded card with some kind of monogram in one corner. He opened it nervously, then stared in astonishment at the copperplate lettering inside.

It read:

Lord Humphrey and Lady Westholme request
the pleasure of the company of

Reginald Bethel

at a Dinner Party to be held at

Dunrovin Manor
Linniker Falls
Nr. Bogwater Creek
West Western Aisles

Jeannette's invitation was identical apart from the substitution of her own name for that of Reg.

Reg looked at Mortimer, looked at the invitation and then back at Mortimer again.

'But who . . . I mean how . . . I mean why . . .?' he burbled, uncertain about which question was more important.

'Let's take them one at a time,' suggested Mortimer patiently. 'As for *who*, Lord Westholme is the head of a rather large mining corporation and possibly the richest man in the Western Aisles. I, for my sins, am his personal secretary. Frankly, my duties with regard to Lord Westholme are minimal to say the least, but her Ladyship keeps me fairly busy one way and another. As for *how*, I believe a certain Professor Ledbetter is responsible for your being here. His experimental work in the field of relative dimensionistics is much admired, and Lord Westholme – at the request of his wife I should add – has for some time now been providing him with the necessary finance. As for *why*, as far I am aware you were brought here solely for the purpose of attending a dinner party shortly to be given by Lady Westholme. She likes to invite a few . . . *unusual* guests, you might say. It impresses her friends.'

Reg stared, his brain chaotic with activity as a million thoughts raced backwards and forwards along its corridors in search of the appropriate desk on which to leave their message. Jeannette's mouth opened and closed in the manner of a fish impersonating another fish, as she struggled to translate her outrage into words. Finally, her tongue found its feet.

'Are you trying to tell me,' she asked with chilling placidity, 'that we've been dragged from the comfort of our own homes, flushed through holes in the fabric of space and time and subjected to danger, hardship and unpleasantness simply in order to attend someone's dinner party?'

Mortimer took a moment or two to digest Jeannette's question, then nodded. 'I would say that was a fair summation of the facts, yes,' he admitted.

'But that's . . . that's . . . outrageous!'

'I do admit,' admitted Mortimer, 'it does seem a little . . . impertinent, shall we say? However, I believe Lady Westholme felt that you might forgive the unceremonious nature of your arrival here in return for the rare – indeed extraordinary – privilege of visiting a world in another dimension. And, of course, a free dinner.'

'She did, did she?'

'She did. I think she felt that the opportunity to experience life on another planet would more than compensate for her lack of etiquette in bringing you here without first acquiring your . . . *permission*, as it were.'

'She did, did she?'

By this time Jeannette's arms were folded tightly across her chest and her right foot was tapping insistently on the polished wood floor, and Mortimer began to experience a rare sense of unease.

'Erm, yes,' he said lamely.

'Then why the hell didn't someone meet us when we first landed here?' exploded Jeannette angrily. 'Why wasn't there a cab waiting to take us to the dinner party? Why, in short, have we just travelled half way across the bloody planet and almost got ourselves killed in the process, if we're only here to make up the numbers around somebody's sodding dinner table?!'

Jeannette, one will have guessed, was miffed.

'Ah, yes, well I'm afraid the Professor was guilty of one or two minor inaccuracies with respect to his calculations.'

'You mean he got it wrong.'

'Not exactly. After all, he got you here. You just didn't arrive where you were supposed to arrive, that's all.'

'And where was that?'

'The Professor's laboratory in the cellar of Dunrovin Manor. Instead of landing there, however, you ended up in Bogwater Creek, and unfortunately by the time I got there you'd already left. I've been trying to catch up with you ever since.'

'Well I wish you'd done it earlier,' grumbled Reg. 'It would've saved an awful lot of time and trouble.'

Mortimer nodded. 'Had it not been for a certain Black Nidge – as I believe he is known – I would undoubtedly have intercepted you a good deal sooner.'

Reg grunted.

'Still, what's done is done,' observed Mortimer

cheerily. 'May I suggest that you accompany me back to Linniker Falls now, where I believe dinner awaits?'

'I hope you're not expecting us to walk,' Jeannette said threateningly.

'Indeed not, miss. I have taken the liberty of hiring a private airoloon. If the wind currents are in our favour we should arrive at Dunrovin Manor by tomorrow afternoon, in plenty of time for the party in the evening.'

'What about this professor chap, though?' Reg wanted to know. 'Will he be able to send us back home afterwards?'

'He brought you here, did he not?' Mortimer reminded him. 'I would assume, therefore, that he has the power to send you back.'

Reg and Jeannette grinned at each other, their faces suffused with the healthy pinkish hue of relief.

'The airfield is approximately fifteen miles from here,' Mortimer announced. 'I suggest we hire a motor waggon from the village and proceed there with all haste.'

'I'll second that,' said Reg, and Jeannette chuckled and slipped her arm through his.

As they reached the bottom of the hill a little under three minutes later, a short, stocky, bearded man leapt out from behind a bush and pointed a blunderbuss at them.

13

Reg, Jeannette and Mortimer peered down the yawning barrel of the blunderbuss in perplexed silence.

Though obviously shocked by the man's sudden appearance, oddly enough Reg and Jeannette found themselves suppressing an urge to giggle. Their assailant (who looked vaguely familiar in some peculiar way) was wearing a heavy black overcoat with the collar pulled up around the ears, the kind of jam jar bottom spectacles one might find in a tacky joke shop on Blackpool promenade and a black woollen bobble hat.

'Hold it right there!' he commanded, which was a little unnecessary since his three victims had by this time come to a halt and were, in fact, already conscientiously engaged in the act of 'holding it right there'.

'I said, hold it—! Oh, you are doing.'

'What, may I ask, is the meaning of this?' enquired Mortimer politely.

'Silence!' bellowed the little man. 'I'll ask the questions!'

Since it seemed reasonable not to argue with a man holding a blunderbuss, they stayed quiet and waited.

A long silence followed, which was broken only by the somewhat minimal sounds of a man pointing a gun and three people waiting.

'Erm, about those questions...' prompted Reg at last.

'What questions?'

'Well, you said you were going to ask us some questions.'

'Silence! How can I ask questions if you keep talking?'

'Sorry.'

The little man scratched his bobble hat thoughtfully. 'Right!' he yelled suddenly. 'Which of you are the Charring Crossers?'

'Who wants to know?' asked Mortimer.

'What?'

'I said, who wants to know?'

'Why?'

'Because I'm afraid we can't divulge that information unless we know who it's for.'

'Oh. Well if you *must* know, it's for Our Leader, Rolf Hilter.'

'Indeed? Mad Rolf Hilter, eh?'

'That's right. And I demand to know which of you are the Charring Crossers!'

'Now what would someone like Rolf Hilter be wanting with two Charring Crossers?' Mortimer asked gently.

'Silence!' yelled the little man. 'I'm only following orders, and my orders are to find the Charring Crossers and take them to Hilter's chateau!'

'But why?' insisted Mortimer. 'What possible use could they be to him?'

The man with the blunderbuss sighed and rolled his eyes. 'Goat, but you're a nosy bugger. For your information, Our Leader wishes to set up a trade agreement with the other world.'

'What other world?'

'The one where the Charring Crossers come from, dumbo. Since the various governments of Urth have seen fit to impose a total arms embargo on our great leader, he is forced to seek suppliers elsewhere.'

'You mean he intends to go to our planet and buy weapons?' said Jeannette incredulously.

'Exactly.'

Reg and Jeannette exchanged a horrified glance, as visions of some demented warlord in possession of the kind of lethal weaponry available on Earth flickered before their mind's eye.

'May I ask what your name is?' enquired Mortimer, seemingly out of the blue.

The man in the bobble hat smiled, and Jeannette suddenly found herself consumed with a passionate and irrational rage. It was such an arrogant, impertinent, self-satisfied sort of smile, that it immediately made her want to push a particularly stiff toilet brush down his throat.

Like a third-rate club stripper, the man slowly turned back the collar of his coat, removed the spectacles and pulled off his hat.

Mortimer nodded slowly. 'I thought I recognized the voice.'

Jeannette looked at him in astonishment. 'You mean you *know* him?'

'This, my dear Jeannette, is "the man in the black

hat". Better known as Jeremiah Beagle, he is chief of Rolf Hilter's secret police and one of the most hated men on the planet.'

Jeremiah grinned as if he'd just been complimented. 'And now, if you don't mind, I'll take the two Charring Crossers.'

'But of course,' said Mortimer, and his hand slipped inside his coat.

'No false mo—' began Jeremiah, but before he could finish the sentence Mortimer had pulled his small pearl-handled revolver from its holster and shot him dead.

'I've been wanting to do that for years,' Mortimer said with quiet satisfaction, and slipped the revolver back under his coat.

*   *   *

The airoloon was originally invented towards the end of Urth's nineteenth century by Professor Lionel Airo, the celebrated scientist and eccentric (who was almost as famous for his habit of insulting pineapples as he was for his work in the field of aeronautical design). His early attempts to achieve powered flight, which involved large numbers of chickens and several hundred yards of elastic, sadly ended in failure and poultrycide, but Airo persevered, and by the age of thirty-five had built his first prototype airoloon. This basically consisted of a large leather bag attached by lengths of rope to a small rowing boat. Aided by several volunteers, Airo carefully filled the bag with milk, and was apparently devastated when the prototype failed to leave the ground. Subsequent experiments using sand, beer, sawdust – and on one occasion, broccoli – produced similarly disappointing results, and it wasn't until his assistant pointed out that all these substances were in fact *heavier* than the air they were supposed to float through, that Airo hit upon the idea of using gas.

Beneath the surface of the Urth lie huge natural reservoirs of heligen (a curious amalgam of helium and hydrogen, which has caused many an unwary pot-holer to suddenly start floating about and giggling in a very high voice), and it was to these largely untapped deposits that Airo now turned. Having first located an adequately sized pocket of heligen, Airo drilled a bore-hole deep into the ground and placed the open end of his 'balloon' over the top of it, thus capturing the outrushing gas. The experiment was a tremendous success (although sadly the assistant whose job it was to stop the balloon from floating off got a little carried away, and was never seen again), and so the age of air travel was born.

Nowadays airoloons are sophisticated and luxurious affairs, with cabins, restaurants and comfortable glass-floored lounges, where passengers can relax with a cold beer and watch the world go by beneath their feet. Suspended beneath huge dirigibles, these magnificent vessels are powered by two large rear-mounted propellers (which are in turn powered by several well fed reptobates) and steered by means of a rudder utilizing the same principle as a ship.

Reg and Jeannette sipped their beers and looked down through the thick glass floor, as the Urth's landscape unravelled far below them like a vast (if somewhat unfamiliar) map. The towns and villages looked like clusters of Lego dwellings, and the occasional vehicles that wound along the dusty roads resembled nothing so much as tiny ants crawling across the page of an atlas. They had passed over the Big Water in the early hours of the morning, and the golden coastline of the East Western Aisles now lay some fifty miles behind them.

Mortimer wandered in and sat down next to Reg.

'Feeling any better?' Reg asked.

Mortimer, who was looking not so much green around the gills as dead, nodded weakly. 'I'll be fine,' he said. 'It's just this damned air sickness. It'll go as soon as we land. Used to get it all the time in the Service.'

'Service?'

'I was a captain in the SHS for several years.'

'Ah, right. Erm, what's the SHS?'

'Special Hair Service. It's an anti-terrorist unit, mostly involved with undercover and counter-insurgency stuff. We used to travel around the Aisles posing as hairdressers and, well, not to put too fine a point on it, "eliminate" the more troublesome of the terrorist agitators.'

'Eliminate?'

'Cleanly and efficiently, of course.'

'Of course.'

'You'd be surprised what an effective weapon a pair of scissors can be, particularly when your victim's sitting in a chair with his back to you expecting a quick trim and tidy up.'

'I can imagine,' said Reg, trying not to imagine.

'What time do we land?' asked Jeannette, returning at that moment from a very pleasant daydream involving a large bronze sculpture and a civic building.

'About three o'clock, western time,' Mortimer told her.

'And how far is it from the airfield to Linniker Falls?'

'No more than ten miles – roughly half an hour by trolley.'

'Good.'

'Why.'

'Because I'm *dying* for a bath.'

Schedules had always been something of a forte with Mortimer, and at three thirty precisely that same afternoon, Reg and Jeannette found themselves standing in the middle of Union Street, Linniker Falls, watching the back of the trolley bus as it disappeared in a cloud of yellow dust. Mortimer brushed several specks of the latter off his coat, and adjusted the brim of his hat.

'So. Here we are,' he observed. 'The Manor is a short walk away on the edge of town, so if you'd care to follow me . . .'

'I'll follow you to the edge of the world if there's hot running water there,' said Jeannette, and the three of them set off up the street.

Dunrovin Manor, the huge sprawling mansion that was the residence of Lord and Lady Westholme, was a masterpiece of architectural insolence, built of local redstone in a mixture of styles ranging from classical Corinthian to Victorian Gothic. It was at once a monstrosity and a marvel, and as they walked up the tree-lined gravel drive towards it, Jeannette didn't quite know whether to wince, giggle or both.

Mortimer strode up to the massive, ornately carved front door, and as he pulled on the short length of rope hanging next to it, a huge bell pealed somewhere deep within the bowels of the house. A moment later the door was opened by a tall, perfectly attired butler, who looked as if he'd spent countless hours in front of a mirror practising peering down his nose at people.

'Hello, George,' Mortimer said.

'Ah, Mr Mortimer,' purred the butler, 'I see you have brought our "special" guests. Do come in, and I'll show you to your rooms.'

Stepping into the house, Reg and Jeannette found themselves in a sumptuous hall of polished wood, with a bewildering number of panelled oak doors leading off it. At the back of the hall was a wide carpeted staircase, at the top of which was a huge stained glass window depicting a dragon in shining armour in the process of slaying a knight.

'If you'd care to follow me,' murmured George,

'your rooms are on the first floor. Bathrooms are en suite, naturally.'

Jeannette had to exert considerable willpower at this point to stop herself running up the stairs.

An hour later, clean, refreshed and attired in the casual slacks and cotton blouses they had found laid out for them on their beds, Reg and Jeannette were shown into the parlour.

'Mr Bethel and Miss Higginbottom, m'lady,' announced George.

Lady Westholme leapt from her chair and advanced on Reg and Jeannette with terrifying vivacity.

'My dears! My dears!' she exclaimed, embracing them simultaneously and smothering them with noisy kisses. 'What a dreadful, dreadful experience you must have had! I simply can't tell you how sorry I am that we didn't catch you in time!'

Reg and Jeannette, whose initial indignation had been tempered considerably by hot water and soap, the imminence of a three-course meal and the prospect of going home, attempted to demur.

'Oh, that's all right,' mumbled Reg, blushing and managing – just – to resist the temptation to wipe his cheek. 'We got here in the end.'

'Oh, but my dear, if only we'd found you before you left Bogwater Creek! You must've had a simply wretched time, travelling all that way for nothing.'

'Well, there were some pretty hairy moments,' admitted Jeannette, 'but looking back on it now, I suppose it was really quite an adventure.'

'But you could've been killed, my dears! I feel too awful about it, I do really!'

'Well, never mind,' said Reg, who had just spotted a maid approaching with a tray of drinks. 'All's well that ends well.'

At that moment George reappeared in the doorway, accompanied by a rather stout, vacant looking woman and an elderly florid faced gentleman.

'Major and Mrs Trumpton, m'lady,' announced George.

Lady Westholme finally relinquished her hold on Reg and Jeannette and flung herself at the new arrivals.

'Biddy! Henry! How delightful to see you again! Come and meet Reg and Jeannette! You'll never guess where they're from.'

'Probably not,' admitted the Major. 'Where are they from?'

Lady Westholme tapped the side of her nose mischievously. 'I'll tell you at dinner.'

Over the course of what was left of the afternoon several more guests arrived, and at six o'clock prompt, the party retired to their rooms to dress for dinner. (Reg and Jeannette were delighted to find that their own by now decidedly grubby clothes had been beautifully dry cleaned in the interim.)

By seven thirty that evening everyone was finally seated around the splendidly decorated oak table, and the diners now numbered ten in all. Lord and Lady Westholme sat at opposite ends of the room, and as well as Reg, Jeannette and the Trumptons, there was a young woman called Cynthia Tweedale-Sloane, a Miss Ditherington, who was head of Linniker Falls Academy for Girls, the Westholmes' nephew, Steven Snotcade-Porterhouse (who had obviously taken rather a fancy to Miss Tweedale-Sloane), and an odd looking little man with an egg-shaped head, who had the unlikely name of Hercules Pierrot.

As George served the soup, Lady Westholme made the necessary introductions, taking obvious delight in leaving Reg and Jeannette till last.

'I know none of you have met Reg and Jeannette here before,' she said, absent-mindedly fondling the huge ruby around her neck, 'but I really think you'll find them most interesting to talk to. You see, Reg and Jeannette' (her voice was now almost a whisper) 'are not from this world.'

'Not from this world?' piped the robust and military voice of Major Trumpton. 'What on Urth do you mean, Hortensia?'

'Exactly what I said, my dear Major. They come from another world.'

'My Goat! D'you mean to tell me they're aliens?'

'In a manner of speaking, yes.'

'But how did they get here? Where are they from?'

'They come from a place called Earth – that's right, isn't it?'

Reg and Jeannette nodded.

'Blessed if I know what you're talking about, Hortensia old girl. If they come from Urth they're not aliens, are they?'

'Ah, but it's a different Earth, Major, in a different dimension. It's *pronounced* the same as our Urth, but *spelt* differently, d'you see? And although they're two completely separate worlds, there are some very surprising similarities – or so Reg and Jeannette have been telling me.'

'I don't know, Hortensia,' said Miss Ditherington. 'You and your unusual dinner party guests! Last time it was those funny little dwarfs who'd come over from the Northern Aisles, and we had to show them how to use a knife and fork.'

'And the time before that', added the Major's wife, 'it was those two handsome young men in the leather trousers who made such lovely flower arrangements.'

'Huh, couple of pansies,' grunted the Major.

'Nonsense, Henry,' said his wife. 'I thought those floral displays were quite delightful.'

M. Pierrot turned to Reg. 'So, from a world in another dimension come you? That is most fascinating. May I enquire how you got here?'

Reg opened his mouth to respond but was cut short by Lady Westholme.

'All Professor Ledbetter's doing,' she announced proudly. 'The man really is a genius.'

'Ah, yes,' said Pierrot, nodding comprehendingly. 'I believe Lord Westholme has been financing the Professor's research for some time now.'

Lord Westholme awoke from a semi-stupor. 'Eh? What's that? Someone mention my name?'

'M. Pierrot was just saying you've been providing

funds for Professor Ledbetter's experiments, dear,' said
Lady Westholme loudly, as if addressing an ancient and
senile relative.

'Who?'

'Professor Ledbetter. You know, he has a laboratory
in the cellar.'

'Oh, him. Professor is he? Yes, well, that would
account for the long white coat I suppose.'

'Anyway,' Lady Westholme went on, 'the Professor's
built this thing, a sort of ray gun affair—'

'It's a Synchronic Radar, Auntie,' Steven cut in, 'not
a ray gun.'

'Is it, dear? Oh well, he's built this Synchronic-thing-
ummy, and it detects unusual things in space—'

'I think perhaps you'd better let *me* explain, Auntie,'
said Steven kindly. 'You're being a little vague.'

'Am I? Oh well, do go on, dear, you know far more
about it than I do.'

All eyes now turned to Steven, who smiled a little
shyly.

'Well,' he began, 'Professor Ledbetter has con-
structed what he calls a Synchronic Radar, which, as
you may have gathered from Aunt Tensy's description,
emits a kind of ray. Now this beam, which is apparently
transmitted somewhere in the ultrasonic sound frequen-
cies, is designed to detect intense synchronistic activity
within the fabric of the universal dimensions, and can
then pinpoint this activity and calculate its exact
location.'

'Come again?' said the Major.

Steven tried a different tack. 'All right then, in simple terms, synchronicity means coincidence. Now when a major coincidence occurs somewhere within the omniverse—'

'What's the omniverse?' the Major wanted to know.

'It's everything. All the universes, all the worlds and all the dimensions that ever existed.'

'Ah,' said the Major, satisfied. 'Big bugger, then.'

'Quite. So anyway, when a massive coincidence happens, the Professor's radar can pinpoint exactly where in the omniverse it has occurred.'

Reg and Jeannette glanced at each other. ' "Figure of a Man, Bending",' said Reg under his breath, and Jeannette nodded.

'Now then,' Steven went on, 'when a Synchronicity Quotient of Mack 10 is achieved (in other words, a really incredible coincidence), it creates instability in the very fabric of space and time, which in turn causes holes to appear in the wall of the Universal Mainframe. Now these holes, which are known as Charring Faults, automatically attach themselves to the nearest opening, say a door, or a window, thereby forming a link between the dimensions. The problem is, the holes only exist for a fraction of a second before closing up again, so the chances of anyone actually walking through a door whilst it's in conjunction with a Charring Fault are slim, to say the least.'

'Good thing too,' muttered the Major, 'otherwise we'd have people popping out of thin air every few minutes.'

'That's true,' admitted Steven. 'The point is, in order for Reg and Jeannette to get here, that's exactly what had to occur. And that's where the Professor's pièce de résistance comes in.'

The Major scratched one of his chins. 'What's that then?'

Steven grinned. 'The Temporal Suspension Beam.'

'Really, Steven,' said Lady Westholme, 'I don't know how you remember all these wonderful names.'

'And what does this Temporal thingy Beam do then?' asked Reg.

'Quite simply,' replied Steven, 'it causes Time to stop. Don't ask me how it works, because I don't know, but whatever you aim it at actually stops moving in Time for as long as the beam is activated.'

Reg wrestled manfully with his confusion, but rapidly found himself pinned in a half-nelson. 'Erm, I still don't quite erm . . .'

'Well,' Steven went on, 'having pinpointed the Charring Faults with his radar equipment, the Professor was then able to direct the Suspension Beam at them and freeze them in Time, thereby holding them in place until they'd served their purpose.'

'So what you're saying', said Reg slowly, 'is that one of these holes, or Charring Faults, attached itself to my bathroom door, and this Professor chap fired this beam at it and somehow . . . *froze* it there until I walked through it and landed here?'

'Exactly.'

'And then he did the same to Jeannette?'

'That's right. You see, up until now, no one had ever known where these holes were going to appear, and they simply didn't last long enough to be of any use to anyone. But using the Synchronic Radar to locate them and the Suspension Beam to hold them in place, inter-dimensional travel becomes possible. It really is quite a breakthrough when you think about it.'

'This is all very interesting,' said Jeannette, 'but if it takes a huge coincidence to create these holes in space, how exactly is the Professor going to get us back? I mean, do we have to create another coincidence here, or what?'

Steven shook his head. 'No, it can't be done. The very act of creating something intentionally renders it uncoincidental.'

'Then how's he going to do it?'

'Quite simple really. Inside your house on Earth the molecules are still reverberating with the echoes of the original coincidence – whatever it was – and even as we speak, holes are opening and closing behind your doors and windows. All the Professor has to do is direct the Suspension Beam at one of them to hold it in place, then you and Reg walk through a special door which is linked up to the machine, and poof! – you're back in your own house.'

'Really? You mean it's that simple?'

'Like falling off a log.'

'Oh, well, that sounds a doddle,' said Reg. 'I'll have a drop more of that red wine if you don't mind.'

'There is one thing that's been puzzling me,' said

Jeannette, sitting back to allow George to remove her empty soup dish. 'How did you know our names?'

'Ah, now that was the best bit,' said Steven, grinning. 'The thing is, when a massive coincidence occurs in a particular dimension, and the subjects of that coincidence then pass into a different dimension, it would seem that an event of corresponding improbability must necessarily take place in the dimension into which they pass. In other words, according to the laws of dimensionamatics, because something truly remarkable happened in your world, something equally remarkable was bound to happen here as well.'

'But what's that got to do with you knowing our names?'

'That's just the point. We guessed them.'

'What?'

'We guessed your names. We knew two people had come through and landed somewhere near Bogwater Creek, but that was all. So when we wrote out the invitations, Auntie and I picked the first two names that came into our heads – and we were right! So there's your coincidence.'

'That's remarkable,' remarked Cynthia.

'Oh I don't know,' said Reg airily. 'Over the last week or so I've learned not to be surprised by anything.'

'Much is possible, even probable,' observed M. Pierrot, 'and never should one rule out the impossible.'

An awkward silence followed this remark, which

was thankfully broken by the timely appearance of George and the main course.

Even the food, which was truly excellent, could not stem the flow of conversation, and over the next hour and a half Reg and Jeannette found themselves at the receiving end of a veritable barrage of questions concerning Earth. What did it look like? What were the people like? What was its history – and could they recommend any good restaurants?

'Ever get any decent wars on this planet of yours?' the Major wanted to know.

'The worst two in our history happened just this century,' Reg told him. 'We call them the First and Second World Wars. The casualty figures ran into the millions.'

'Really?'

'Absolutely. During the First World War one side alone lost over 600,000 men during the course of a single battle.'

'Good grief! Now that's what I *call* a war.'

'Well, it sounds simply dreadful to me,' said Lady Westholme. 'All those brave young men giving up their lives – and for what?'

'Well,' said Reg, 'ostensibly it was to save the world from tyranny, but I sometimes wonder if it was worth it.'

'Of course it's worth it!' insisted the Major. 'Surely you'd rather die gloriously on the battlefield than live in a world ruled by some demented despot?'

'Well, I can't say I've given it much thought,' admitted Reg.

'Well you should, lad, you should, because if – I say, I think I've just gone blind!'

'No you haven't, Major,' said Steven's disembodied voice. 'The lights have just gone out.'

14

The lights had indeed just gone out, and because George had conscientiously snuffed the candles as he removed the cheese board, the room was now in total darkness. There was a scuffing and scraping of chairs on the wooden floor as people rummaged through pockets in search of matches, and a female voice cried out suddenly in the blackness.

'Who was that?' demanded the Major.

'Me,' said the voice.

'Who's me?'

'Hortensia.'

'What's up old girl? Not afraid of the dark are you?'

'No, but . . . someone, something, *touched* me.'

'Touched you?! By Goat, I'll have 'is pancreas out if I catch 'im! Who was it?'

'I don't know, I couldn't tell, I—'

At that moment the lights came on again, and everyone blinked and peered at each other suspiciously.

'My dear Lady Westholme,' said M. Pierrot, 'you are not harmed in any I hope way.'

'No, no I'm fine,' she said, patting one of her cheeks lightly. 'It's just that I felt something touch the back of my neck, and it startled me.'

'But who could have done it?' asked Cynthia. 'We're all sitting down apart from George, and he was at the other end of the table when the lights went out.'

Lady Westholme tried to compose herself. 'Well, I don't suppose it matters. It was probably just my imagination – the shock of the lights going out, or something.'

'Forgive me, Madam,' said M. Pierrot slowly, 'I may be mistaken – though that is rare, I admit – but were you or were you not a moment ago wearing a beautiful ruby on a silver chain?'

Lady Westholme's hand instinctively went to her lower neck and clutched at . . . nothing. The ruby was gone. Her beautiful Cullinan Ruby, presented to her by her late father on the occasion of her marriage, had disappeared into thin air. The sentimental value of such a thing could not be calculated. The financial value, on the other hand, could, and Lady Westholme's mind was already wandering through the niches of her Hepple-black bureau, trying to remember whether the ruby was separately covered on the house insurance policy. With a sinking heart, she realized that it was not.

'Ye Goats!' bellowed the Major. 'This is intolerable! Someone deliberately turned out the lights and stole Hortensia's ruby! I demand that the culprit declare himself! Come now, someone in this room is guilty, and I insist that they confess to this heinous crime!'

Everybody looked at everybody else, their faces pink with suspicion and embarrassment.

Lord Westholme chose that particular moment to wake up again. 'What's going on?' he demanded drunkenly. 'Why's everybody looking guilty? Has somebody farted?'

'The lights went out, Uncle,' Steven explained, 'and whilst they were off someone stole Auntie's ruby.'

'What, you mean that monstrosity of a jewel she wears around her neck?'

'The Cullinan Ruby, yes.'

'Ah well, can't be helped. Never liked the damned thing anyway.'

'Humphrey!' cried Lady Westholme. 'Whether you liked it or not is immaterial. That ruby's worth thousands!'

'Is it? Oh, well, that's different then. All right, who nicked it? Come on now, hand it over. Can't be doing with pilfering, particularly where valuables are concerned.'

Lord Westholme peered around the table expectantly, and everyone squirmed.

'Well *I* haven't got it!' Miss Ditherington exclaimed suddenly. 'Surely it must be one of the aliens, Hortensia. I mean, hevvan knows what they get up to in their *own* world! This sort of thing may be quite acceptable there.'

'Could be working as a team,' suggested the Major. 'One of 'em swipes it, then the other one eats it in case they're searched.'

'Madam,' said M. Pierrot quietly, 'if you would allow me, I believe I may be able to assist you in clearing up this little matter.'

Lady Westholme turned to the little man gratefully. 'Oh, M. Pierrot, can you really? I can't tell you how relieved I'd be. This whole thing has to be some foolish prank, surely nothing more.'

'It is no prank, Madam, of that I can assure you. Consider the facts.'

'Yes?'

'One moment you are wearing your precious ruby. Suddenly the lights go out, and when again they come on – pssht, the ruby is gone.'

'Erm, yes?'

'But Madam, do you not see what this means? The truth, it is staring you in the nose.'

'It is?'

'But of course. In view of the facts which just I have recounted, there is only one conclusion to be reached.'

'Is there?'

'Absolutement. Someone, Madam, deliberately turned out the lights, and whilst the room plunged into darkness was, stole the Cullinan Ruby from around your neck. It was the hand of the thief himself that you felt there in the darkness!'

'But that's just what *I* said,' pointed out the Major.

'Quite so, Major Trumpton,' agreed Pierrot, 'and you were of course correct.'

'But who *did* it, man? That's the point. Who stole the ruby?'

'Ah,' said Pierrot, leaning back in his chair, 'that, my dear Major, is the million doily question.'

'But M. Pierrot,' said Cynthia, 'you are one of the most famous detectives on Urth. Surely you can solve the mystery.'

Pierrot sighed. 'Very well then,' he said, placing his hands together in front of him, 'if we are to the bottom of this going to get, we must employ the little grey cells. Now then, including George, there are eleven people in this room, and we must assume that one of them is the guilty party. So, let us consider the suspects in turn. First and foremost, I think that I myself may be discounted, do you not agree?'

'But why, M. Pierrot?' asked Steven. 'Surely in a case such as this we should discount no one, not even you?'

'Don't be ridiculous, M. Snotcade-Porterhouse. I am the great Hercules Pierrot. I *solve* crimes, I do not commit them.'

'That's right, Steven,' agreed Cynthia. 'M. Pierrot can't possibly be a suspect, otherwise the story wouldn't work.'

'What story?'

'Well, I mean, it just wouldn't be right.'

'Oh, all right then, so M. Pierrot is out of the running.'

'Thank you,' said Pierrot with a little bow. 'Now then, I think we can also discount Lord and Lady Westholme themselves. After all, why would they steal their own ruby?'

'Could be an insurance job,' suggested the Major, then yelped as his wife nudged him savagely in the ribs.

Pierrot turned to Lady Westholme. 'I believe I am right in thinking, Madam, that the ruby is not insured separately from the other contents of your house.'

'Why no, that's true, but how did you know?'

'It is my business to know these things, Madam,' said Pierrot primly. 'So, we have established that the Westholmes and myself are blameless in this matter. There is one other person who can immediately be discounted, and that person is . . . Miss Jeannette Higginbottom.'

Jeannette started. 'Me? But why? I don't understand.'

'Miss Higginbottom, if you look down you will observe that your napkin is still tucked into the waistband of your skirt, where you yourself placed it – an old habit no doubt. You will also observe – forgive me for pointing it out – that the other end of your napkin is lying on the table in front of you, and for the last five minutes, your wine glass has actually been standing on it. Consequently, if you had left your seat at the time of the blackout – and this you would have had to do in order to remove the ruby from Lady Westholme's neck – your wine glass would have been pulled to the floor where it would have shattered. But as we all can see, your wine glass is still intact – indeed, it is still standing on your napkin.'

Unable to suppress yet another blush, Jeannette lifted her glass quickly and pushed her napkin back into her lap.

'Brilliant!' cried Mrs Trumpton. 'What powers of observation!'

'Thank you, my dear Mrs Trumpton,' said Pierrot, and bowed. 'So, including the butler, that leaves seven people. But before we consider the people themselves, let us consider this: the blackout – and I timed it myself – lasted for *precisely fifteen seconds only*! And that, my friends, is a very short space of time indeed. Who, then, could have been nimble enough to get up from his chair, make his way round to Lady Westholme – in complete darkness, mind you – remove the Cullinan Ruby and get back into his seat before the lights came on again?'

'Have to be someone pretty quick on their pins,' admitted the Major.

'Quick indeed,' agreed Pierrot. 'In truth, Major, only two people could possibly have had time to commit the crime, and they are the two people sitting closest to Lady Westholme. However, those two people are, as you can see for yourselves, myself and Miss Higginbottom, who we have already established are beyond suspicion. The fact is, my friends, *no one sitting at this table could have removed the ruby and got back to their seat in complete darkness in just fifteen seconds!*'

'Then what exactly are you saying, M. Pierrot?' asked Steven.

'I am saying, M. Snotcade-Porterhouse, that only one person could have removed the ruby so rapidly and remained undetected, that person being the only one who was not sitting down at the time.'

'You mean . . .?'

'Yes, that is exactly what I mean. *The butler did it!*'

There was a shocked silence as all eyes turned to George, who was standing discreetly to one side near the head of the table.

'I can't believe it,' said Lady Westholme at last. 'My dear M. Pierrot, George has been with us for, for ... well actually, not all that long now that I come to think about it.'

Pierrot nodded in a satisfied manner, then turned to the butler. 'And you, Monsieur, what do you have to say for yourself?'

George shrugged impassively. 'I did not steal the ruby, sir.'

'Now come on, George old boy,' urged the Major. 'If you took the damned thing you might as well own up to it. You've been rumbled, d'you see?'

'Please, Major,' said Pierrot, 'do not derange yourself.' He turned back to the butler. 'And as for you, George, I *know* that you did not steal the ruby.'

George stared. 'You do, sir?'

'Yes, I do. However, I put it to you, George the butler, that you are not in fact George the butler at all, *but his twin brother, Eric!*'

There was a startled gasp from the assembled diners, and the colour drained from the butler's shocked face.

'But, but ...' stuttered Lady Westholme.

'It is so, Madam, I assure you,' said Pierrot smugly. 'Fortunately, I had the foresight to anticipate this nasty crime, and I am confident that even as we speak, the real George has already been apprehended by the two policemen I posted at the gate.'

At that moment the dining room door opened, and two burly looking men in long raincoats propelled Eric's disgruntled looking twin brother into the room.

He sailed serenely across the wooden floor and came to rest by the mantelpiece.

'Why Pierrot,' cried Steven, 'that's remarkable! Tell us, how was it done? How did the blighters pull it off?'

Pierrot gave a Gallic shrug. 'Quite simple, really. If you had been a little more observant during the course of the meal, you would have noticed, perhaps, that George is wearing roller skates.'

They all looked, and were amazed to see that Pierrot was quite right.

'It was these same roller skates,' he went on, 'which enabled him to move from one end of the table to the other with such rapidity, knowing full well that the noise of the wheels would be drowned by the scraping of chairs as people searched for matches.'

'But where does the twin brother come into it?' Steven wanted to know.

Pierrot gave one of his little bows. 'I will explain. At a pre-arranged moment, George's twin brother, Eric, enters the room, switching off the lights as he does so. He then walks straight to the other end of the table and takes up his position near to Lord Westholme.'

'Eh? What? Did somebody – ouch!'

'At the same time, George skates rapidly in the opposite direction, snatches the ruby from Lady Westholme's neck and proceeds out through the door, switching the lights on again as he goes. When again we all can see, our eyes tell us instinctively that George has never moved, because he is standing exactly where he was when the lights went out. What we *don't* know, is that this is *not* George the butler, but his identical twin brother, Eric.' Pierrot tapped the side of his nose. 'But me, Pierrot, I know.'

'But how, Pierrot?' insisted Steven. '*How* did you know?'

Pierrot twirled his splendid moustache. 'A little earlier today, soon after I had arrived, I went in search of the bathroom, and on passing the scullery I happened upon a peculiar sight. What I saw was George the butler, meticulously eating his way through a basket of carrots. Now what, I thought to myself, would a man want to eat all those carrots for? Unless, of course, *he wanted to improve his night vision for some reason!*'

'Brilliant!' declared Steven. 'What a deduction!'

'And then when I saw George serving at table in a pair of roller skates, I immediately knew what was afoot. I am just thankful that by then I had already requested the two police officers to take up positions by the gate.'

'I suppose we owe you our thanks yet again, M. Pierrot,' said one of the officers grudgingly. 'It would've looked bad for us if these scoundrels had got away with the famous Cullinan Ruby.'

Pierrot bowed, twirled his moustache and tried not to look smug, a feat he had thus far in his life failed to master.

After the excitement of dinner came the even more exciting prospect of watching Reg and Jeannette make the Charring Crossing back to their own dimension. Only an inveterate dinner party giver like Lady Westholme could have thought up such a spectacular climax to the evening for her guests, and as she led them all down the cellar steps to Professor Ledbetter's laboratory, she was positively bursting with silent magniloquence. What an evening! What a party! The unique kudos of two guests from another dimension, then the theft of the Cullinan Ruby with Hercules Pierrot right there on the spot to solve the crime. And now they were about to see Reg and Jeannette step back through the dimensions into their own world. How on Urth would she ever top this one?

As they reached the bottom of the stone steps, a tiny little man in a long white lab coat trotted over to greet them. The top of his head was completely bald, but long, frenzied strands of white hair exploded from each of his temples. His misshapen nose looked far too big for his face, and perched on the end of it were a pair of tiny, silver-rimmed spectacles. It is also perhaps worth mentioning that he was completely bog-eyed.

'This is Professor Ledbetter,' Lady Westholme told the assembled guests, 'possibly the greatest scientist on Urth.'

'Oh, please, Hortensia,' said the little man, 'you flatter me. My work is a mere bagatelle compared to that of men like Halibut Weinstein. Why, without his Theory of Irrelevantivity my own experiments would have come to nothing.'

'Come now, Professor. Weinstein may have come up

with the theory, but it's you who have put it into practice and made travel between the dimensions possible.'

'Oh, well, it was nothing really . . .'

Reg wandered across the laboratory to where a perfectly ordinary looking wooden door was standing on its own, apparently leading nowhere. The frame was held in place by four diagonal wooden stays, and from an electrode embedded in the wood itself, a length of cable snaked across the floor to a large and exceedingly complicated looking piece of machinery. Reg wandered around the door a couple of times, then opened it tentatively and peered through, half expecting to see his bathroom on the other side of it. He was a little disappointed to find that what was visible through the door was exactly what logic stated *should* be visible, to wit, the other end of the laboratory.

Jeannette wandered over, followed by the Professor, Lady Westholme and the little group of dinner guests. (Lord Westholme had by this time slid under the dining room table and sunk into a coma.)

'Is this the door, then?' asked Jeannette.

The Professor patted it affectionately. 'This is indeed the door, my dear. When the Temporal Suspension Beam is activated, you and Mr Bethel will step through this historic portal and, as if by magic, disappear from view.'

'With all due respect,' ventured Jeannette, 'it doesn't *look* very historic. I mean, it's just a few bits of two by two and an ordinary wooden door. It's not even painted.'

'Decoration is not necessary, my dear. It is an opening, an aperture, and once it is aligned with one of the Charring Faults in the Universal Mainframe, it will become a gateway between the dimensions.'

Jeannette looked at it doubtfully. 'Well, if you say so.'

'Trust me,' said the Professor, and grinned good naturedly. He turned to Lady Westholme. 'Everything is in place, madam – when do you wish me to activate the beam?'

'Oh, well, that's up to Reg and Jeannette.'

Reg shrugged. 'Well, I suppose now is as good a time as any,' he said, glancing at his watch. 'I mean, it is sort of going home time, anyway.'

'Excellent, excellent!' declared the Professor, and bounding across the room to his beloved machine, he began pulling levers and flicking switches. The lights dimmed slightly and the room was filled with a low, harmonic hum, as the Temporal Suspension Beam gathered energy.

At that moment a maid appeared on the cellar steps, clutching Reg and Jeannette's virulent nylon rucksacks.

'Sir, Miss,' she said in a timid, maid-like sort of way, 'I thought you might be needing these.'

The rucksacks were duly passed over, and grinning nervously at each other, Reg and Jeannette slipped their arms through the straps. The weight of the packs against their shoulders, though minimal, felt somehow comforting and familiar.

They turned to Lady Westholme and her little group of expectant guests.

'Well, thank you for a lovely dinner,' said Jeannette. 'It's been quite an evening.'

'It's been quite a fortnight,' added Reg.

'Oh my dears!' gushed Hortensia, dashing across and kissing them both noisily. 'If only Mortimer could have found you before you left Bogwater Creek!'

'Oh, that doesn't matter,' Reg assured her. 'I mean, looking back, it really has been the adventure of a lifetime. Of course, when we get home nobody will believe a word of it, but who cares? *We* know it happened.'

'Well, goodbye then,' said Lady Westholme, looking as if she was about to burst into tears, 'and good luck.'

'Yes, cheerio, safe journey and all that,' called the Major, and the little group of dinner guests began to wave, which, due to the fact that they were currently standing in what had until recently been the wine cellar of a large country house, looked decidedly peculiar.

The Professor consulted a series of dials and made some minor adjustments to the controls of his machine. Finally, he nodded to himself and turned to Reg and Jeannette.

'According to the Synchronic Radar, I am currently locked on to a Charring Fault somewhere inside Mr Bethel's house. That will be satisfactory, I take it?'

'Perfect,' said Reg.

'Good.' The Professor made a minute adjustment to one of his dials. 'Well, everything is aligned. You may step through the door whenever you wish.'

Reg and Jeannette glanced at each other nervously.

'I'd better go first,' said Reg, 'just in case.'

Jeannette nodded. 'See you back at your place, then.'

Reg reached out tentatively and turned the handle of the door. As it slowly swung open he experienced a thrill of acute disappointment, akin to that of reaching into a coat pocket and feeling something soft and papery and ten pound note-like, then pulling out a month-old Sainsbury's till receipt. The view through the doorway hadn't changed one iota, and Reg was beginning to have serious doubts about the Professor's 'gateway between the dimensions'. If this didn't work he was going to feel a right pillock, and he glanced enquiringly at Ledbetter. The diminutive boffin merely nodded and grinned and stuck out his thumb.

Oh well, thought Reg, here goes.

With a brief cheery wave to Lady Westholme and the other dinner guests, Reg reached behind him and took hold of Jeannette's hand, and one after the other they stepped through the door.

15

Like inhaling deeply from a bottle of amyl nitrate then falling naked from a great height into a vat of cold porridge, the sensation of passing between dimensions sent Reg's mind scurrying into the darkest corner of his skull, where it cowered and bit its nails apprehensively. The human brain was simply not designed to withstand this kind of cerebral battering, and the one inside Reg's head was beginning to wonder why it continued to put up with it. If Reg wasn't careful, his mind decided, it was going to nip out for a loaf of bread and simply not come back, and if that left Reg staggering about and blithering like an idiot, well, it served him right for mistreating it.

Slowly, as the effects of the Charring Crossing began to wear off, Reg's mind pulled itself together and calmed down a bit. After all, Reg's head wasn't such a bad place to be when you got right down to it. It was warm, and quite cosy, and he fed it with information on a reasonably regular basis. Besides, if it left Reg it would only have to find someone else's head to inhabit, and who knew where it might end up? The idea of finding itself inside the skull of some minor Brussels bureaucrat suddenly brought Reg's mind to its senses, and it sidled back into position sheepishly, trying not to blush.

As sentience slotted slowly into place, Reg peered

around in bewilderment. He was vaguely aware of holding something in his right hand, and turning around he was slightly surprised to discover that it was Jeannette. They stared at each other for several seconds, blinking and trying to focus.

'Have we, I mean, are we . . . did we make it?' asked Jeannette at last.

'I think so,' said Reg. He gazed around the room and nodded. 'Yes, I think we made it.'

Jeannette followed his gaze and wrinkled her nose. 'Where the hell are we though?'

'Erm, it's er, it's my bedroom,' said Reg awkwardly, aware of that faint but distinctive odour which only mature French cheese and overripe socks can produce. 'Sorry about the mess.'

He let go of Jeannette's hand and proceeded to lurch around the room, plucking items of clothing from the floor and stuffing them into the dirty washing basket.

'Meant to tidy it up,' he explained breathlessly, 'but I left in a bit of a hurry, if you see what I mean, ha ha, didn't really have time, sorry.'

Jeannette slid the rucksack from her shoulders and let it slip to the floor, then kicking off her shoes, flopped down on the bed.

'Oh Reg, don't worry about the mess. I couldn't care less. We're home! We're back in England, back on Earth!'

Reg dropped a particularly fetid pair of sports socks into the basket, then sat down on the bed and slipped off his own rucksack. 'You're right,' he agreed. 'I can hardly believe it. I feel as if I've been away for years.'

'Me too,' admitted Jeannette.

'I wonder . . .' Reg glanced at the digital alarm clock on his bedside table and gasped. 'My God,' he said slowly, 'it's like in the Narnia books.'

Jeannette peered at him. 'What?'

'It's like we've never been away.'

'What are you talking about?'

'Time!'

'Time?'

'Yes! According to the clock, we've only been gone a few seconds! Even though we spent nearly two weeks on Urth, practically no time at all has passed here!'

'Honestly?'

'Yes, it's incredible! Here's me thinking the police would be out looking for us, and no one will even have missed us.'

'Oh well, at least my mum won't have been worried then.'

Reg gazed around the room in wonder. 'I say, Jenn, we didn't dream it all, did we?'

'I hope not,' said Jeannette, 'because if we did, it means I've never met you, in which case, what the hell am I doing on your bed?'

'Good point,' conceded Reg. 'It's just that it all seems so unreal now that we're back home.'

'I know. It's like coming back off holiday. By the time you've been home a day, you feel as if you've never been away.'

Reg lay back against the pillow and closed his eyes. Jeannette snuggled up to him, laying her head against his chest.

Reg sighed. 'I could sleep for a week,' he said drowsily.

'Me too.'

'It really was some adventure—'

numbers

'—though, wasn't it?'

'It certainly was.'

'You realize, of course, we won't—'

something about the numbers

'—be able to tell anyone.'

'Absolutely not. They'd think we were nuts.'

'Completely—'

something about the numbers on the digital alarm

'—bonkers.'

was wrong

Reg sat up abruptly, sending Jeannette sprawling across the bed.

'Reg? What is it?'

'The numbers are wrong.'

'What?'

Reg snatched the alarm clock from his bedside table and peered at it. Jeannette leaned across and stared over his shoulder at the digital display.

'Reg,' she said quietly, 'why are the numbers the wrong way round?'

He looked at her, and she realized with alarm that he was edging towards panic. He suddenly threw the alarm clock down, leapt off the bed and ran over to the bookcase.

'Reg, what's going on?' asked Jeannette, an element of fear creeping into her voice.

Reg snatched a book at random and almost pulled it in half in his frenzy to get it open. He stared at the page in front of him for several seconds, then slowly he lowered his arms and the book fell from his hands. He turned towards Jeannette, his face blank and his eyes glazed.

'Reg, please tell me what's wrong,' she pleaded.

'Backwards,' he said dully. 'It's all backwards.'

'You mean the writing? In the book?'

'Everything. The writing, the numbers – everything's the wrong way round.'

'What does it mean, Reg? What's happened?'

Reg shook his head. 'I'm not sure – but I think we'd better take a look outside.'

'Outside? But why? Reg, you don't think . . .?'

With an effort, Reg pulled himself out of his daze. 'Only one way to find out,' he said, and headed for the door. Jeannette leapt off the bed and followed him.

As he reached the bottom of the stairs, Reg stepped carefully over the thing that was lying there, and bounded down the hall. He reached the front door, unfastened it and flung it open. Jeannette arrived a few seconds later and peered over his shoulder.

They stood in silence for almost two minutes, staring out over the vast dusty plain in front of them, its barren emptiness illuminated by two silver moons. In the distance a cluster of town lights twinkled, and a million unfamiliar stars glittered in the black sky. From the direction of the town and still some half a mile away, a little line of lanterns weaved its way towards them.

Reg let out his breath in a long shuddering sigh. 'We're back on Urth,' he said quietly. 'You know that, don't you?'

Jeannette slid her arm around his waist. 'Yes,' she said softly, then added, 'and there's a dead body at the bottom of your stairs.'

THE END . . . ish